The Quest to the Uncharted Lands

THE QUEST TO THE UNCHARTED LANDS

JALEIGH JOHNSON

DELACORTE PRESS

Text copyright © 2017 by Jaleigh Johnson
Jacket art copyright © 2017 by Owen Richardson
Jacket lettering copyright © 2017 by Tobias Saul
Map illustrations copyright © 2017 by Brandon Dorman

All rights reserved. Published in the United States by Delacorte Press, an imprint of Random House Children's Books, a division of Penguin Random House LLC, New York.

Delacorte Press is a registered trademark and the colophon is a trademark of Penguin Random House LLC.

Visit us on the Web! randomhousekids.com

Educators and librarians, for a variety of teaching tools, visit us at RHTeachersLibrarians.com

Library of Congress Cataloging-in-Publication Data
Names: Johnson, Jaleigh, author.
Title: The quest to the uncharted lands / Jaleigh Johnson.
Description: New York : Delacorte Books for Young Readers, 2017. | Summary: "Stella's parents are on the first expedition to the uncharted lands of Solace, but Stella doesn't want to be left behind. Stowing away aboard the ship, she finds a mysterious boy who is also hiding, and he's keeping a very big secret. She must decide whether to trust him or risk the fate of the expedition"— Provided by publisher.
Identifiers: LCCN 2016028802| ISBN 978-1-101-93312-1 (hardback) | ISBN 978-1-101-93314-5 (glb) | ISBN 978-1-101-93313-8 (ebook)
Subjects: | CYAC: Fantasy. | BISAC: JUVENILE FICTION / Fantasy & Magic. | JUVENILE FICTION / Social Issues / Friendship. | JUVENILE FICTION / Action & Adventure / General.
Classification: LCC PZ7.J63214 Que 2017 | DDC [Fic]—dc23

The text of this book is set in 12-point Goudy Old Style.
Jacket design by Katrina Damkoehler
Interior design by Ken Crossland

Printed in the United States of America
10 9 8 7 6 5 4 3 2 1
First Edition

This one's for the boys:
Tim, Jeff, and Todd.

We may not have a big blue box
or the Iron Glory, *but that hasn't*
stopped us from exploring the
world together.

City of
Kovall

Beldt
Grasslands

Hiterian Mountains

UNCHARTED
LANDS

THE WORLD OF
SOLACE

Scrap
Towns

S.T. 16

Archivists'
Strongholds

MERROW
KINGDOM

The 401's Journey

Cutting Gap

DRAGONFLY
TERRITORIES

Mining
Country

Noveen

☙ ONE ☙

W hen the *Iron Glory*'s engines rumbled to life for its journey to the uncharted lands, it marked a new future for the world of Solace. Confetti swirled, kings smiled, and thousands cheered.

Except Stella Glass, who was busy crouching on her hands and knees in a cypress grove, burying smoke bombs.

She rummaged in her alchemy case for some matches, trying to ignore the clutch of nerves in her stomach. Stella's first love would always be medicine, and she intended to become a full-fledged healer someday like her parents, but she had to admit, the alchemical sciences tickled her imagination also. It wasn't just the potential to make things go *boom*—although that was fantastic. There was a subtle art to alchemy, one that could be put to so many different uses. The smoke bomb was one of her favorites. A cooked concoction of saltpeter, sugar, and saleratus offered infinite possibilities. No boom required.

With her thumb, Stella dug a shallow hole at the base of the closest cypress tree and carefully placed one of the smoke bombs in it. She stood up and walked over to another tree about ten feet away, repeating the process until she'd created a rough square in the grove.

The next part of her plan was trickier. She'd measured the fuses of the smoke bombs so that each one was roughly three inches longer than the last. If she started with the longest fuse, this would theoretically allow her enough time to light each one, disappear from the grove, and join the massive crowd gathered on the palace grounds to watch the airship take off.

Four smoke bombs, though harmless, made for one big distraction, and Stella couldn't risk anyone seeing that she had been the one responsible for setting them off. She'd guessed at how long it would take for the fuses to burn down based on experiments she'd done in the field behind her house. She thought she'd given herself enough time, but her experiments were never exactly the same and she couldn't be certain. Yet one more variable to contend with, one more way her plan could go wrong.

Stella sat back on her heels and peeked between the trees to catch a glimpse of the *Iron Glory*. Sunlight reflected in blinding ribbons off the ship's metal skin.

It rested on its landing gear in a roped-off field on the west side of the palace. The air was heavy with the reek of sulfur as steam clouds leaked from its stern. It was a strange mix, part sky-sailing ship and part balloon. Its long hull was a full five stories tall, with a set of propellers to guide it. A single mast and crow's nest rose from the main deck, stripped down with no sails or rigging. Instead, it flew banners proudly displaying the Dragonfly territories' colors of green and gold and the Merrow Kingdom's blue and yellow.

But most impressive of all was the envelope that held the ship's lifting gas. Locked in place by dozens of metal cables attached to the main deck, it towered over the rest of the ship like a huge pearl. The envelope's milky-white fabric resembled silk, with a strange iridescent quality that made it sparkle in the sunlight. Stella didn't know exactly what the material was, only that it had been designed to withstand both subzero temperatures and the most punishing winds.

Good thing too, because the vessel was going to take Stella's parents and thirty-seven other brave humans, chamelins, and sarnuns all the way across the Hiterian Mountains to the uncharted lands of Solace.

Farther west than anyone had ever explored before.

A journey full of unknowable dangers.

The Dragonfly territories had planned the expedition and paid for the construction of the airship. Because of that, the honor of launching the ship belonged to King Aron, in his capital city, Noveen. But it was the Merrow Kingdom's scientists who had designed the *Iron Glory* and mapped the route for the journey.

Neither king was taking any chances with security. Stella had counted over a dozen palace guards stationed around the airship, and those were just the ones on the ground. A pair of chamelins circled the sky, their keen eyes watching for trouble. In their shape-shifted forms, they had the arms, legs, and torso of a human, but their skin was a leathery deep green, their faces ridged and elongated, reminding Stella of a lizard. A pair of batlike wings sprouted from their backs, holding them aloft on the air currents.

Stella could just make out the laborers hauling the remaining cargo up a ramp into the belly of the ship, a steady stream of crates bearing research equipment and survival supplies. Meanwhile, King Aron stood before the doors of the palace, waving to the crowd and speaking to the Merrow family, including their children. The captain and first officer of the *Iron Glory* were also there, and in a few minutes, the king would make a speech as the ship's crew prepared to leave on their glorious expedition. The whole atmosphere was like a festival, and the crowd watched and murmured excitedly in anticipation.

Stella turned back to her smoke bombs. She held the matches in her hands and took a deep breath.

This was it. All her weeks of planning, lying awake at night for hours, worrying over the details she might have missed, wondering if, when the moment came, she would actually have the skill and courage to pull this off, or if she would be caught and forced to stay behind.

No, she wouldn't let that happen. Her parents were setting off on a journey into unknown territory. She had to go with them.

Because how would she bear it if they never came back?

The matches shook in Stella's hands. She closed her eyes and forced down the sudden panic that swept over her. *It's all right,* she told herself. *Pretend this is nothing more than an experiment in the lab. Follow the steps—one by one.* Everything was in place. She just had to strike the match and begin.

Opening her eyes, Stella felt a veil of calm settle over her. She lifted her hands and struck the match, and with a crackle, a bright flame sprang to life in front of her eyes. Before she could change her mind, she touched it to the fuse.

A bead of orange engulfed the string and started to burn. Stella jumped to her feet, running to the next one, and the next. When all four fuses were lit and burning toward the smoke bombs, she stuffed the matches into her alchemy case and moved quickly out of the grove and across the palace lawn, careful to hurry but not run.

In her head, she began to count. From the experiments she'd conducted, she judged that she had about forty seconds before the smoke grew thick enough to attract someone's attention. Forty seconds to weave through the crowd and get to the ship.

Now thirty.

Twenty.

With ten seconds left in her count, a scream tore through the humid afternoon air.

"Fire! Someone, help! Fire!"

Stella sped up her pace. One by one, faces in the crowd began turning from the ship toward the grove. To keep up appearances, and because she wanted to see how visible the smoke screen was, Stella turned with them. A jolt of satisfaction went through her when she saw the thick gray clouds twisting toward the sky, obscuring the speared tips of the cypress trees.

More panicked shouts rang out, the crowd ahead of her thinning as people either ran toward the smoke or tried to back away to a safe distance. Palace guards shoved people aside as they ran toward the imaginary fire.

Stella turned back to the ship. The way was suddenly clear in front of her. The laborers who'd been loading cargo had gone to help put out the fire. There wasn't a guard in sight to block her way or a chamelin watching from the sky. Her stomach pitched, but Stella forced her feet to keep moving, counting her steps in her head.

One.

She reached the rope line barring everyone from the ship.

Two.

She ducked under, rising to her feet on the other side.

Three.

The cargo bay of the ship loomed before her, dozens of crates still arranged in neat piles on the lawn. Casting one last furtive glance around her, Stella ran up the gangplank and into the dark belly of the ship.

The *Iron Glory*, flagship of the Dragonfly territories and symbol of its fragile peace with the Merrow Kingdom, was going to be the first vessel in Solace history to make it across the Hiterian Mountains to the uncharted lands.

And Stella Glass wasn't letting her parents go without her. She would be the first stowaway to see what was waiting on the other side of that range.

⪦ TWO ⪧

S he'd done it.

Giddy with success, Stella squeezed behind a tall row of crates at the back of the cargo bay. Based on her research of the ship, the safest place to hide and set up camp was in this left corner. The crates in that section held gifts that the kings intended to offer to the inhabitants of the uncharted lands. That part of the cargo had been loaded first, packed into a corner and sealed with padlocks. Since nothing in those crates would be used during the journey, the crew had no reason—and, Stella hoped, no desire—to squeeze back there to get to the cargo. That made it the perfect place for a hideout.

Large, round windows dotted the upper walls of the bay letting in just enough light for Stella to see as she sat down behind the crates and pressed her back against the wall. On the other side of that wall was the engine room. Its proximity warmed the air, and the smell of sulfur tickled Stella's nose. Growing up in a lab, she was used to the smell but not to the darkness, and the stifling heat burned her lungs.

Panting, Stella shifted and leaned against the towering crates instead. It didn't help. The walls of the cargo bay seemed to shrink suddenly, closing in around her. Black spots popped in front of her eyes, and Stella had to brace her hands against the floor to keep from toppling over.

Not now, she thought, her body trembling. *Please, not now.*

Darkness sometimes triggered a panic attack. Once it started, there was no stopping it.

When Stella was five, she'd accidentally locked herself in her grandparents' root cellar. It wasn't long before her parents found her, but in that time, night fell, and Stella never forgot the terror of lying on the cellar floor in the pitch-black, the smell of damp soil making her imagine she'd been buried alive. Helpless, she'd curled into a tight ball and listened to mice and insects scurrying around her.

Not many things truly frightened Stella, but tight spaces were high on the list. She'd known that was going to be her biggest challenge, hiding out down here in a humid little corner of the ship, but she'd had no idea the panic would envelop her so quickly.

She closed her eyes, leaned her head back against the crates, and took several deep, steadying breaths. Normally, when the attacks came on, she imagined herself in the middle of a flower-filled meadow or some other wide-open, pleasant space. But this time she found herself thinking of this morning, when she'd said goodbye to her parents before they boarded the *Iron Glory*.

In her mind, she was standing in her mother's arms, chin hooked over her right shoulder, trying not to cry.

Why had it been so difficult? She'd shared hundreds, probably thousands, of hugs with her mother since she was a little girl. Hugs that meant goodbye, hugs that said welcome back, hugs that soothed an injury or congratulated a new discovery in the lab. She'd tried to pretend this one was like all the rest.

But it wasn't.

Because this was a hug to send her mother and father soaring into the sky on a ship that would carry them thousands of miles away from Stella.

This hug whispered *Change*.

Stella had felt the word sink deep into her bones. It whispered of a journey, of places unknown, of a future that looked different day by day.

Change, change, change, it'd echoed in her mind. *Nothing will ever be the same.*

Stella tried to block out the memories, but they were relentless. This wasn't making her feel any calmer.

By having her parents join the *Iron Glory*'s crew, King Aron was as good as declaring them among the best healers and scientists in the Dragonfly territories. Maybe even in all of Solace. Naturally, he had to have the best, for the good of the kingdom. He'd praised their research on infectious diseases, declaring that it would be invaluable when the expedition encountered new people and environments on the other side of the mountains.

Stella clenched her hands into fists. It all sounded like a compliment, but she'd learned that when the king said a person was invaluable and he asked them to do something "for the good of the kingdom," what he really meant was that it wasn't a request they could refuse.

So her parents had had no choice but to join the expedition. And since no children were allowed on the ship—it was too dangerous, the king had said—they'd been forced to leave Stella behind in the care of her grandparents. But as much as Stella loved her grandmother and grandfather and knew she would be safe with them, they weren't enough. She needed to be with her parents, to make sure they were safe.

She'd written a letter for her grandparents to find later, once the ship was too far away to communicate with the city. She'd tried to explain why she had to do this, begging them not to worry and to forgive her for running away.

Stella curled her body into a protective ball, just like

she had that day in the root cellar. *You're all right,* she told herself, wiping the sweat from her forehead. She hadn't been left behind. She was here now, safe and hidden, about to embark on an adventure unlike anything she'd ever known in her small corner of the world.

Breathe, Stella. In and out. You're strong enough to do this. Nothing in the dark can hurt you.

After a few minutes, Stella opened her eyes and sat up straight. The heat was still stifling, but she found she could tolerate it now.

Time to get down to business.

If she was going to live back here, she needed to set up camp.

Stella's hideout was little more than a pocket between the backmost row of crates and the wall of the engine room. She couldn't stretch her arms all the way out from her sides without hitting either the crates or the wall, but she could live with that. The important thing was that the area was large enough to fit her and her few selected possessions without being seen by crew members.

Which reminded Stella, she needed to *retrieve* her supplies as soon as the ship took off. She'd been particularly proud of that part of her plan. Her parents had arranged to have certain medical supplies from their lab shipped to the palace and loaded along with the other cargo. Never one to waste an opportunity, Stella had hidden a box of her own clothing, food, water, and a few toiletries among her parents' things. Having memorized where each portion of the ship's cargo was stored from the manifest, she knew she could get to it quickly, before anyone unpacked it and noticed the additional items.

So far, everything—well, everything except for her panic attack—was going according to plan. After she set up camp, all she had to do was stay out of sight until the ship reached the uncharted lands. Only then would she reveal herself, when there was no chance the ship would turn around to take her home.

She wondered how long it would be before the ship launched and imagined standing at one of the windows watching the ship rise, the rush of excitement she'd feel as the ground dropped away from her feet.

She'd watched the *Iron Glory* make test flights in the months leading up to the voyage. Right before dawn, when the world was still dark and the stars were just beginning to fade, she'd stumble out of bed, dragging a thick cotton blanket behind her. After a quick stop in the kitchen for a cup of cocoa, she would slip out to the backyard while her parents slept or worked in the lab.

The ship would take off from a field behind the factory where workers had spent the last year and a half building it, which just so happened to be visible from Stella's yard. Sitting on the cold, dew-soaked grass with her blanket wrapped around her shoulders, Stella would squint up into the distance, admiring the dozens of lanterns illuminating the main deck. So captivated was she by the sight of the great airship rising into the sky amid clouds of billowing steam that Stella didn't care that her pajama bottoms would be soaked by the time she got up. She was too busy pretending that the ship was a fallen star rejoining its brothers and sisters in the sky.

Maybe that was why the airship fascinated her. In one of the old languages, Stella's name also meant "star," and it made her feel connected to the ship, as if they both belonged in the sky. It was a fanciful thought, and Stella didn't usually think about impossible things like that, except on those nights when she watched the *Iron Glory* fly.

On those nights, it'd been easy to believe in the impossible.

Daydreaming, Stella closed her eyes and let the ship's engines lull her into a half sleep. She wondered what the Hiterian Mountains would look like from the air. In the North, people told stories of rivers of crystal-blue ice running through them like veins, of the sun reflecting off the unbroken snow so brightly it could strike a person blind. There was even talk of hidden cities, people who made their homes in the cold wasteland at the heart of the mountain range, where it was thought that no living thing could survive. Stella knew they were just campfire tales, but still, a tingle of excitement ran down her spine when she thought of what they might see from their high vantage point.

Lost in her imagination, she drifted into a deep sleep.

A sonorous *boom* jerked Stella awake. For a moment, she froze in confusion, taking in the unfamiliar surroundings. She'd forgotten where she was. Then it all came back to her in a rush. The windows on the wall above her didn't offer much light, and she couldn't tell where the sound had come from. She glanced around the small space, disoriented and frightened that she might have been discovered. Had the palace guards decided to search the ship after the false fire? Were they about to drag her out from behind the crates?

Stella went very still. She listened, but there were no footsteps, and she didn't hear the booming sound again. The cargo bay was quiet except for the deep, constant rumble of the ship's engines.

It'd probably been someone passing through the cargo bay, Stella reasoned. The crew would be very active now. She had no idea how long she'd been asleep, but she could tell by the bobbing motion of the ship and the slight churning in her stomach that they were in the air. Stella scowled to herself. All that excitement and she'd missed the takeoff completely.

How could she have been careless enough to nod off?

The stress of carrying out her plan, combined with the fact that she hadn't slept at all the previous night, must have exhausted her more than she'd realized.

Still, the sound she'd heard troubled her. It hadn't been loud, but it'd been deep and so . . . close. Cautiously, Stella rose to her feet and stepped out from her hiding place. The cargo bay was deserted. No one was working down here. The sound must have come from the engine room.

Stella moved along the rows of crates toward the staircase. Maybe someone had dropped a tool and that had made the booming sound.

No, that wasn't right. Now that Stella was fully awake, her memory was coming back. It hadn't been a mechanical sound, but some kind of pulse. She'd felt it reverberate in her bones. She probably wouldn't have if she hadn't been sleeping near the wall.

When she reached the base of the stairs, Stella hesitated. She'd promised herself she wouldn't risk going near where the crew would be. Secrecy was vital to the success of her plan. If anyone came out of there and into the hallway, she would be seen, and the ship's security team wouldn't rest until they'd rooted the stowaway out of her hiding place.

But what if the sound signaled a problem with the ship? What if no one else had heard it, and even now, pressure was building in one of the boilers, threatening to explode? Stella gripped the rail tightly and gazed up at the dark silhouette of the doorway that led into the hall.

Maybe she'd just take a quick look, make sure all was well.

Slowly, Stella climbed the stairs, straining to hear footsteps or nearby voices. All too quickly, she reached the top. On either side of the landing was a support column as wide as her body. Stella hid behind the left one, built up her courage, and then slowly peered around the column into the hall.

Her heart stood still.

In the middle of the hallway, partially hidden by the clouds of steam seeping up from the engine room, was a boy.

THREE

Stella swallowed a gasp and slid into a crouch behind the column, trying to make her body as small as possible. Luckily, the boy didn't appear to have seen or heard her. When Stella's vision adjusted to the dim gaslights flickering along the walls, she realized that the boy's eyes were closed. His brow was furrowed tight, as if he was concentrating—or in pain.

While she watched, afraid to move for fear of discovery, the boy slowly turned to face the wall that separated the hallway from the engine room. He lifted his hands and pressed his palms flat against the wall. He swayed, as if unsteady on his feet.

Stella's mind whirled with questions. What in the world was going on here? Who was this boy, and what was he doing on the ship? Did the crew know he was aboard? Stella guessed that this boy was about her age.

He had dark hair and wore an old, stained knapsack on his back.

Could he be another stowaway? Stella bit her lip in consternation. Nowhere in her plans had she allowed for something like that. Who would? *Two* stowaways on the same ship? What were the odds?

And such a strange stowaway. He was in plain sight, standing there in the hallway. His hands pressed against the wall as if he were trying to push through it, and yet, at the same time, he seemed vulnerable, as if the wall were the only thing holding him upright. Was he injured or about to faint? For a moment, Stella's healer instincts took over, and she took a half step toward the boy before she stopped herself.

Bad idea, Stella. She didn't know anything about him. She couldn't just jump out from behind the column and yell, *Hold it right there!*

So she stayed where she was, muscles tense, waiting to see what the boy would do.

The minutes ticked past, and Stella's uneasiness grew. They were so exposed here, too close to the busy areas of the ship. She was beginning to think the boy would stay there as still as a statue forever.

And then his hands began to *glow*.

Stella gaped as pale golden light outlined the boy's fingers and shot up his wrists all the way to his elbows. The gaslights on the wall danced and guttered, as if the light was somehow sucking power from them. Stella must have gasped, because finally, the boy moved, turning his head in her direction.

He opened his eyes.

They were also glowing.

Golden radiance completely obscured the whites and irises of the boy's eyes, spilling down his cheeks like shimmering tears. The light was so bright that Stella flinched and pushed back from the column, teetering dangerously close to the edge of the stairs. She wanted to turn and run, but fear filled her boots with lead. All she could do was stand and stare at the boy.

Could he see her? Through that blinding glow, it was impossible to tell.

"Wh-what's going on?" Stella's voice barely rose above a whisper. "Who are you?"

"It's . . . all . . . r-right," the boy said haltingly. His gaze fixed on her as he spoke, but the light in his eyes was too intense. It made Stella's own eyes water, and she had to look away. "Just d-don't . . . touch me. *Please.*" The boy gasped out the last word, his voice weakening.

The *please* made a tiny crack in the veil of terror that had fallen over Stella, and again her healer's instincts took over. She squared her shoulders, pushed aside her fear, and swept him with an assessing look. "Are you hurt?" she asked. "What's happening to you?"

"I'm f-fine." The boy spoke with a slight accent Stella

couldn't place—northern Merrow Kingdom, maybe. He stood up straight, lifting his hands from the wall, and the golden light slowly faded from his skin. His eyes darkened to a rich brown. They were actually quite pretty, Stella thought, but she didn't have time to appreciate them, for suddenly they rolled back in the boy's head. He was about to pass out.

Without thinking, Stella darted forward and caught him, her arms encircling his chest. That was a mistake. He sagged against her, and his weight dragged them both down. Scrambling aside so he wouldn't fall on her, Stella managed to protect the boy's head by propping it against her shoulder. They both kept sliding until she ended up on her knees in the middle of the hallway with the boy flat on his back, his head awkwardly cradled in her lap.

The whole thing happened so fast that shock replaced most of Stella's terror. What in the world was going on here? She was tempted to pinch herself to see if she was dreaming. But Stella knew what she'd seen. The boy had been *glowing*, as if lit from within by a powerful lantern. How was that possible?

Stella considered her options. She had some spirits of hartshorn in her alchemy case, a concoction of ammonia and deer horn whose fumes might be pungent enough to wake the boy, but if he was badly hurt, the shock to his system could be dangerous. She made a quick inspection of his head and chest but found no injuries, and when she checked the pulse at his neck, it was strong. That was a good sign. Having nothing else to go on, Stella guessed that exhaustion had caused him to pass out.

But what had exhausted him? Was it that strange light spilling from his hands and eyes? A chill passed through Stella at the memory of the boy staring at her with that blinding gold gaze. She'd lived in Noveen her entire life, and in that time, she'd encountered many people who were different from her. There were the sarnuns with their tentacle-like feelers and their gift of speaking mind to mind. And the chamelins shifted their bodies from human shape to lizard-like creatures with wings. Yet this boy had just done something she'd never seen before. It frightened and fascinated her at the same time.

Come on, Stella, concentrate, she chided herself. She could figure things out once she was safe in the cargo bay. Any moment, one of the crew could come walking down the hallway and discover them. She looked down at the unconscious boy. "If you won't wake up on your own, I'm going to have to drag you," she whispered, half hoping her voice might make him stir. But the boy remained inert, his shaggy dark hair hanging in his eyes.

Dressed in plain black trousers and a shirt, with a gray linen vest that had been patched many times with crooked stitches and different colors of fabric, he looked tall. Although he was not much bigger than she was, Stella already knew he was heavy.

She considered the steep flight of stairs standing between them and her hiding place back in the cargo bay. A weary sigh escaped her. "Well, this is going to be interesting," she said.

It took time, but Stella managed to drag the boy's dead weight down to the cargo bay. The stairs seemed to go on forever, and by the time she limped to the bottom, she was spent.

She had to wrench the back row of crates farther away from the wall to create space for them both in her hideout, and there still wasn't much room to maneuver, but Stella eventually managed to lay the boy out on the floor near the wall, and she sat down beside him, her back against one of the crates. Now that they were out of sight and out of immediate danger, Stella relaxed.

But she wouldn't let herself rest for long. Scooting closer to the boy, she stripped the dirty knapsack off his back so that he could lie more comfortably. Then, making sure he was still fast asleep, she left him while she went in search of the crates of medical supplies where she'd stashed the rest of her own belongings.

Stella pulled out a copy of the cargo list she'd transcribed from one sent to her parents, and set off in search of where the exact crates were stored. As she walked the aisles, she noted where others of interest were located, too. If she was careful, she could pilfer small quantities of food from the ship's supplies without anyone being the wiser, but she'd also brought her own store of food and water. Once she'd found the correct crate with her supplies, she opened it as quietly as possible, pulled them out, and then repacked the medical equipment so that it would look as if nothing had been disturbed.

When she returned to her hideout, the boy was still unconscious, but at least he hadn't moved or made a sound to alert someone to his presence. Stella sat down beside him and unpacked a couple of blankets from her supplies, covering him with one of them and using the other as a pillow that she wedged beneath his head. Then she lit a candle, as the sunlight from the cargo bay windows was slowly fading into night. Soon it would be pitch-black in her tiny corner, and Stella was *not* going to spend her first night here curled up in a trembling ball. Just to be safe, she lit an extra candle, filling the small space with warm, buttery light. That done, she turned her attention back to the boy's condition.

His eyelids fluttered slightly in his sleep. Stella wondered, if she lifted one of them, would she be blinded by that golden light she'd seen earlier? She shivered and drew her hand back.

Oh, stop being so squeamish! She was a healer and an alchemist, and she needed to analyze the situation without letting her fear get in the way.

No, the boy's eyes would likely be normal, she decided, because his hands were no longer glowing. Stella lifted a corner of the blanket to uncover his right hand. She laid her own palm over his and gasped in surprise.

His hand was warm, much warmer than the rest of his body. Stella's skin tingled where she touched him, as if dozens of tiny needles were pricking her fingers. She jerked her hand back, rubbing her fingers together to dispel the sensation. Wherever that gold light had come from, it was still affecting the boy somehow.

Unsure of what to do next, Stella reached for her alchemy case, but her gaze fell on the knapsack lying beside the boy on the floor. Maybe there was some clue to his identity hidden in there.

She grabbed the sack and unknotted the leather cord that held it shut. When she peered in, her brow furrowed in confusion. She'd expected to find survival supplies similar to what she'd brought with her, but besides a single food pack, a couple of rumpled shirts, and an extra pair of trousers, there were only three other items.

She pulled them out one at a time. The first was a neatly folded bundle of shimmering black cloth, much finer and more cared for than the wadded-up shirts she'd put to the side or the tattered clothes the boy wore. Stella laid the bundle down to inspect later. Next was a piece of paper that looked as if it had been folded and refolded hundreds of times until it was about to fall apart. Finally, at the very bottom of the sack was a small, round object about the size of a walnut shell but much heavier.

When Stella held it up to the candlelight, she realized it was a tiny statue fashioned in the shape of a beetle.

At first glance, the figure appeared to be made of iron, but examining it more closely, Stella noticed the metal had a distinctly reddish sheen to it, which suggested tarnished copper. But she was no metallurgist and therefore couldn't be sure. The artist who'd made the piece had put an astonishing amount of detail into the design. Its outer wings shimmered red, while the beetle's head glinted a lighter shade, almost pink. The antennae jutting from it were so thin and delicate that Stella was afraid they would break off in her hand. She gently touched one of the beetle's legs with the tip of her finger and was surprised to find that it felt quite strong. She almost believed that if she set the little statue on the floor, it would skitter away.

But why have something like this when he carried so little else with him? It must be a keepsake or something important to the boy, for though it was beautiful, Stella could see no practical use for it. Carefully, she set the beetle down on the floor—looking back at it once just to make sure that it wasn't actually going to scurry away— and reached for the bundle of black cloth.

The fabric was beautiful, dark and glittering like a star field on a cloudless night, but it had a strange, *wrong* texture. It puddled in her lap, slicker and heavier than cloth should be. Up close, it looked as if hair-thin strands of metal had somehow been woven into the fabric. Stella gently shook it out to get a better look.

Unfolded, she was surprised to find that the piece of cloth was actually a bodysuit, similar to what a bee-keeper might wear. Long, thick sleeves ended at the wrist in a pair of detachable gloves, and trousers flared at the ankles as if to cover the wearer's shoes. A hood attached to the back of the shirt collar, and from that, a veil came down over the face, thin enough to see through. Hook and eye clasps ran up and down the back of the suit so that a person could step into and out of the outfit easily.

Stella couldn't even begin to guess what the boy thought he needed with a beekeeper's suit on board an airship bound for the Hiterian Mountains. They were thousands of miles from the nearest bee.

Confused and frustrated, she reached for the last item, the worn piece of paper. An impressive collection of mysteries about the boy swirled in her head, and she could only hope that the paper might explain at least one of them.

Unfolding and smoothing the creased paper out on the floor, Stella found a short note written in Trader's Speech, the most common language in Solace, although, the words were so sloppy she could barely read them, as if the person who'd written the note had been in a terrible hurry.

I hope you find this because it means you got away. I'm so sorry. We couldn't wait. I'll tell them everything. It's my fault. I'm so sorry.

The letter was unsigned—questions piling on questions—and another mystery added to the list.

Stella rummaged in the bottom of the knapsack to make sure there was nothing else, but other than the extra clothes and food, those three objects appeared to be the sum total of everything the boy owned. Looking from the beetle to the cryptic note and then to the bee-keeper suit, Stella sighed helplessly.

He was a stowaway, and he glowed with a strange power she'd never seen before. Whatever he was doing here, it could mean trouble for the ship and its crew.

She needed answers, and the only way she was going to get them was to talk to the boy.

Quietly, Stella opened her alchemy case and searched among the packets of herbs and powders until she found the vial containing spirits of hartshorn. The healer in her still wanted to let the boy rest and recover his strength, but a stronger warning hummed in her veins that she couldn't ignore.

That didn't mean she'd act recklessly. In addition to the spirits of hartshorn, Stella removed a round metal compact from her case. It was small enough to hide in her right hand, and the clasp that held it shut was easy to manipulate. She could open and close it one-handed in less than a second. Inside the compact was her best weapon of self-defense. With it in her right hand and the spirits of hartshorn in her left, Stella began to feel a bit more confident in what she was about to do.

Before she could change her mind, Stella uncorked the vial and held it under the boy's nose, releasing the scent of the spirits.

≫ FOUR ⩽

The pungent vapors of the hartshorn worked instantly. The boy jerked awake, coughing and sputtering, his head whipping from side to side as he tried to take in his surroundings. When his gaze found Stella, his chest heaved. Panic filled his eyes, like a wild animal staring at an open cage.

Despite her own anxiety, Stella felt a rush of sympathy for the boy. She hated to see anyone so afraid. "It's all right," she whispered, setting the vial on the floor and laying a hand on the boy's shoulder to stop him from thrashing and throwing off the blanket. "You're safe. You're all right."

Quick as a lightning strike, his hand came out from beneath the blanket and snatched her wrist. He yanked her forward until their noses were almost touching.

"What happened?" The boy's voice was raspy from sleep and fear. "Where am I?"

"Let me go!" Stella yelped, trying to squirm out of his grip. She held the compact in her free hand, but she didn't dare use the weapon this close to him, not without risking its effects on herself.

The boy didn't move, and Stella berated herself for being so careless. She shouldn't have woken him so suddenly. Now, with the crate at her back and the boy right in her face, she had no easy escape if he decided to attack her in the small space. Again, she tried to jerk free, but the boy only tightened his grip. What was she going to do now?

The boy stared at her while she struggled, and gradually, his dark brown eyes lost some of their panic and wildness. Maybe he realized there was no immediate danger, or maybe he noticed that she was starting to panic too, for suddenly, he released her and sat up, scooting back against the wall. The blanket she'd covered him with tangled around his waist. He glanced down at it, his forehead furrowed in confusion, and then he looked back up at Stella.

Silence fell over the cargo bay while the two of them studied each other. With the boy pressed against the wall and Stella leaning into the crate, it was as if someone had drawn an invisible line between them. In Stella's mind, that line said, *Do not cross or there will be trouble.* She opened her mouth a couple of times to say something, but each time she couldn't get any words out. The boy didn't try to speak at all. He simply watched her, his gaze sharp, as if she were a puzzle and he were trying to assemble all the pieces at once.

Finally, Stella couldn't stand it any longer. She crossed her arms over her stomach, rubbing her wrist, which still ached from where he'd grabbed it. "Are you going to hurt me?" she blurted out, voicing her biggest concern first. She readied the compact, just in case.

Hearing the question, the boy's expression changed dramatically, his face crumpling and his eyes widening in shock. "No!" he said, and then, in a quieter tone, "Of course not. Why would you think . . ." His voice trailed off as he noticed her now cradling her wrist. His eyes softened at the corners. "I'm sorry. I didn't mean to hurt you."

His apology certainly sounded sincere. Then again, he might say anything to try to put her at ease.

Her expression must have betrayed her inner suspicion, because the boy raised his hands as if he was surrendering and tried to move even farther away from her, but the wall behind him wouldn't allow it. More slowly now, he took in their surroundings. "Where are we?" he asked. "Is this the cargo bay?"

"Yes," Stella said shortly. Now that she'd gotten over some of her fear, she remembered that she wanted answers too. She wasn't interested in his questions. "What are you doing on this ship?" she demanded.

The boy had been looking her in the eye, but now his

gaze dropped. He rested his hands in his lap and seemed to be thinking over how to answer her.

Or how to lie.

"I know you're not part of the crew. You don't belong here," she stated preemptively.

"Fair point," he said at last. "You're right. I'm not part of the crew, and I *really* don't belong here." A smile tugged at his mouth, as if he was laughing at a private joke. But the grin faded quickly, and a shrewd look came into his eyes that Stella didn't like. "You know, I could accuse *you* of the same things," he said. "There aren't supposed to be any kids on this ship, so you shouldn't be here either. You snuck on board just like I did, and now you're hiding, just like I am. Isn't that right?"

Stella gritted her teeth. Well, he'd figured that out fast. "What's your name?" she asked, ignoring his question.

"Cyrus," the boy answered, a little too quickly.

Stella raised an eyebrow. "Is that your real name?"

He hesitated and then shook his head. "No."

Now Stella was annoyed. "We're never going to get anywhere with fake names and questions you won't answer," she said.

"I agree," Cyrus said. Then, unexpectedly, he grinned at her. "Maybe we should stop the interrogation right here."

"I'm not *interrogating* you," she snapped, but that

only made him smile wider. Stella's cheeks burned with anger and embarrassment. Was he laughing at her? Did he think this was all a big joke? "I don't know who you are, but if you're here to stop this ship or hurt anyone on it, I swear I'll turn you in," she said, knowing as she spoke the words that they were true. "I don't care if it means they find me too."

"I—" The boy stopped and stared at her flushed face in surprise. "I believe you," he said, and he wasn't grinning anymore. "But why would you think I'm here to hurt the ship?"

"Isn't it obvious?" Stella gestured to the metal walls surrounding them. "This ship—this whole expedition— only came about because of a joint agreement between the Merrow Kingdom and the Dragonfly territories. We're exploring the world together and maintaining the peace back home at the same time."

But there were still those in both kingdoms who weren't so quick to forget the Iron War. The war had ended in a treaty—with no clear winner on either side— after the death of old King Easmon Merrow. On the day his son formally ascended to the throne, he immediately pushed for peace talks, an end to all the suffering. Unlike his warmongering father, the new king had no desire to invade and conquer their southern neighbor.

King Aron of the Dragonfly territories had agreed to the talks, and after a long, drawn-out negotiation, the war came to an end. The resource it had been fought over—precious iron—would be traded openly between the two kingdoms again, and the Merrow Kingdom agreed to reduce the size of its military and weapons manufacturing. Widespread relief accompanied the announcement of the outcome, but it would take the land and the people a long time to heal, and not everyone was ready to forgive and move forward.

Stella recalled that there had even been protests reported outside the royal palaces of Merrow and Dragonfly in the weeks leading up to the *Iron Glory*'s launch. Some dissenters called the expedition a fool's mission undertaken with the enemy.

"If someone wanted the Merrow Kingdom and the Dragonfly territories to go to war again, sabotaging this expedition would be the best way to do it," Stella said pointedly.

"I see." Cyrus regarded her thoughtfully. "But if you were worried I was here to hurt the ship, you could have easily turned me in to the crew while I was unconscious. Yet you didn't. Maybe that means you really don't think I'm a threat. Or maybe just a little threat?" He held up two fingers an inch apart.

Stella frowned. If nothing else, he was a very pushy boy. "I'm still deciding," she said.

"Would it make any difference if I told you I could actually *help* the expedition?" Cyrus asked, wearing a hopeful expression now.

Help them? The boy with the lying tongue, the

annoying grin, and hands that spontaneously glowed? No, Stella hadn't considered that possibility, though it was the best lie he could have used to try to gain her trust.

"It *might* help if you'd explain what you were doing in that hallway and why your hands and eyes were lit up like suns when I first saw you," Stella said.

A much heavier silence fell over the cargo bay this time.

"Ahhhh," Cyrus said, drawing out the word as if he'd suddenly forgotten how to put a sentence together. "Yes, you've got a *great* point there. That light probably scared you, didn't it?"

Stella nodded vigorously.

"So if I could explain my . . . er . . . my trick . . . would it make you feel better?"

Again, Stella nodded, though she thought he was only stalling.

"It's nothing dangerous," Cyrus assured her. He held out his hands, palms up. A flash of light passed over his skin and vanished, as if he'd caught a sunbeam and then just as quickly let it go. "It's a power I have. I can shield things, strengthen them—that's what the gold light is. I was using it to try to protect the ship, specifically the engine room."

"How?" Stella whispered, fascinated and unsettled by the brief reappearance of the gold light. Was that what had made the sound that had woken her earlier—the strange pulse she'd felt? "How does it work?" she asked.

"The power comes from inside me, and then I twist and turn it to the size and shape I need. Sometimes it feels like I'm building a wall or a net. I can't really explain it any better than that," Cyrus said, lowering his hands. "It's just something I've always been able to do."

But Stella had a feeling he could explain more. He just didn't want to. He was hiding something. "Why were you trying to protect the engine room?" she prodded. "And why did your power make you pass out?"

"Oh, that." Cyrus flexed his fingers, making Stella wonder if they were still hot to the touch. "It was just a precaution. I was trying to put a permanent shield around the engine room because if something were to go wrong on the ship, that's where it's most likely to happen. It didn't work, though. The engine room is too big for me to shield for the whole trip. I fed too much of my power into it, and it weakened me. I don't usually pass out, but I couldn't help it this time. Also, I sort of have to shut out the world while I'm using it. It takes me a few minutes to come back afterward, so I'm . . . not good for much else. I'm rather helpless."

By the look on Cyrus's face, Stella guessed that helpless wasn't a condition he enjoyed. He was silent for a minute, and then he rolled his shoulders back and forth, as if shaking off something unpleasant. He fixed another grin on his face. "So, now that the interrogation's over," he said, "have you decided whether you're going to turn me in?"

Stella didn't know what to say. Hearing him describe his strange power, she was almost as unsettled as she'd been when she saw his glowing eyes.

Yet, for some reason, she sensed he wasn't dangerous. Evasive—yes. Irritating—definitely. But now that he was awake and coherent, she was sure that whatever else happened, he *wasn't* going to hurt her. Maybe it was because he'd expressed such shock when she'd suggested it. Or that he'd teased her about questioning him.

But even if Cyrus didn't intend to hurt her, he was almost certainly lying to her, and that could turn out to be just as bad.

"Give me one good reason why I shouldn't," she said.

Cyrus cleared his throat and gave her a solemn look. Or maybe he was just being dramatic. Hard to tell. "Because the *Iron Glory* will never make it over the Hiterian Mountains without me," he said.

She'd been prepared to listen to a reasonable argument, but at that announcement, Stella felt her mouth fall open in disbelief. "How can you say that?" she demanded. "Do you have any idea what this ship is capable of? It's the first long-range flying vessel of its size ever built—and by the best machinists in Solace!"

"By the best craftspeople, you mean," Cyrus corrected her. "The Merrow Kingdom and their machinists designed it, yes, but the pieces were put together by common laborers in Noveen's factories."

Stella threw up her hands in frustration. "The point is you don't know what you're talking about. The *Iron Glory* is the greatest ship ever built."

"Hang on, let's not talk crazy here. I agree it's a *decent* ship," Cyrus said, a cocky grin spreading across his face. He splayed his fingers against the floor, like a healer resting his hand against a patient's heartbeat. "I ought to know; I was one of those factory workers who helped build it."

"You?" Stella sputtered. "Worked on the *Iron Glory*? *You* did? Then how can you say—"

"I said she's a good ship, just not the best in Solace." Cyrus's patronizing grin made Stella want to throw him out a window. "Look, it doesn't matter," he added. "I swear it won't survive the journey without my help. You hand me over to the crew and they'll lock me away somewhere for being a stowaway. If they do that, I can't help. That's all there is to it."

"Prove it," Stella challenged him. "You say we're doomed without your help, so tell me why, *and* prove to me that you won't be the cause of whatever's going to happen."

"That part's easy," Cyrus said. "In about five days, the *Iron Glory* is going to run into an ice storm over the mountains. So unless you think I can control the weather, you'll see that the danger has nothing to do with me."

"I don't see how you can predict ice storms either," Stella said. "But this ship has been designed to navigate through the most extreme temperatures and climates."

Cyrus shook his head, and the haunted look that came into his eyes chilled Stella through her skin and straight down to her bones. "You've never seen a storm like this," he said softly. "You've never felt wind gusts that could knock you off your feet, ice shards that cut skin. The reason I know we're going to run into a storm is because the storm is *always* there, hanging over miles and miles of the Hiterian Mountains like a permanent cloud of death. It's the reason why no explorers have ever made it over the mountains. None of you are prepared for what you're about to face."

He was frightening her now, and Stella hated being frightened. She preferred anger to fear. Anger didn't paralyze her. Anger spurred her to act—sometimes rashly, but at least it meant she was *doing* something. "If it's that bad, what makes you think *you're* prepared for this storm?" she asked, her voice choked as she battled through her fear.

"Because I've already been through it once," Cyrus said, "when I traveled here from what you call the uncharted lands."

≈ FIVE ≈

At Cyrus's declaration, Stella burst out laughing. It was completely absurd, without a doubt the most outrageous lie she'd ever heard, and nothing less than what she'd expected from the irritating boy.

Yet, instead of joining in with her laughter and admitting that he'd pushed the joke too far, Cyrus just stared at her, his expression serious and a little bit sorrowful.

In the face of that, Stella's laughter died. No, it couldn't be true. He was just playing with her, laughing at her again. She could feel her anger stirring. "You're a liar," she said.

Cyrus shook his head. "I'm not lying—" He paused. "What's your name? You never told me."

It was the last thing Stella had expected him to ask. She considered lying about her name, just as he had, but what would be the point? *She* had nothing to hide. "Stella Glass," she said.

"Nice to meet you, Stella Glass." He held out his hand for her to shake. She hesitated, then took it. "I promise you I'm not lying, and I'm not here to hurt anyone," Cyrus said. "I'm just trying to get home."

Stella sifted through her scattered thoughts, trying to ignore the imprint of heat Cyrus had left on her hand. It wasn't a painful sensation, but it was an unsettling reminder that something wasn't right about him.

But what if he was right about the storm? If it hit when he'd predicted, the ship would be deep in the Hiterian Mountains where no one had ever been. She knew from her studies in school that many explorers had tried to hike over the mountains to see what lay on the other side, and the few who hadn't been killed in the attempt had returned describing impassable heights, avalanches, and freezing temperatures that no human, chamelin, sarnun, or other being would be able to withstand. Seen in that light, the boy's story about a storm to end all storms didn't seem so far-fetched.

But if he was telling the truth about the storm, that meant he was also telling the truth about being from the uncharted lands, and that was a revelation that left Stella's head spinning.

"All right, let's pretend—*pretend*," she emphasized, "that I believe you. How did you get here from the uncharted lands?"

"On an airship like this one," Cyrus said. "Well, maybe not *exactly* like this one, but close enough. My people came in secret on three different expeditions spread over five years."

Five years? Stunned, Stella tried to imagine it. If he was being honest, that meant that the entire time people on her side of the world had been preparing to mount an expedition to the uncharted lands, there had already been strangers from that mysterious place in her part of Solace.

Although if she could put aside her shock and look at the situation logically, was it so hard to believe? Surely there must be explorers in the uncharted lands, just like there were in the territories. And they were bound to be just as curious about what lay on the other side of the mountains as Stella's people.

"But where's your ship?" she asked. "And why hide yourselves? Why didn't you just tell us you were here?"

"Because we weren't sure what to expect," Cyrus explained. "And we didn't know how you'd react. My people have explored other lands before yours. Their first expedition went to a group of islands far away in our northern sea. They went in airships, and when they landed on the beaches, the people there were afraid. They'd never seen an airship before, nothing close to that level of technology. Because they were scared, they attacked the explorers and drove them away. So now, whenever we go to new lands, instead of just barging in and introducing ourselves, we hide our ships and try to blend in, observe, and report what we find." His face clouded, as if he was remembering something painful. "I came over on the final expedition a year ago, but something happened and . . . I wasn't able to go back with the rest of the explorers, so I looked for another way home.

"When I found out King Aron was building the *Iron Glory* for an expedition to the uncharted lands, I knew I had to be on board. I got a job at the factory where the ship was being built so I could get familiar with it, find places to hide. I wanted to be ready when the time came."

That didn't prove his story, but it explained how he'd gotten on board, Stella thought. If he'd worked at the factory and helped build the ship, he probably knew his way around it as well—if not better—than she did.

"So that's why I'm here," Cyrus said. His expression had turned bleak. "I have a family in the uncharted lands. They might think I'm dead. I *have* to return to them, no matter what it takes."

Hearing the conviction in his words, Stella again felt a rush of sympathy for the boy. Everything he'd told her, outrageous as it sounded, had the ring of truth. She *wanted* to believe he was really from the uncharted lands.

Maybe that was the problem—she wanted to believe his story too much. What if she was wrong? What if the powers he claimed to have were really just an elaborate trick?

In that moment, Stella found herself wishing more than anything that her parents were here to help her. Even though they were just three decks above her, down a twisting corridor to the medical bay, they might as well have been a hundred miles away. But if there was danger, their lives and the lives of the rest of the crew might just depend on the decision she was about to make.

Restless and worried, Stella rose to her feet. She did her best thinking when she could pace, but the tiny camp didn't give her much room to get a good circuit going. Stupid, cramped space. Already she hated it.

"What are you doing?" Cyrus asked. He also stood up, but Stella could see he was shaky on his feet.

"I'm thinking," she said, scowling at him. "Don't interrupt."

His expression darkened. "You're going to turn me in, aren't you? After everything I told you, you still think I'm lying!"

"I didn't say that," Stella snapped. "It'd just be nice if you could give me a little more proof, that's all."

"I don't believe this!" Cyrus banged his fist against a crate. "We're on a ship full of explorers who *want* to find people from the uncharted lands. If you'd stop being stubborn and afraid for five minutes, you'd see that you've found one!" He sighed and raked a hand through his tousled hair. "Look, I'm sorry," he said. "I didn't want it to come to this. I wanted you to trust me, but the truth is, I won't let you turn me in. I've come too far to have you stop me."

Stella's stomach did a flip, but she forced herself not to betray her fear. She raised an eyebrow. "Oh, really? Just a few minutes ago you said you wouldn't hurt me."

He scowled fiercely. "I'm *not* going to hurt you," he said. "Just stop you, that's all."

"I see." Casually, Stella put her hands behind her back and released the clasp on the compact. "And how are you going to do that, exactly?"

"Well, I am bigger than you," Cyrus said, stating the obvious.

"Hmmm." Stella cocked her head, pretending to consider that, when really she was gauging the distance between them, trying to decide if she should use the compact now or try to get farther away from him. "So your plan is to . . . what? Keep me tied up in the cargo bay for the whole journey to the uncharted lands? That seems a bit harsh, don't you think?"

Now he was flustered, his face turning bright red. "I haven't ironed out all the details yet," he said, taking a step forward.

Too close, Stella thought.

In one quick move, she snapped the compact shut, turned, and took off running, scraping her shoulders as she squeezed through the narrow gap between the crates. Cyrus gave chase at once, but as he'd said, he was bigger, and so it took him longer to shove his way through the tight spot.

The cargo bay was like a maze, rows and rows of crates and equipment, with very little open space except in the center of the room, where the ship's massive gangplank rested. Weaving among these obstacles, Stella ran in the direction of the opposite wall, trying to outrun Cyrus while she came up with a plan. Unfortunately, Cyrus knew the ship as well as she did and could find his way around almost as easily. It was only a matter of time before he caught up to her. She just needed to get far enough away from him to use the compact safely.

But maybe she shouldn't be trying to outrun him at all. That gave Stella an idea. She turned left, ducking down the nearest row of crates. She grabbed the lip of one of them and hauled herself up, crouching on top. Quickly, she flipped open the lid of the compact, her hands shaking with nerves. Inside was a shallow dish filled to the brim with a greenish-white dust.

Cyrus flew around the corner, charging toward her just as she was taking a pinch of the dust between her thumb and forefinger. Careful not to inhale the stuff herself, Stella threw it down in a cloud that hit him squarely in the face.

Cyrus staggered back, waving his hands in front of

him, but he'd already inhaled most of the dust. "What did you—" But his words were lost in a fit of sneezing. He wiped his face. His eyes were red and streaming, which speared Stella with guilt, but she was also a little worried. The dust should have taken effect instantly. "What is this stuff?" he said, glaring up at her.

"Something I learned to make during my studies," Stella explained. The dust was a nasty substance in its own right, although those who used it weren't admirable people. Anything made from it should only be used when there was no other choice.

Cyrus's glare deepened to a look of absolute fury. "I've seen this. Slavers use it to paralyze their victims so they can capture them quietly. Is that what you're trying to do?"

"No!" Stella insisted. "I would never use it like slavers! I modified the ingredients and turned it into a knockout powder for self-defense."

"You . . . modified it? You mean you're an alchemist?" Cyrus blinked in surprise, forgetting that she had just attempted to immobilize him. With the remnants of the dust settling in his hair and eyebrows, his expression was almost comical, but the last thing Stella wanted to do was laugh.

"And a healer," she added defensively, though she didn't feel like one at that moment.

"I don't believe this." Cyrus took a step forward

and staggered, his legs giving out as the powder finally started to take effect. He fell to his knees, clutching the side of the nearest crate. He looked up at her, but behind the anger, a look of deep hurt shone in his eyes. "I'm such an idiot," he said, his voice trembling. "I thought maybe you were different, but you're just like him, just like all of them. I should have known."

Stella didn't know whom Cyrus was talking about, but his words were like knives. "I'm sorry," she said, "but you didn't give me a choice."

"Please." The boy cast around with a look of desperation, as if searching for something to save himself. He raised a hand toward her, though he was too far away to reach her. "The suit!" he cried. Hope replaced some of the desperation in his eyes. "Take it . . . Put it on. Move slowly . . . You'll s-see I'm telling the truth."

Then he fell forward onto the floor, out cold again.

For a moment, Stella just crouched on top of the crate, waiting to make sure he was truly unconscious. She closed the lid of the compact and sealed it, then climbed down from the crate and kneeled next to Cyrus to check his pulse. Still strong. He'd suffer no permanent harm from the dust.

But what was she going to do with him now?

If she turned Cyrus in, she would be giving herself up too. The ship was still close enough to Noveen that it would probably turn around and take them both back to the city for good. Her journey would end before it had truly begun.

She also wasn't sure what the crew would do with Cyrus. What was the punishment for stowing away on board an airship to the uncharted lands? What would happen to the mysterious boy and his strange stories?

A tiny voice inside her whispered, *What will happen if he was telling the truth?*

Stella let out a frustrated sigh, bent down, and, for the second time that day, dragged the unconscious boy back to her hiding place.

When they were safely behind the crates again, Stella immediately noticed Cyrus's knapsack, its contents scattered all over the floor. He must have tripped on it when he chased after her. The black beekeeper suit lay in a heap near her alchemy case.

Put it on. Move slowly. You'll see I'm telling the truth.

Cyrus's words echoed in her mind. What had he meant? How was the suit supposed to prove he was from the uncharted lands?

Stella walked over to the discarded garment and lifted it by the collar, holding it up in front of her. It was too large for her—she could tell by looking at it—but it would be easy enough to slip over her clothing.

Fine, but what if it was a trick? Stella instinctively held the garment as far away from her body as she could. Maybe the suit was some kind of trap the boy wanted her to fall into. But if that was its purpose, it was the most impractical trap in the world. It required the person to *willingly* put the suit on. And if it really was an elaborate snare, why would the boy choose to carry it and so little else with him? It didn't make sense.

Stella turned the suit over in her hands. Before she could talk herself out of it, she stuck her left arm into the sleeve. As she'd expected, the fabric glided smoothly over her clothing. Her hand emerged into the glove fastened to the end of the sleeve. Stella bent her arm and wiggled her fingers. So far, she felt normal, and there didn't seem to be anything sinister about the garment. Somewhat reassured, she put her right arm into the other sleeve and pulled the rest of the suit on over her clothes. Then she reached behind her to fasten up the back. Her hands worked awkwardly in the gloves, but finally she managed to secure all the clasps. She put on the garment's hood, tucking short, wispy black strands of hair behind her ears. Finally, she draped the gauzy veil over her face so that her entire body was hidden inside the strange suit.

Now what?

Stella stood there, holding her hands in front of her face, watching the starry black cloth shimmer in the candlelight. Waiting for something to happen. It was already warm in the cargo bay, but the suit quickly made the heat unbearable. Beads of sweat trickled down her face as she stood there, feeling more foolish with each passing minute.

The boy had just been toying with her, Stella thought. Frustrated and embarrassed, she reached up to tear the veil from her face.

And discovered that her hand and arm had vanished.

⇝ SIX ⇜

S tella stared at the place where her arm should have
been. She brought her hand close to her face. Slowly,
she flexed her fingers one by one. Nothing. Stella looked
down at herself and let out a shocked squeak at what she
saw—or rather *didn't* see.

Her whole body had vanished.

But that was impossible! No substance had the power
to make someone invisible. As far as she knew, not even
the archivists, who studied strange objects that fell in the
meteor storms up north, had ever encountered anything
like this.

Stella was sweating all over now. She clenched her
fists at her sides and forced herself to calm down and
think about the situation. So she was invisible, but how?
Maybe something in the suit's material—that strange,
lightweight metal that was woven into the fabric—was

mimicking her surroundings, causing her to blend in so completely that it looked like she'd disappeared.

Move slowly, Cyrus had said. Maybe that was a clue to how the suit worked. Stella raised her hand again, but instead of following Cyrus's instructions, she waved it back and forth in front of her face. A ripple passed through the air before her eyes, like a stone thrown into a still pond, and for just a second, she glimpsed the outline of her hand.

So that was the secret. Move slowly and the suit had time to shift itself to match whatever background she stood against. If she moved too quickly, the distortion in the air would cause her to reappear. The power had its limits, but the suit was still a marvel.

And an especially useful tool for sneaking on board an airship to return home to the uncharted lands.

Stella walked over to where Cyrus lay unconscious, still under the effects of the knockout powder. She looked down at him, imagining bright gold light spilling from his hands and eyes. He'd said he used it to shield things.

Now this wondrous suit had turned her invisible.

How much more proof did she need?

None, Stella decided. As outrageous as Cyrus's story was, she believed it. He really was from the uncharted lands. He'd come over the mountains in secret, and now he was trying to return home to his family. What was more, there was a storm out there getting closer and closer to the *Iron Glory* and its crew, and Cyrus was the only one who could get them through it safely. She couldn't turn him in. She had to take a chance and let him help.

Stella swallowed a spike of fear and prayed she was doing the right thing.

She removed the invisibility suit, folded it carefully, and put it back in Cyrus's knapsack, along with the rest of its spilled contents. Then she sorted through her supplies, taking a rough inventory of how much food and water there was and if she could stretch it for two people.

She'd brought a handful of apples, three oranges, and some cheese to eat early in the trip before they spoiled. Using a small pocketknife from her alchemy case, she sliced up one of the apples for her and Cyrus to share when he awakened. She also got out a wedge of yellow cheese, which she cut into bite-sized chunks. She put the food on a small metal plate she'd brought as part of her meal kit and opened one of her water containers so they'd have something to wash it all down with. It wasn't a feast by any means, but she'd been prepared to eat sparse meals for the next couple of weeks. Although considering the storm, she began to wonder if the journey wouldn't take longer than she'd anticipated.

Her stomach rumbled at the sharp, crisp scent of the apple, and Stella was just contemplating taking a slice when Cyrus stirred and opened his eyes. He blinked, blearily shaking off the effects of the dust. Suddenly, he bolted into a crouch, looking around as if he expected an enemy to leap out at him from one of the dark corners of the cargo bay.

His eyes rested on Stella and filled with confusion. "What's going on?" he asked. He sounded a little groggy, but Stella knew that would pass.

She held the plate of apples and cheese out to him, hoping that the offering of food would go a little way toward helping him forgive her for using the powder on him.

"Hungry?" she asked.

A growly noise answered her, coming from Cyrus's stomach. Stella smiled and waved the plate, inviting him to take some food. His gaze never leaving her face, Cyrus crawled over to the plate and grabbed an apple slice, then sat down across from her. He raised the fruit to his mouth but hesitated, his eyes narrowing, as if he thought the food might be poisoned.

Stella supposed she deserved that. She took a wedge of cheese, popped it into her mouth, and chewed. Once she'd finished, she ate an apple slice, savoring its tart juices. Swallowing, she glanced at Cyrus, one eyebrow raised as if to say, *See how I'm not trying to hurt you?*

It seemed to work. Cyrus stuffed the apple into his mouth, devouring it in quick chomps. With another pang of guilt, Stella wondered how long it had been since he'd last eaten.

They shared the food in silence for a few minutes while Stella tried to decide what to say to him. She was still coming to grips with the fact that he was from the uncharted lands, a part of Solace that was completely unknown. She had so many questions bubbling up inside her. What was it like where he lived? Was his home in a city or out in the wilderness? How big were the uncharted lands? Was everyone there human, like she and Cyrus, or were there sarnuns and chamelins too? It was impossible to decide what to ask first. Luckily, Cyrus saved her by speaking first.

"You didn't turn me in," he said. It sounded like a question.

Stella shook her head. "I put on the suit," she said, hoping that would explain things.

He'd been about to take another apple slice off the plate, but his hand froze midair. "You did?"

"The invisibility effect is astonishing." She took another apple slice and then slid the plate over to him to encourage him to eat more. "Is the material in the suit . . . magical?" She didn't know if that was the right word, but she couldn't think of another way to describe the mysterious substance that powered the garment.

"You could call it that," Cyrus said. "The suit is made of a material called aletheum. As far as I know, the substance doesn't exist in your part of Solace, so I guess it would seem like magic to you. Even we don't fully understand all the things it's capable of."

Magic. Stella's scalp prickled, and more questions crowded her mind. She could have asked dozens just about aletheum. An entirely new material. Was it metal? Cloth? A hybrid? What else was it used for?

Cyrus popped another wedge of cheese in his mouth, speaking around it. "Does this mean you believe me?" he asked.

Stella dragged herself out of her thoughts, met his eyes, and then looked at the floor. "Yes, I believe you," she said. "And I'm sorry I used the knockout powder on you."

He nodded, a look of relief softening his face. "I didn't give you much choice," he admitted, and Stella thought she heard a smile in his voice. "I'm impressed, actually. Not many people can catch me off guard like that."

Stella took the last apple slice off the plate, but she stopped before taking a bite. "Do you hear that?" she asked.

A high, keening whistle echoed from beyond the ship's walls. At first, Stella thought it was the wind, but then the sound changed, coming in short, quick bursts like pistol shots.

"It sounds like it's coming from the main deck,"

Cyrus said, standing and cocking his head to listen. "Maybe the crew is signaling someone to—"

"Wait," Stella said, holding up a hand to quiet him. "I think there's something else out there."

The whistling abruptly cut off, and now the air beyond the ship's walls was filled with the sound of furious wingbeats, like a swarm of locusts bearing down on them. Stella ran to the row of crates nearest the windows and shoved one of them flush against the wall. Climbing on top, she stood up so she could see what was happening outside. Cyrus scrambled up beside her.

"Oh, that can't be good," Stella said, her breath fogging the glass.

In the distance, a flock of birds arrowed straight toward the *Iron Glory*. Their bodies were the same pale silver as the moon, lighting up the darkness like frightful beacons. There must have been hundreds of them, each the size of a red-tailed hawk. As they got closer, though, Stella could see that their bodies were nothing at all like a hawk's. They were shaped more like fish, scaled, silver and wriggling, with membranous wings that tore through the air and brought the flock even with the ship.

"What are they?" Cyrus said, pressing his face to the glass, straining to see as the birds flew past the window.

"Nightcallers," Stella said. "They nest in the mountains and glow like they're filled with moonlight. Most times they fly at night, but I've never seen so many at once before. They're drawn to high-pitched sounds and bright colors because they mimic the colors and calls of the smaller birds they prey on. It puts them in a frenzy."

"So that whistle we heard—"

"Was like a dinner bell," Stella said. "Watch out!"

The birds were coming faster now, slamming against the hull of the ship, but one of them aimed straight for their window.

"Get down!" Stella jerked Cyrus to his knees as it punched right through the window, showering them with shards of glass.

Stella looked up in time to see the bird careening wildly around the cargo bay before it smashed into a crate and fell to the floor.

Jumping down, Stella ran to where it lay. The bird was stunned but clearly not dead. It flopped on its belly, wings spread crookedly across the floor.

"Careful," Cyrus said, coming up beside her. "Wow, those things are strong."

"And dangerous," Stella confirmed. She pointed to the thing's scaled body. "Their scales are like sandpaper or sharkskin. You can cut yourself handling them."

"Give me a second." Cyrus ran back to their hideout and emerged a moment later with one of his spare shirts. He tossed it over the stunned bird to quiet it, then carefully picked it up off the floor.

They went back to the window, and Stella carefully

swept the glass off the top of the crate. She held the bird beneath the shirt while Cyrus climbed up. Then she handed the bird to him so he could release it safely out the broken window.

Stella climbed up beside Cyrus just in time to see the bird dip and corkscrew through the air before rejoining its flock, which was now soaring up, higher above the ship.

Circling the *Iron Glory*'s gasbag.

"No!" Stella cried. Grabbing Cyrus's spare shirt, she punched out the remaining chunks of glass so she could lean out the window into the cold night wind, trying to get a glimpse of the gasbag.

"Careful!" Cyrus yanked her back inside. "Those things are still swarming."

"But their beaks are even sharper than their bodies!" Stella shrugged off his arm. "They'll tear up the gasbag in minutes if we don't get them away from the ship!"

She jumped off the crate and ran to get her alchemy case. Rummaging through it, she found her matches and a pair of small green cubes, which she stuffed into her trouser pockets. When she rejoined Cyrus, he was batting more of the birds away from the broken window, cursing as their scales sliced a long cut on his hand.

"Are you all right?" Stella looked at the gash, but it wasn't deep. She could help him bandage it later. "I'm going out there," she told him.

"What?" Cyrus grabbed her arm. "Are you crazy?"

"There's a ladder attached to the side of the ship, about two feet away from the window," Stella said, leaning out to show him. "I just need to get their attention, draw them away from the ship before they puncture the gasbag."

"Stella, the gasbag will be fine," Cyrus said, refusing to let go of her arm. "I told you I helped build this ship, remember? Well, I put some of the aletheum—the same material in the invisibility suit—into the ship's gasbag to strengthen it. The birds won't be able to peck through it."

"So you say, but have you ever seen a flock of nightcallers on the hunt?" Stella demanded, waving her arm out the window at the zigzagging birds.

Cyrus clenched his jaw. "No, but I—"

"Cyrus, my parents are on board this ship," Stella said, jerking free of his grasp.

That got his attention. Cyrus went very still. "I didn't know that," he said, his voice dropping.

A wind gust from the broken window blew Stella's hair around her face. She raked it back, reached in her pocket with her other hand, and pulled out the cubes. Fuses curled from their centers like cherry stems. "I didn't just stow away on the *Iron Glory* for the fun of it," she said. "I knew the expedition would be dangerous, but if I can help keep them safe, I'll do whatever it takes."

She climbed up onto the window ledge, and this time Cyrus didn't try to stop her. Bracing herself against the frame, and careful to avoid any more of the jagged glass shards, Stella leaned out into the darkness, wind, and screeching nightcallers.

SEVEN

Stella tried not to look down, but her eyes were irresistibly drawn to the yawning darkness spread out below her. Even with the aid of the moonlight and the dizzying glow of the flocking birds, she couldn't see all the way to the ground. Wisps of cloud drifted around the *Iron Glory*'s hull, and a freezing wind went deep into her lungs with every breath she took.

You're not going to fall, she told herself, though she knew it might turn out to be a lie.

"Cyrus," she called back through the window without turning around.

"I'm here." She felt his hand at her waist, bracing her against another wind gust. "Can you reach the ladder?"

"Yes," Stella said. The metal ladder was directly to her right, but at that moment, it seemed like it was a mile away. "Keep swatting the birds away if you can, but protect your hands."

Before she could change her mind, Stella flung out a hand and grabbed the closest ladder rung. The metal bar was freezing, and Stella wasn't wearing gloves. Not a good plan, but she wasn't backing down now. Leaning forward, she stepped off the window ledge and hauled herself onto the ladder.

Out in the open air, away from the protective heat of the cargo bay, she got very cold very quickly. Stella's whole body trembled and her teeth chattered. Nightcallers screeched in her ear, circling her head and skipping off the metal skin of the hull. Tightening her grip on the ladder, Stella forced herself to look up, not down, and began to climb.

The main deck was at least forty feet above her, but Stella didn't need to go all the way up there. For one thing, any crew members brave or stupid enough to be out on deck among the birds might see her, and for another, the closer she got to the heart of the flock, the more likely it was that they'd knock her off the ladder and the ship altogether.

She just needed to climb high enough to attract the flock's attention, and she couldn't do that hanging out the window below. The birds responded to high-pitched sounds, but they were also drawn to bright light, and luckily, Stella had something that could produce both.

The ladder creaked below her, drawing Stella's attention away from the nightcallers.

It was Cyrus. He'd climbed out the window and was coming up the ladder behind her.

"What are you doing?" Stella yelled, to be heard above the howling wind. "Get back inside!"

"I can't let you risk your neck out here alone!" Cyrus said, pulling himself up. "Besides, this ship is my only ticket home. I'm not letting it crash." He had his spare shirt balled up in his fist and used it to swat a nightcaller away from Stella's leg.

Stella didn't have time to argue with him. She kept climbing until she was about twenty feet up from the broken window. The nightcallers were so thick around her now she could barely see. She didn't think she could risk going any higher.

Hooking an arm around the ladder rung, Stella reached into her pocket and pulled out the matches and one of the cubes. Getting the match lit in this wind was going to be a challenge.

"Come up next to me," Stella called down to Cyrus, scooting over on the ladder to make room. When he was even with her, she held up the match, prepared to strike it against the ship's metal skin. "Once I get the fuse lit, it'll go off like a firework. I'll hold it as long as I can, then throw it and hope the nightcallers will see it and forget all about the gasbag."

Cyrus shook his head. "They'll swarm you," he said. "Let me do it. I can give you light without the fireworks." He waved his hand for emphasis.

Stella scowled at him. "And have you pass out and fall off the ship to your death? I don't think so. This'll work. Trust me."

Without waiting for him to agree, Stella struck the match, huddling over it to protect the flame. It took her several tries, but finally, the flame caught and held long enough for her to light the fuse.

"Watch out!" Stella warned Cyrus as she raised the cube above her head.

The fuse burned down, and the top of the cube hissed and spat a shower of red sparks that lit up the sky. Stella turned her face away as they spewed upward in a flaming tower that climbed higher and higher.

"It's working!" Cyrus cried. "Here they come!"

Stella risked a glance up at the gasbag and saw he was right. The nightcallers were gathering, spiraling down from the *Iron Glory*'s gasbag toward the light and hissing sparks at them.

Closer . . .

And closer . . . until finally there was nothing but a sea of sleek bellies filling her view.

Stella hurled the cube as far out into the night as she could. A second later, it exploded, shooting off a dozen tiny red fireballs that spun away in all different directions, filling the air with a high-pitched shriek as they streaked away into the darkness.

The nightcallers, unable to resist the spectacle, twisted and dove after them, following the fireballs away into the night. Stella didn't even need to use the other cube. She stuffed her matches back into her pocket, and she and Cyrus climbed back down to the broken window.

When they were safely inside the cargo bay, Stella surveyed the damage. Thankfully, no more of the birds had gotten into the bay, but there was broken glass everywhere.

"We can't even sweep it up or the crew will know someone's here," Cyrus said. When Stella didn't reply, he added, "I got a good look at the gasbag while you had your light show going, and I didn't see any damage. As long as we don't attract a flock that big again, we should be fine."

Stella nodded absently. She was staring up at the broken window, lost in thought.

"What is it?" Cyrus asked, his boots crunching on glass as he came to stand beside her. "What's wrong?"

"I was just thinking, whoever blew that whistle, or whatever it was, had to have seen the size of that nightcaller flock," Stella said. "They would have known it would draw them in."

Cyrus shrugged. "Maybe it was one of the security officers, or one of the deckhands who didn't know what they were."

Stella wasn't satisfied. "That's just it—they're *trained* to know. The crew has been training for months. You don't make mistakes like that on an expedition like this. And the whistle itself—those short bursts—almost as if . . ." She couldn't finish the thought. It didn't make sense.

Cyrus said it for her. "You think whoever it was might have been calling in the birds on purpose?"

"I don't know," Stella said. "I hope not, but . . ."

She finished the thought in her head. *But not everyone in the Merrow Kingdom or the Dragonfly territories wants the mission to succeed.* Not long ago, she'd even accused Cyrus of being a threat to the ship.

Maybe they actually hadn't found the real threat yet.

Stella shook those dark thoughts away. They had no proof, and Cyrus was probably right. It'd probably just been a deckhand who got careless and didn't know what he was doing. She was tired and cold and letting her worry get to her.

As they made their way back to their hideout, Stella tried to change the subject. "You said this ship was your only way home, but how did you get stranded here?" she asked. "You told me you couldn't go back with your expedition, but you didn't say why."

"You're right. I didn't," Cyrus said abruptly. He wouldn't meet her eyes as they squeezed back behind the crates, where Stella's candles were barely burning, swimming in wax. "Just like you didn't say why *you* stowed away until now. So you're here to protect your parents?"

He'd dodged her question, but Stella let it pass. "They're all that matters," she said. She reached into her alchemy case for a bandage and handed it to Cyrus for the cut the nightcaller had given him. "My whole life, I've lived in one tiny corner of the world, and that was enough," she went on. "I had my parents, my books, and my alchemy experiments. I didn't have much time for anything else—for friends or for dreaming of visiting other places. I didn't think I needed to.

"But then I saw the *Iron Glory* fly," Stella said, her voice dropping. "It made so many more things seem *possible*, and the world just seemed to get bigger overnight. Then suddenly, my parents were leaving to be part of that world, and it felt like a piece of me had been torn out. What if something happened and they never came back? It probably doesn't make any sense, but . . ." She faltered. How could she expect him to understand what she felt? They barely knew each other.

But Cyrus smiled, and there was no teasing in it, only a hint of sadness. "It makes sense to me," he said. "I'm an explorer too, remember? We're just coming from different directions, meeting in the middle."

She hadn't thought of it like that, but he was right. No matter what secrets Cyrus kept, they had this in common. They were explorers. "I meant what I said, though," she went on. "I'll do whatever it takes to protect my parents. If there's really a terrible storm out there—"

"There is," Cyrus interrupted, his face solemn. "And I promise I can guide us through it. As long as no one gets in my way, I can protect the ship."

"I won't get in your way," Stella said. "In fact, I'm going to help you."

His eyes widened, but then he shook his head. "Not a good idea. I work better on my own."

Stella didn't believe that for a second. "You said so yourself: when you use your power, you have to shut out the world and sometimes pass out. It means you're vulnerable. I can watch over you during that time."

He held up a hand, and that annoying grin was back on his face, the one that made Stella want to toss him overboard. "All right, I admit, as an alchemist, you've got a special set of skills and tricks," he said. "Plus you can handle yourself."

Stella snorted. Handle *him* was more like it.

"And you were incredibly brave out on that ladder," Cyrus continued. "But this storm is something you've never dealt with before. You'll just end up making things more difficult for me."

"Which makes things more *fun* for me," Stella said, giving him a sugary smile. "Don't forget, those *tricks* you mentioned also got me on board this ship without anyone being the wiser. I didn't even need an invisibility suit. I'm sorry, Cyrus, but whether you like it or not, I'm in this too."

Cyrus opened his mouth to argue, but then seemed to change his mind and snapped it shut. He sighed, the air hissing between his teeth. Stella took that for as much of an agreement as she was going to get.

However, her satisfaction quickly faded. She might have accepted that Cyrus was from the uncharted lands, but that didn't mean she trusted him. She sensed he wasn't telling her everything about his power, and that worried her, especially in light of what had just happened with the nightcallers.

Stella had collected so many unsettling mysteries— about this strange boy and about the expedition. But she was nothing if not a patient explorer, and she vowed to unravel every one of them, no matter how long it took.

EIGHT

After three days of fixing up the window and attempted snooping around their level, Stella still hadn't gotten the hang of sleeping in the cargo bay. She woke from a restless, miserable night's sleep to the smell of dust and wood filling her nose. She opened her eyes, but it was too dark to make out her surroundings. Was it dawn yet? She tried to raise her arms to stretch and bumped her hands against some kind of obstruction.

Stella blinked, her eyes adjusting to a dim light shining down from somewhere above her, but she didn't understand what she was seeing. A wooden ceiling, inches from her face. She turned her head and found a wall right at her nose. A ball of panic knotted her stomach, and a whimper rose in her throat.

She tried to turn, to sit up, but she was trapped. Someone had locked her inside one of the storage crates.

Light slanted in through cracks in the wood. There was no way out. The box was the size and shape of a coffin, the walls closing in on all sides.

"Let me out!" she screamed, but her voice came out a muffled whisper. She couldn't catch her breath. There wasn't enough air in the box. Frantic, she pounded the crate with her fists, kicking and thrashing, hoping someone outside in the cargo bay would hear her. She didn't care who it was.

"Help me! Please, somebody help me!"

"Stella, be quiet," a soft voice whispered in her ear.

Stella's body jerked. She thought she recognized the voice, but she couldn't remember where she'd heard it before. She thrashed harder, her heart beating wildly. She was making enough noise for the whole ship to hear. Why didn't somebody come?

"Stella, please," the voice begged, more urgently this time.

Wait, she remembered that voice now. It had a name, though it wasn't his real one.

Cyrus.

He was here in the cargo bay with her. But why didn't he open the box and let her out? Had he been the one to trap her? Again she opened her mouth to scream.

"Stella, open your eyes!"

Stella woke to find herself sprawled on the floor of the cargo bay. Cyrus's hand covered her mouth, his other hand pressing down on her shoulder. He was crouched beside her, but he wasn't looking at her. His head was cocked, and he appeared to be listening to something.

Then Stella heard it too. Voices in the cargo bay, crew members talking, and the banging and scraping of crates and other heavy objects being moved around.

Slowly, awareness came back to her. She wasn't trapped in a box. She'd just passed another night in the cargo bay of the *Iron Glory*, hidden away behind a stack of crates in a tiny makeshift camp near the engine room.

But the dream had felt so real. She must have cried out in her sleep, and Cyrus was trying to calm her, afraid one of the crew might hear the noise and come over to investigate.

Stella forced herself to relax and reached up to touch Cyrus's arm to let him know she was awake and that she'd heard the noises. He looked down at her, nodded, and took his hand away from her mouth. Stella looked up at the pale gray light filtering in through the high windows. She guessed it was just after sunrise. The crew was down here early to start their day.

The voices and sounds of movement drifted closer to their hiding place. Stella tensed. Beside her, Cyrus went utterly still.

"I'm telling you, it wasn't an accident," one of the crewmen was saying. "I know a chop-saw cut when I see one. Hey, are you listening to me?"

The sound of metal clanging against the floor made Stella jump. "You've been flapping your mouth for the past hour, Kal," said another voice, tight and full of anger. "I don't mind so much you doing it down here when we're alone, but you keep yapping in front of the crew and you'll start a panic. You heard what the captain said: no jumping to conclusions and no accusations against *anyone* until we know for sure it was sabotage."

Stella barely managed to stifle a gasp. Cyrus met her eyes and mouthed *sabotage*, as if he couldn't believe it either.

"Well, if it wasn't done on purpose, it's the shoddiest workmanship I've ever seen," the crewman Kal muttered. "Those cables should have been checked and double-checked before takeoff. They're what're keeping us tethered to the gasbag. Should have known better than to trust the Dragonfly territories to build this ship."

"See, right there, you're letting your mouth just go and go without checking with your brain first," the other crewman said. There was more loud clanging, and Stella guessed he was throwing tools around the cargo bay. "If someone really is trying to sabotage this mission, don't you think the very first thing he or she wants to accomplish is to get us at each other's throats? And you just want to help things along, don't you?"

"Aw, Dain, you know I didn't mean anything by it," Kal said. "I just don't like it, that's all. I want this mission to succeed as much as the next guy, but we're barely in the air three days and this happens. It's not a good omen, is all I'm saying."

"I know," Dain said, his voice quieter now. "But it's no use worrying until we find out more. Come on, let's go get some breakfast, and then I want to check the gasbag again. I've been seeing some odd cloud patterns. Think we might be headed into rougher weather soon."

Their voices gradually drifted away, and then came the sound of boots pounding on the metal stairs before the cargo bay fell quiet.

Stella sat up and brushed damp hair out of her eyes. She was bathed in sweat from the nightmare, her shirt soaked, but she was too caught up in everything she'd just heard to care.

Cyrus said it before she could. "If what we just heard is right, it means someone tried to cut the cables holding the *Iron Glory*'s gasbag or weaken them so they'd snap on their own."

Dread churned like a poison in Stella's gut. "You think it might be the same person who used that whistle on the deck, the sound that lured in the nightcallers?"

Cyrus's jaw worked, his mouth set in a grim line. "Yes," he said. "I think you were right to be suspicious. I think someone *is* trying to sabotage the ship."

"But that's crazy," Stella said, desperate for it not to be true. "We're flying over frozen mountains right now. If we crash, we're dead, and so are they."

"Maybe whoever it is doesn't want the ship to crash,"

Cyrus said. "Maybe he just wants to damage it enough so that we have to turn around. Or maybe . . . maybe he's crazy, and he doesn't care what happens to him."

Neither of those possibilities boded well for the mission, especially with the heightened tensions between the Merrow and Dragonfly crew members.

"We have to do something," Stella said. "If someone's trying to sabotage this ship, we can't just sit around and wait for him to strike."

"What are you suggesting?" Cyrus asked. "It sounds like the crew is already investigating, and there's not much we can do from down here."

Stella crossed her arms. "Says the boy who has an *invisibility suit* in his knapsack," she said dryly. "We're in the best position to search for the saboteur because he *or she* will never know we're there, and we're not part of the ship's personnel."

"That's true," Cyrus acknowledged, "unless you have another nightmare and someone ousts us from our hiding spot."

Stella flinched, but she quickly recovered and gave him a frosty look. "Thanks for bringing that up," she said. "Don't worry. It won't happen again."

She reached for her alchemy case and pretended to rummage through it, organizing the vials and powders for the hundredth time since she'd snuck on board the ship.

It was easier to ignore her fear of tight places during

the day, when the cargo bay was filled with sunlight. But at night, it was different. The crates loomed larger, the air grew hot and stale, and the walls pressed in on her. In the darkness, lying on a hard metal floor, Stella missed her bed back home. She missed Noveen and the sounds of the city at night. Here, she lay awake for hours, listening to the creaks and groans of the ship. Its swaying motion made her light-headed and sick. Even now, when the wind was calm and she could barely feel the ship moving, Stella found she had no appetite.

She risked a glance at Cyrus and caught the skepticism in his eyes. "You don't believe me?" she asked.

"Just seems like the nightmares are getting worse, not better," he said, frowning. "From where I'm sitting, you're one bloodcurdling scream away from bringing them all running down here."

"I know!" Irritated and embarrassed, Stella slammed the flap of her alchemy case closed. "It's not as if I can control my dreams. I don't mean to make all that noise." Bad enough she'd risked being caught, but she'd had to have a nightmare in front of Cyrus. Cyrus, who acted so sure of himself, never seemed bothered by the motion of the ship, and who over the past three days had demonstrated the appetite of four starving chamelins. Did *nothing* ever shake him up? It was infuriating.

"Whatever's bothering you, we can fix it," Cyrus said reasonably. "What is it you're dreaming about?"

"Nothing," Stella said curtly. She didn't want to talk

about this with him. "They're just dreams. They don't make any sense."

"You're lying," he said. "I can tell. Come on—spill the secret. Or are you afraid I'm going to shout it up and down the halls of the ship?"

Stella clenched her jaw. The boy was insufferable. "I dream about being trapped in a box," she said, and shuddered at the memory, the dream still fresh in her mind. "It's like a coffin. I can't get out."

"You're claustrophobic," Cyrus said, nodding as if he understood. "Some of the other members of our expedition felt the same way too. They couldn't stand being belowdecks on the airship and could only relax when they were topside." He snapped his fingers. "That's what you need—fresh air. You take the invisibility suit first and make a sweep of the ship for the saboteur, and we'll tackle two problems at once."

Stella gazed with longing at the high windows and the pale sunlight filtering through them. "It would be wonderful to walk around on deck," she said. To be surrounded by miles and miles of endless, cloud-filled skies.

"So it's a plan." Cyrus beamed. He was already pulling the suit from his knapsack. "We'll do a walking lesson first, to give you a feel for how the suit works," he said, holding the suit out for her, but Stella hesitated before stepping into it.

Cyrus was offering her an incredible gift. He could have insisted on using the suit himself and left her behind in the cargo bay. Instead, he was offering her a chance to stand on the deck of the *Iron Glory* and feel the wind on her face. It wasn't something she'd expected from him, a boy she barely knew and didn't entirely trust. "Thank you," she said quietly. "For helping me, I mean. It's nice of you, Cyrus."

He shrugged as if it was nothing special. "Like I said, I can't afford to get caught down here. If this solves the problem, it's great for everyone."

Of course, Stella thought, trying not to let the disappointment sting too much. It wasn't that he cared about her comfort. He just didn't want her endangering their hiding place.

"Besides, I can't sleep at night with you thrashing around and making a fuss," Cyrus went on, shooting her a grin. "You kicked me last night."

She rolled her eyes. "I did not."

"I have the bruises to prove it!"

She could tell he was joking, but his words made Stella wonder. "Don't you ever have bad dreams?" she asked. "What do you do to chase them away?"

"Nothing," Cyrus said. He shrugged again. "I don't have nightmares, or if I do, I never remember them."

"Really?"

"Yeah. Guess I'm just lucky." He held the suit out again. "Come on, if you're going to do this, you need to get practicing. We're wasting time."

Stella let the subject drop and focused on getting into

the invisibility suit and following Cyrus's instructions on how to move around. He was a good teacher, more tolerant than she'd expected, but a couple of times she glanced at him out of the corner of her eye and noticed that he appeared lost in thought, a sorrowful expression on his face. When he caught her looking, he just pasted that bright grin on his face and found some subject to tease her about.

But Stella saw through him as easily as he'd seen through her. He'd been lying earlier. He did have night-mares that he remembered. If that look on his face was anything to go by, they were bad ones, though he never betrayed any hint of distress during the night.

Unlike her, he must have learned to bury his fears deep.

≈ NINE ≈

After a couple hours of practice, Stella had mastered the art of moving around in the invisibility suit. It turned out that the hardest part wasn't making herself walk slowly. She was used to being patient and meticulous when conducting alchemy experiments in her parents' lab, and she was able to apply the same discipline to using the suit.

The tricky part was controlling her other movements. Gestures like turning her head too quickly or lifting an arm too fast would create a ripple in the air and reveal the outline of her body. The effect only lasted a few seconds, but as Cyrus pointed out, a few seconds was all it would take for a crew member to spot her if anyone was looking her way. Stella imagined it would give the unfortunate man or woman a terrible shock, like seeing a ghost.

Once Cyrus was satisfied that she had the basics

down, Stella practiced on her own for the rest of the day while he cleaned up and organized the supplies in their hideout, occasionally throwing out comments or suggestions on her movements.

As sunset neared, Stella finally headed topside, excitement humming within her.

It was everything she'd imagined.

She stood on the main deck of the *Iron Glory*, leaning over the bow railing as mile after mile of snowcapped mountains passed beneath her.

A dozen or so crew members moved up and down the deck, watching the skies, performing navigational tasks, or just getting a breath of fresh air like she was. A frigid breath, at that. Every one of the crew wore heavy winter coats buttoned to their faces, thick hats, and gloves to protect their hands. The temperature had been steadily dropping over the last twenty-four hours, and it was well below freezing now.

Gripping the rail, Stella found herself lost in a misty white world as the airship drifted into a cloud bank. Mountain terns soared up alongside the ship, quicksilver specks of brown that basked in the warm air currents emanating from the propellers below. The small birds were much more relaxing to watch than the frenzied, frightening nightcallers. And then, just when Stella thought they were truly adrift in the mist, the clouds broke apart, again revealing the vast plains of snow and stony peaks spread out below.

That view of the Hiterian Mountains brought tears to her eyes.

We've never seen the world like this, Stella thought. In just a few days, the *Iron Glory* had already ventured farther into the mountains than any explorer from Stella's part of the world had ever been. No matter what else happened on their journey, she would never forget the sight of those mountains. She felt as if she were standing at the very top of the world. Not bad, considering she'd expected to spend the entirety of the journey stuffed away in the ship's cargo bay.

It would have been the perfect moment, if only she could have shared it with her parents. Their absence was an ache inside her that refused to go away. If anything, the revelation that the ship was in danger had made it worse. Stella worried about her mother and father all the time. What were they doing right now? Were they thinking of her, missing her as much as she missed them? Or were they happy to be away, sharing in the adventure of a lifetime . . . without her?

There was one way to find out, Stella concluded, her hands tightening on the rail as she looked down at her invisible form. She didn't know why she hadn't thought of it immediately. She needed to make a sweep of the ship anyway. There was no reason she couldn't pay a secret visit to her parents along the way.

First she had to make a circuit of the main deck. Stella turned and cautiously headed for the stern, where a group of crew members were gathered around the cables attached to the ship's gasbag. She crept as close as she dared to eavesdrop on their conversation, but it didn't take long to confirm the truth of what she and Cyrus suspected.

As Kal and Dain had said, four of the metal cables attached to the ship's gasbag had been sawed almost all the way through. If the crew hadn't seen it in time, the cables likely would have snapped, and the resulting strain might have brought the whole ship down.

The idea of four identically frayed cables was enough to convince Stella that there was a saboteur on board.

Not on my ship, she vowed, stepping away from the group and heading for the hatch that would take her back to the cargo bay. Not while her parents were on board. She and Cyrus would search the ship top to bottom every day if they had to, but they would find whoever was responsible for this.

Standing at the hatch, Stella took one last look at the sky, which had burst into sunset colors. They were so beautiful it was almost painful to watch. The orange light of the fading sun deepened to crimson in a fiery line along the horizon, and for the first time in her life, Stella realized that there were certain shades of red that could only truly be appreciated in the sky.

She turned away from the sunset and headed below.

Out of the open air, it was harder to move around. Stella made her way with agonizing slowness down a narrow hallway, pressing her flank against the left-hand wall as two men rounded the corner up ahead and came toward her. Thankfully, one walked ahead of the other, so they passed her with plenty of space between them. Patience was the key. If she hurried, that was when it was riskiest and she would likely be discovered.

She made her way down to deck three, which included the bridge and the observation lounge. There was more traffic here than Stella was comfortable with, but it was also the deck where the medical bay was located, where her parents would be.

Stella's heartbeat sped up with each slow step she took in that direction. She wanted to see them so much, needed to hear their voices, even if they had no idea she was in the room with them. Now more than ever, with a saboteur on board, she wanted to feel safe again, if only for a little while.

In her excitement, Stella abruptly realized she'd quickened her step. The air shimmered, briefly showing the outline of her left leg. *Careful!* She stopped for a moment to try to calm down. It was then she heard a voice up ahead of her in the corridor. It sounded like it was coming from the bridge, which was nearby.

A moment later, a man and a woman stepped out

a doorway on the right-hand wall and began walking down the hall toward her. Stella recognized them both at once: the *Iron Glory*'s Captain Keeler and his first officer, a sarnun woman named Drea. The captain's frizzy, thinning gray hair and dark eyes stood in sharp contrast to his companion's milky-white eyes, not to mention the glistening blue feelers sprouting from her head and draping in graceful waves down her back. They both wore the uniform of the Dragonfly territories, green jackets with gold epaulets, but their clothes were rumpled, and the captain looked exhausted.

No surprise there. Likely neither one of them had slept since they heard there was a saboteur aboard.

Unfortunately, the captain and the first officer were walking side by side down the hall and were taking up most of the space. As quickly as she could without betraying her presence, Stella flattened herself against the wall. She held her breath as the two highest-ranking officers glided past her, the captain speaking in a low voice. Stella was able to catch only a few sentences.

". . . a full report from every deck within the hour," Keeler was saying. "And I want to know if the gasbag was damaged."

When she replied, Drea put her thoughts directly into the captain's mind, so of course Stella couldn't hear them. But sarnuns also communicated emotion with their feelers, and the first officer's feelers were rigid against her back. Stella knew from talking to sarnun scientists, friends of her parents, that the gesture meant that Drea was upset.

After they'd passed by, Stella resumed her snail's pace down the hall, until finally she reached an open doorway with a placard on the wall that read: MEDICAL BAY.

Her mother's voice echoed from inside the room.

"Hand me the broom," she was saying, her voice tight with anger. "I need to sweep up this glass before someone steps on it and slices their foot open."

"It's behind you, Eliza. Against the wall," Stella's father answered, also from inside the room.

Stella blinked to clear the tears from her eyes. If she closed them, she could almost pretend it was a normal day in the lab and she was just coming to ask her parents when they were going to stop for dinner. She even caught the scent of her mother's lavender perfume drifting out into the hallway.

Cautiously, she peeked around the doorway. A pair of examining tables were arranged side by side at the back of the room, along with a more comfortable-looking cot with a pillow and blanket. White cupboards lined the right-hand wall, and below them, a length of countertop covered in test tubes and jars of medicines and herbs. Her mother stood in front of the counter with the broom—it was almost as tall as she was—and was sweeping shards of glass from a broken test tube into a pile while her father crouched on the floor, ready with the dustpan. Stella's mother wore an expression of fury that caught Stella off guard.

"Please calm down," her father said as Stella crept into the room. She positioned herself in the corner closest to the doorway, where she could listen and not chance either of them bumping into her accidentally.

Her mother slammed the broom down on the pile of glass with a loud crunch. "You really think I can be calm after what we just heard? The captain confirmed it, Martin. The cables were cut. One of the crew—people I thought were our *friends*—is sabotaging the ship."

"I know," her father said quietly. "I just can't bring myself to believe it. We've worked side by side with these people for months. If you'd asked me yesterday, I'd have said I'd trust them with my life."

"One of them is a traitor—to both Merrow and Dragonfly." Her mother's face was red with outrage. Stella didn't think she'd ever seen her this angry before.

"The captain will find whoever's responsible," her father said. His voice softened. "You know, if we were at home right now, we'd have roped Stella into helping us clean up this mess."

Stella stiffened at the mention of her name. Her father was obviously joking, trying to distract her mother from her fury. But it was Eliza's reaction that truly shocked her. Instead of chuckling, she stopped her sweeping, laid her forehead against the broom handle, and burst into tears.

"Oh, Eliza," her father said, dropping the dustpan and wrapping his arms around his wife. "I'm sorry. I didn't mean to upset you. I was trying to take your mind off the bad news."

Without thinking, Stella stepped forward, hands reaching, wanting to comfort her mother too. Then she remembered where they were. She was so close, and yet so helpless, it was almost too much to bear. She curled her hands into fists and made herself edge back into the corner.

"It wasn't supposed to be like this," Eliza said, pressing her face against her husband's shoulder. "This ship is supposed to be indestructible. The king *assured* us. It's the only reason I was able to leave Stella at home without it tearing me to pieces."

"I don't think the king realized there'd be a traitor among us," Stella's father said, stroking his wife's long dark hair in a soothing gesture. "I don't think anyone really knew what we were getting ourselves into."

Stella's mother pulled back just far enough to look up at him. Her eyes were haunted. "Martin, if we don't catch this person, he could bring down the ship. We'd never see Stella again. She'd be an orphan."

A change came over Martin then. It was as if

something . . . broke, starting from the inside and working its way out. His shoulders slumped, and he bowed his head, now leaning on his wife for support. But not until the moisture dripped down his face did Stella realize he was crying.

"I know," he said, his voice trembling. "I've worried about that every day since we left, but there's no going back now. We have to focus on what's ahead of us, do everything we can to get back to her."

Stella closed her eyes and shrank into her corner. She couldn't bear to see her parents in such pain. Her father had *never* cried before, at least not in front of her. And her mother . . . Stella would gladly have listened to her shout and rage and throw the broom. That was the small, fierce woman she knew and loved. But these frightened people—she'd never seen this side of her parents before.

And it was all because of Stella. Her parents were terrified that they wouldn't make it back to her. They were afraid of the same thing Stella had been for months. But why had they never told her just how scared they were?

Because they hadn't wanted her to be any more frightened and upset than she already was, Stella realized. In that moment, she wished more than anything she could cross the room and throw her arms around her parents. They could have shared the fear. Maybe then it wouldn't have hurt so much. Maybe she wouldn't have felt as if they were abandoning her.

Stella sighed softly. Her father was right. The past couldn't be changed. The important thing now was to find the saboteur before he could doom the expedition or cause a permanent divide among the crew.

Stella crept slowly out of her corner and inched toward the door, careful not to step on any broken glass that might make a sound under her feet. Her parents pulled apart and went back to their cleanup, but Stella noticed that they stayed close, as if they were lending each other strength.

We'll protect you both, Stella promised her parents silently. *Cyrus and I. We're all going to get home.*

Stella slipped out of the medical bay and retraced her steps down the hall. For the moment, the area was deserted. *The crew must be at their stations*, she thought. *Just as well.* It allowed her to move a little faster than she normally would have, though not fast enough to make her visible.

She moved from deck to deck, methodically searching for . . . what? That was the question. A crew member acting suspiciously? Something out of place? Maybe some sign of the tools the saboteur had used to slice the *Iron Glory*'s cables. Chop saws weren't easy things to hide, even on a ship this size.

But after about an hour of painstakingly combing the

corridors, Stella had found nothing unusual. Her stomach rumbled and her feet were sore. She didn't want to stop searching, but she needed to get back to the cargo bay to let Cyrus know she was all right.

Discouraged, Stella moved down the corridor toward the closest set of stairs that would lead her back down to the cargo bay.

Just ahead of her on her right, a door slowly opened, and a man peered into the hall, looking in both directions before stepping out. He had heavy jowls and brows, sideburns that ran in two thick rows down either side of his face. In his hands, he held a box of matches.

A prickle of uneasiness tugged at Stella's scalp. The man looked like he was checking the hall to make sure it was empty before he came out of the room. Was there some reason he didn't want to be seen? And Stella didn't recognize his face. She'd met many of the crew members during the preparations for the expedition, though she didn't know all their faces from memory.

The man closed the door and leaned against it for a second, gazing in both directions again before he turned and hurried for the stairs.

As the echo of his footsteps slowly faded, Stella resumed her walk down the hall. She paused in front of the door the man had come out of, hoping it would give her some clue to his position on the ship.

The sign on the door said STORAGE.

Curls of white smoke bled from a crack beneath the door, the scent of burning cloth and chemicals filling her nostrils.

The man with the matches had started a fire.

≫ TEN ≪

Stella yanked open the small storage closet. The door banged against the opposite wall. Boxes stacked up to the ceiling on the right side of the closet, but on the left there were a bunch of cleaning supplies, a mop and bucket, and a pile of dirty rags in the corner. Orange flames ate up the dry cotton, turning them to curled black husks. Every second that passed, the fire inched closer to the boxes.

The *Iron Glory* might have been a metal ship, but there were still enough wood and gaslight systems on board that a fire could turn deadly in minutes.

Stella stamped on the rags with both feet to put the fire out. She kicked the blackened remnants and ashes into the corner, as far away from the stack of boxes as possible. By the time all the flames had died, she was breathless and trembling inside her suit.

When she was sure the fire was out, Stella peeked out

the closet door. The hallway was still deserted. There was no sign of the saboteur or the rest of the crew.

Stella's thoughts raced. If the man was still nearby, he'd know soon enough that his fire hadn't spread. Which meant he might try again, and Stella had no idea where he'd gone.

She scanned the walls, searching for the gaslight lines. In her studies of the ship, she'd learned there was an alarm system running alongside the gaslights that would sound bells throughout the ship in case of an emergency like this. She needed to warn the crew.

There! High on the wall was a red button next to a gray metal bell. Stella ran to it, stretching up on her toes to jam the heel of her hand into the button.

A deafening clang filled the hallway, ringing in Stella's ears. Seconds later, it was picked up on the decks above and below her as other crew members heard the bell and sounded their alarms. Soon the whole ship echoed with the sound.

Stella left the closet door open and moved as quickly as she dared out of the corridor and back to the cargo bay. She wanted to stay and make sure the crew found the evidence of the fire, but she would be vulnerable. The corridors would be full of people soon, making it almost impossible to move around without someone bumping into her.

Footsteps pounded on the stairs above her, but Stella made it back to the cargo bay ahead of them.

Cyrus was waiting for her behind the crates, pacing back and forth as if he might wear a trench into the floor. When she pulled off the hood of her suit and became visible, he jumped back, banging his elbow against the wall of crates.

"You scared the life out of me," he hissed, keeping his voice low. Before Stella could answer, he put his hands on her shoulders, surprising her into silence. "Are you all right? What happened? I heard the alarm, and I was afraid they'd caught you."

"I'm sorry," Stella said. "It was the only thing I could think of." They sat down on the floor, and she quickly filled him in on the fire and the man she'd seen.

Cyrus's face paled. "I didn't think he'd try anything again so soon, especially with the crew on alert. But it seems like he's determined to bring us down."

"He'd be crazy to try again today," Stella said, pointing to the ceiling. "It sounds like the whole crew is on the move up there."

One by one, the alarm bells were shutting down, but shouting voices and footsteps echoed above them. The crew had obviously found the remnants of the fire. They'd be searching the rest of the ship for more piles of burning rags.

Stella prayed they wouldn't come rooting all the way back to the corner of the cargo bay.

"Could you tell which one of the crew it was?" Cyrus asked.

Stella shook her head. "I don't know them all," she said. "I met the captain and first officer, some of the main deck crew, and most of the scientific team. It wasn't any of them."

"There's another possibility," Cyrus added. "He might not be part of the crew at all. He could be a stowaway, like us."

"Three stowaways hiding on one ship," Stella said skeptically. "What are the chances anyone could pull that off?"

"Well, we have an advantage with your alchemy set and the invisibility suit," Cyrus pointed out. "Who knows what the saboteur has?"

"And we're heading into a storm," Stella said, fighting off panic. "What are we going to do?" For once, she wouldn't have minded hearing Cyrus's jokes or his teasing, anything to take her mind off what was in front of them.

"Same thing we planned," Cyrus said decisively. "You're right. The crew will be doubly on their guard now, so the saboteur will have to lie low while they search for him. In the meantime, you and I will focus on the storm and getting the ship through it."

"All right." Stella nodded. Plans were good. Preparation was set. It made her feel calmer, more in control.

Cyrus was right. She'd made a promise to protect her parents, and the best thing she could do for them now was to focus on what was ahead.

On the impending weather.

⇒ ELEVEN ⇐

After a couple of more restful nights—thanks to the fresh air she'd gotten—Stella was back on the *Iron Glory*'s main deck, watching the skies and going over the plan in her head.

"I have to be on the ship but outside its walls for my protective shield to work," Cyrus had explained. "It's kind of like making a net and then casting it over the outside of the ship. You'll wear the invisibility suit and keep watch. Warn me if anyone's coming, though I'm hoping none of the crew will be stupid enough to come outside once the storm hits."

Stella had bitten her lip and refrained from reminding him that the two of them were going to be the stupid ones outside in the storm. Instead, she'd asked, "But why can't *you* wear the suit so no one will see you? Will you be running around a lot, moving too fast for the suit to keep up?"

"No, I'll be staying in one place and holding very still, but for what I'm going to do, I can't be wearing the suit. It causes . . . interference with my power."

Stella wondered what he'd meant by "interference." The whole idea of his protecting the ship with his strange powers fascinated her, and she wanted to know how they worked. Where had he gotten this gift? What were the limits of his power? But every time she tried to ask questions, Cyrus managed to change the subject. Obviously, he didn't trust her all the way.

Stella tried to tell herself that was fine. It wasn't as if they were friends or anything. She wasn't quite sure what they were. Allies, maybe? But definitely not friends. Friends knew each other's real names. She'd tried and failed again the night before to get Cyrus to tell her, so she'd resorted to guessing games.

"Bostwick? Brent? Baris?" she'd ask.

"None of those," Cyrus would inevitably reply. "Do I really look like a Bostwick to you?"

"Conal? Darwin? Edward?" Even being thorough and starting at the beginning of the alphabet, she'd gotten all the way to "P" before getting tired at her lack of success. "Peregrine?"

"Peregrine? Isn't that a falcon?"

She'd shrugged. "Maybe your parents really like birds. Now, stop interrupting. Peter? Patreol?"

He'd sighed loudly. "Are you going to keep this up for the whole journey?"

Stella'd smiled. The best part of the game was how much it annoyed him.

Still, they managed to get along, even in the cramped quarters of the cargo bay, and there were even a few moments it seemed like they could be friends, if it weren't for . . . something. It wasn't just that she didn't know his real name. Cyrus's eyes were full of secrets, and every time it looked like he might be on the verge of sharing one of those secrets with her, his eyes became shadowed, and he withdrew into his thoughts and didn't speak.

He refused to answer any of her questions about him at first, or he'd pretend not to hear her. This frustrated Stella to no end, but eventually, she started to recognize a pattern to his refusals and silences. Whenever she asked him for information directly related to where he was from, like what the name of his hometown was or how big the uncharted lands were, he'd refuse to answer or just give out vague details like, he lived in a big house in a big city. But he was willing to talk about the expeditions that had brought him and dozens of others to her part of Solace over the last five years.

"We were chosen for the missions for many of the same reasons as the crew of the *Iron Glory*," he had explained as he bent over one of Stella's maps of the ship. "We each have a set of skills that helps us survive. Some of us are healers or navigators, and others are just good at blending in."

Remembering that comment, Stella couldn't help the little shudder that passed through her. Who were these people from the uncharted lands, these strange visitors who had been spying on them for years? Could they be dangerous? What was the *Iron Glory* going to find once they crossed the mountains?

Lost in her own thoughts, Stella almost stepped into the path of a woman in a bright green coat who was pacing the deck. Stella stood perfectly still as the woman walked past her, inches away from bumping her shoulder. Then the woman stopped and gripped the railing, looking out over the stern as Stella had been doing. Probably checking to see how much ice had formed on the ship's hull.

Ever so slowly, Stella backed away, putting some distance between herself and the woman so she wouldn't turn suddenly and walk into her. Rubbing her gloved hands together for warmth, the woman glanced around, making a cursory inspection of the deck and looking right through Stella as she did so.

Stella held perfectly still as the woman's gaze passed over her. Any minute, she expected her to let out a shriek and point. *There she is! Stowaway! Stowaway!*

Or worse. *Saboteur! Saboteur!*

But in the end, the woman just yawned, stamped her

boots for warmth, then turned around and walked back toward the hatch that led down to the lower decks. Stella watched her go and tried to banish the rubbery-leg feeling that swept over her.

No amount of practice with the invisibility suit would ever familiarize her to people looking straight through her.

Once she was sure no one else was headed her way, Stella returned her gaze to the mountains, hoping the view might calm her.

A line of hateful clouds loomed on the horizon, a slash across the sky like a scar.

Stella cringed. There it was—the storm, bearing down on them with frightful speed.

She wasn't the only one who'd noticed the oncoming danger. Shouts went up all over the deck just then, and the lookout in the crow's nest rang the warning bell, its coppery tones cutting through the frigid air.

"Storm coming! Everyone below deck! To your stations! Go! Go! Go!"

Even they know it's bad, Stella thought. She clutched the rail, unable to look away from the ominous clouds signaling that it wasn't any ordinary storm.

As she stood there, a blast of frigid wind struck her full in the face. The temperature on deck had plummeted just in the last minute, and the dark scar on the horizon was growing, a hideous monster crawling toward them.

Turning, Stella watched as the crew went single file through the hatch to the lower decks, the last man slamming the metal door behind him. Minutes later, the door opened slowly, and Cyrus poked his head out and looked around. "Stella?" he called softly.

"I'm here," Stella answered, lifting her veil so she became visible. "You can come out. The deck's clear."

"Good." Cyrus stepped out on deck and shut the hatch. He was dressed in a heavy coat and hat that they'd scavenged from one of the supply crates, a scarf wrapped around his neck, but no gloves. He had his knapsack on his back and a long metal bar in his hand, which he'd found in the cargo bay. He wedged it between the door and the deck. "I don't think this will hold if someone really wants to open this door," he said, "but it could discourage people from coming up here during the storm."

"How long do we have before it hits?" Stella asked, pointing at the cloud line.

Cyrus squinted at the horizon, and his face paled. "Ten minutes, maybe, but probably less," he predicted.

Stella's heart sank. *So soon!* How long would it take Cyrus to put up his protection barrier around the *Iron Glory?* She followed him across the deck to the mast, where a ladder led up to the crow's nest.

"How did we come upon the storm so quickly?" Stella asked as Cyrus prepared to climb. "One minute the skies were clear, and the next, they turned black."

Cyrus paused with his hand on a ladder rung. His knuckles were already red from the cold. "I'm not exactly sure how it works," he said, "but the storm is always in the same place and spread over so wide an area of the mountain range that we can't fly around it. Luckily, our ships are made of aletheum top to bottom, so they were able to make it through without too much damage to the hull. Our scientists believe that the storm is some kind of artificially generated climate."

"Artificial?" Stella echoed in disbelief. "But if that's true, then . . . what . . . or *who's* making it? And why?"

Cyrus shrugged. "Someone on the ground? Maybe there's a hidden city down there that doesn't want trespassers. That's one theory the scientists have."

A city in the frozen heart of the mountains. Stella had heard stories about such a thing, but she'd thought they were just that—stories. "That's impossible," she said. "People couldn't survive down there, living in freezing temperatures, cut off from the rest of the world."

"Maybe, but I wonder. The world's a lot bigger than you think it is, Stella," he said soberly. "Like you said, up to now, you've been living in one corner of it." He hesitated, as if he wasn't sure how much he should say. "I think there are a whole bunch of other lands out there, beyond our seas, just waiting to be discovered. And if that's true, maybe there are other things that aren't so 'impossible' going on right under our noses."

Cyrus glanced up at the crow's nest. "I need to hurry and get up there. Stay down here on the main deck and keep watch. I'll be back as soon as I can."

"Wait a minute," Stella said, putting a hand on his shoulder to stop him. "You didn't say anything about needing to go up in the crow's nest alone."

"There's not much room," Cyrus said. "But it's the highest point on deck, which makes it easier to cast the protection net, so that it covers every part of the ship."

"But *you* won't have any protection from the storm," Stella argued. "And the last time you used your power, you passed out!"

"That was nothing," Cyrus said, scowling. "I just released too much power too quickly trying to make a permanent shield. I'll be weak for this, but I won't pass out again. Now, I have to go. If I don't get this protection net set up, the ship won't make it, and my way home is sunk. I'm not about to let that happen." He pulled away from her and started to climb the ladder.

Stella sighed, frustration gnawing at her. Cyrus acted so sure of himself, yet by her count, he'd only been through this storm one other time. She wasn't about to trust him to do this alone.

Pulling the veil back down over her face, she waited for the suit to activate and then grabbed the closest ladder rung and started to climb.

Though she was invisible again, Cyrus must have

heard her footsteps on the ladder, for he looked down and glared at her—or at the empty air where she should be. "I said stay down there and keep watch!"

"We don't have time to argue about this," Stella said curtly. "I can keep a much better lookout from up in the crow's nest, and I can watch your back at the same time. I promise not to get in the way. Is that good enough for you—Quentin? Quartus? Quill?" She grinned, though he couldn't see it.

Cyrus snorted. "Fine—I surrender. Just stop the name game, and watch yourself. It's going to get rough up here."

That was the only warning Stella had before the clouds reached out to swallow them.

⇒ TWELVE ⇐

The sky darkened to a false night, and a gust of wind tore at Stella's suit, finding every tiny gap in the metal fabric. She clutched the ladder rung tighter. She felt weightless, adrift in a cold, dark nightmare. The frigid air burned in her lungs. Above her, the repaired cables holding the ship's gasbag creaked and strained as the envelope bobbed and twisted at the whim of the wind. But the *Iron Glory* fought its way forward, into the storm.

Finally, after it seemed like they were climbing to the top of the world, the pair reached the end of the ladder and came up through the floor of the crow's nest. It was a small, round platform protected by a double railing, a space just big enough to fit four people crowded together. Above them, the banners of the Merrow Kingdom and the Dragonfly territories snapped violently in the wind.

Cyrus flailed his hands until he found her arm. He turned her and pointed to a spot on the floor of the crow's nest a few feet away. "Crouch down there and hold on tight to the railing!" He had to shout above the howling wind. "Remember, if you move, I won't know where you are! I'll be right here next to you." He rubbed his bare hands together for warmth and then held them up so she could see them. "You can watch my back, but you can't touch me while I'm using my power, you understand? When you see the gold light, *don't touch me.*"

His face was dead serious, with no trace of his usual careless smile. He'd said the same thing to her in the hallway when they'd first met. "Don't touch me." Stella opened her mouth to ask why, but at that instant, the ship shuddered, rocking beneath them, and she had to grab the railing for balance. "All right!" she shouted in agreement. She crouched where he had directed her and got a firm grip on the railing. From this vantage, she had a view of every corner of the deck below.

"Here we go!" Cyrus arranged himself beside her and grabbed the railing with his bare hands, wincing as his fingers curled around the freezing metal. How could he stand the cold?

Stella got her answer a second later when a halo of golden radiance outlined his fingers, slicing through the darkness and bringing with it a wave of heat that flowed over her and instantly made her feel as if she were standing next to a roaring campfire.

The last time Stella had seen Cyrus use his power there hadn't been this warmth. What was different? Was he protecting the ship's hull from ice? Creating a shield that would last through the storm? Or just using more power than he had before?

Whatever he was doing, it seemed to work immediately. The ship steadied beneath them as the light flowed down the mast and spread across the deck in liquid gold waves, creating a buffer that absorbed the worst of the storm's blows. It would still be a rough ride, but she thought the ship could handle it.

Cyrus had been telling the truth. He could get them through this.

Hope surged in Stella, but she didn't have time to savor it, for just then, a loud clinking, like hundreds of pebbles bouncing off metal, filled her ears, and then the pebbles were falling on her, stinging her skin even through the thick suit.

Of course, they weren't pebbles. Stella bent over the crow's nest railing and watched the ice shards fall, faster and thicker until the deck was coated white and the clinking sound became a roar.

The wind attacked.

The first gust hit Stella from behind, knocking her against the crow's nest railing. The *Iron Glory* groaned and listed starboard. Next to her, Cyrus balanced on his knees, gasping as the wind, the ice, and the tilting ship all fought to break his concentration. Stella automatically reached out, wanting to grasp his shoulder, but at the last second remembered what Cyrus had told her.

"Don't touch me."

Reluctantly, she pulled her hand back and glanced up at the sky. They were surrounded by the storm now, the darkness and falling sheets of ice making it hard to see. A clanging sound drew her attention below. The metal bar Cyrus had used to wedge the hatch door shut had been knocked away by the wind and was now rolling around on the deck.

It hardly mattered, Stella thought. None of the crew would dare come out here now, and she was beginning to think she and Cyrus might have made a terrible mistake taking on the storm by themselves.

But there was no time for regrets. Another wind gust ripped down on them with a roar like a locomotive. This time Stella couldn't hold on to the railing. The wind tore her hands away and the world spun as she fell onto her side. Crying out, she rolled and wrapped her arms around the mast where it came up through the middle of the crow's nest floor. Tilting her head, she had a dizzying view down the ladder to the deck of the ship and, beyond it, the darkness of angry clouds and falling ice.

She twisted and craned her neck to check on Cyrus. He was behind her now, one hand gripping the railing and the other flailing, hurling gold streaks into the sky. She cried out as his fingers slipped, but at the last second, he tightened his grip and slammed his other hand down on the rail, steadying himself. His eyes glowed dull gold. Pain and exhaustion twisted his features, and Stella felt a jolt of fear that had nothing to do with the storm.

What would using all this power do to Cyrus?

She opened her mouth to call out, ask him if he was all right, when suddenly, Stella caught movement out of the corner of her eye, a small, bright glow like a blue star, very different from the light of Cyrus's power. It was coming from the deck below. Wrapping one arm securely around the mast, Stella scooted forward to get a better look down the ladder.

Below them, a lone figure stood at the bow of the ship. He was bundled in a thick coat and hood. He had one hand on the bow railing, feet slightly spread to brace himself on the icy deck. In his other hand, he held a metal rod that was about the length of his arm. A blue light danced at its pronged tip. Stella had never seen anything like it before. It looked like a torch that burned with blue fire.

As she watched, the figure raised the rod and tipped his head back to look up at the crow's nest. The blue light illuminated his face beneath his hood.

"No," Stella whispered. She couldn't hear her own voice above the wind, just felt the vibration in her chest along with her stuttering heartbeat. "It can't be."

But it was—the man who'd started the fire in the

storage closet. She recognized the heavy jowls and side-burns. It was the traitor. He'd risked coming out onto the deck during the deadly storm.

And he was moving right toward the crow's nest, his gaze fixed on Cyrus.

THIRTEEN

"Cyrus!" Stella called out, trying to get the boy's attention, but he was huddled over the crow's nest railing, oblivious, the golden light outlining his arms up to his shoulders now. The rest of the *Iron Glory*, including its gasbag, was glowing a faint gold as well, every part of the ship shielded by Cyrus's power.

Stella didn't want to interrupt Cyrus—what would happen to that golden protection if it cut off in the middle of the storm?—but the saboteur now stood at the base of the ladder. He turned his hooded gaze upward and looked directly at her.

Stella froze. Could he *see* her? No, he was looking through her, just like the woman on deck earlier.

He was coming up the ladder. He had to move slowly through the wind and ice, all while cradling that strange metal rod, but it would only be a minute or two before he was nose-to-nose with Stella.

He still couldn't see her. He was coming after Cyrus, but why?

Because Cyrus is protecting the ship, a tiny voice inside her whispered.

But that didn't make any sense. How could the saboteur know Cyrus was using his power to protect the ship? How could he know the power of the storm?

Unless . . . maybe he'd also been through it before.

The realization jolted Stella, almost causing her to lose her grip on the railing. But what if it was true? What if the saboteur wasn't from the Merrow Kingdom or the Dragonfly territories? What if he wasn't part of the crew at all?

Another stowaway from the uncharted lands, just like Cyrus.

Except this man wanted to kill them.

What was she going to do? Stella's mind raced, going over the contents of her alchemy case, which she'd hidden inside the invisibility suit. No use trying the knockout powder. The pelting ice would turn it into wet clumps, rendering it useless. She'd never get a smoke bomb lit for the same reason, and that would only be a temporary distraction anyway. The one advantage she had was concealment. The saboteur didn't know she was waiting for him at the top of the ladder.

Maybe that was enough. If she could surprise the man, knock that strange, glowing rod out of his hand, at the same time it would let the saboteur know that there was someone up here hidden, defending Cyrus. It might be enough to scare him away.

The man didn't have to know that Cyrus's protector was a young girl half his body weight. No, best to keep that fact to herself.

But watching the man climb up the ladder, closer and closer—it was all Stella could do not to retreat. The light crackling at the tip of the metal rod outlined the man's face in a stark blue. And his eyes . . . they were blood-shot and empty. It wasn't just that he couldn't see her. His eyes held no emotion at all.

Why are you doing this? Stella thought, fighting off despair. *Why are you trying to kill us?*

And then she had no more time to think, for he'd drawn close enough for Stella to hear his harsh breathing. He held the metal rod parallel to his body, careful not to get its tip too near his face.

Now or never, Stella told herself, working up her courage.

Trembling, she reached down through the hole in the crow's nest floor. Slowly. Slowly. It was vital that the man see no distortion in the air, have no inkling she was only inches away.

Her hand passed beneath the crackling blue light,

and through the suit, Stella felt the hairs on her arm stand up, as if drawn to the glow. A part of her feared it, and yet the scientist in her was fascinated, wondering how it worked and from where it drew its power. It was like a tiny, trapped lightning bolt.

Then the saboteur was right in front of her. One more step up the ladder, and they would bump heads.

Swallowing her fear, Stella grabbed the metal rod just below the glowing light. She'd intended to wrench it out of the man's grip, hurl it down to the deck, then pull back into the crow's nest before he could react or figure out what had happened.

At least, that was the plan.

Stella was still envisioning it in her head when the light at the tip of the rod flashed in a brilliant halo, blinding her. The man jerked and cried out, his hand slipping from the ladder rung. At the same instant, a shock wave went through Stella's hand, traveling all the way up her arm. Pain followed the sensation, a sharp, trembling agony. She tried to pull her hand back, but it was as if her palm had been fused to the metal rod. Through her glove, her hand burned.

She screamed.

Below her, the man screamed too, fumbling on the ladder to secure his grip, but he was slipping, the wind tearing at him. Half blind, Stella fell forward onto her stomach, her upper body hanging down through the hole in the crow's nest. She still couldn't let go of the rod, and the man's grip on it dragged her down. She blinked her vision clear in time to see him lose his footing on the ice-slick ladder. His bloodshot eyes widened, and his face . . . his face . . .

Changed.

There was a ripple, as if the man had been submerged in a pool of water. When it cleared, his flesh tightened, the age lines around his mouth disappearing. The sideburns on his face receded to his temples. Years peeled away from his face, until a much younger man with blond hair and a mustache stared back at Stella. Only his eyes were the same, still bloodshot and empty of every emotion except pain.

Before Stella could react, the man's hands slipped off the ladder, and he fell, plummeting toward the deck. He managed to keep hold of the metal rod, finally ripping it from her grasp.

Freed, Stella wrenched herself up through the hole and collapsed on her back on the floor of the crow's nest. She clutched her injured hand to her chest. It still throbbed painfully, but not nearly as bad as when she'd grabbed the rod.

She stared up at the dark sky, the veil of the invisibility suit pressing against her face. Suddenly she felt as if she were suffocating. With her uninjured hand, she wrenched off the veil and hood, ignoring the cold shock of wind that hit her in the face. With the suit compromised, the rest of the invisibility effect faded, and her body shimmered into view. "Cyrus!" she yelled.

"I'm here!"

She heard his voice first, and then Cyrus's face swam into view above hers. His eyes were back to their normal brown color and full of concern. "What happened?" he asked. "I saw a light flash, and then you screamed, but I couldn't see you until now. Are you all right?"

"I think so." Gingerly, she detached the glove from the suit and pulled it off to look at her injured hand. A large, raw blister ran the length of her palm. "It was the traitor," she said, her voice unsteady. "It came from his . . . weapon or something. It was a long metal rod with a blue light at the tip. He was coming up the ladder, so I reached down, and when I touched the rod . . ." Her voice trailed off as she remembered that burst of agony and the transformation that she never would have believed if she hadn't witnessed it happening inches from her own face.

Cyrus's face paled, his whole body tense. "You say he had a rod with a blue light at the tip? And you *touched* it? Let me see!"

"I'm fine now." But Stella sat up, letting Cyrus help her lean back against the mast. She uncurled her fist and laid her open palm in her lap so he could look at the angry blister. "I have salves in my alchemy case that'll take the pain away and help the wound heal," she assured him.

Biting his lip, Cyrus nodded. "Good, then it's not as bad as I thought. Those weapons . . . well, they affect people differently."

"You've seen one before?" Stella demanded.

Cyrus nodded grimly. "In my part of the world," he said.

So she'd been right. The saboteur was from the uncharted lands.

"He fell off the ladder and onto the deck, but right before he did, his face changed," Stella said. She described the shocking alteration before realizing. "Is he still down there?"

"I'll look. Stay here," Cyrus said, squeezing her shoulder gently. "Don't move."

He stood up, grabbing the crow's nest railing for balance, and looked down at the deck, shielding his eyes against the swirling ice. A moment later, he returned to kneel beside her. "I don't see him anywhere down there," he said. "The fall was sure to hurt him. You probably scared him off—and saved my life."

If he'd felt anywhere near the pain Stella had, she wasn't surprised that the man had retreated. "He was coming after you," she said. "Who is he? *What* is he?"

Worry and sorrow pinched Cyrus's face. "He's from the uncharted lands, like me," he confirmed, his voice barely audible above the wind. "He and others like him were on the expedition I came over on. They're called the Faceless. They have the power to change their appearances. It helps them blend in."

"He's not trying to blend in!" Stella shouted, fear rising in her. "He's trying to crash the ship! Why?" She grabbed Cyrus's arm with her good hand, squeezing hard until he winced. "He wants to kill everyone on board, including himself. That's insane! Who does that?"

"I don't know why he's doing this!" Cyrus said, his voice and temper rising to match hers. "Our expeditions were just supposed to observe you, not to interact with you and certainly not to hurt you! We wanted to see what your people were like, learn about your culture and society before we made contact for the first time. We were just being cautious, I swear." He held up his hand to stop any further arguments. "Look, we won't find any answers up here in this storm! I'm exhausted, and we need to get you back to the cargo bay and treat that wound."

Stella opened her mouth to protest, but he was right. The blister on her hand was starting to throb. At that moment, the safety of their warm, dark corner of the cargo bay sounded like bliss. "What about the ship?" she asked. "Did you finish the protection net?"

Cyrus nodded. "Another half hour or so and we should be clear of the storm," he said. "We're going to make it through. Now let's get off this crow's nest before someone decides to come up onto the deck to check the skies."

And in case the Faceless man came back. He didn't say it, but Stella knew Cyrus was as worried and scared as she was. She could see it in the shadows under his eyes.

He helped her stand, and Stella followed him to the crow's nest ladder. She didn't know what made her look toward the horizon at that moment, but she was just in time to see a wall of darkness bearing down on their port side. Another storm cloud, the largest she'd yet seen. She opened her mouth to call out to Cyrus, when suddenly, the wind gusted violently, and Stella felt the world falling out from under her.

The *Iron Glory* moaned and listed starboard. Stella screamed as the crow's nest tilted sharply sideways. She slipped on the ice-slicked floor and fell, her ribs hitting the railing. She twisted and wrapped her arms around it to keep herself from tumbling off the ship and hurtling thousands of feet to the frozen ground.

Beside her, Cyrus was in worse shape. The crow's nest had turned almost horizontal. He skidded and scrambled to find a handhold against the sloping floor, but there was nothing to grab. All at once, golden light shot from his hands, as if he was trying to use his power to stop himself from falling. It didn't work. The light illuminated his body as he slid through the opening beneath the crow's nest railing. It was all happening too fast. He was going to fall.

At the last second, Stella reached out her injured hand and grabbed him by the forearm. Pain shot up her arm as his weight yanked her against the railing, but she had a secure grip on it with her other hand. Cyrus's legs dangled in the empty air above a terrible abyss. He stared up at her, eyes wide and terrified.

"It's all right," Stella gasped. "I've got you."

Only then did she remember the golden light that bled from Cyrus's hands. It had snaked its way up his forearm and now enveloped her hand as well.

His warning rang in her head like an alarm bell.

Don't. Touch. Me.

But I can't let him go, she thought. *He'll die.*

The world shimmered around her.

And then went black.

≥ FOURTEEN ≤

Where am I?

Darkness enveloped Stella, and panic wasn't far behind. What was happening? Had she and Cyrus fallen to their deaths from the crow's nest? She didn't want to believe it, but at that moment, it seemed the only explanation for the *nothingness* she was experiencing.

Stella felt no pain, no searing chill from the storm. The terrible roar of the wind was gone, leaving behind an eerie silence. She drifted in it like a boat with no anchor.

Then, out of nowhere, a faint golden light appeared in front of her, and a stinging sensation in her hand pierced the nothingness. Looking down, Stella saw her hand gripping Cyrus's forearm, just as she had done a moment ago when they dangled from the crow's nest. Strangely, the darkness obscured the rest of Cyrus's body, and the link between them—hand to arm, with no clothing covering them—was all that Stella could see.

Oh, please, please don't let us be dead, she thought. Her mother and father . . . when they found out, it would destroy them. She could picture the two of them, their shock and bewilderment when the captain came to the medical bay to give them the news.

Not Stella. Not our daughter. How could she be dead? She's not even here. *She's at home, safe with her grandparents, where we trusted her to stay.*

No, it was worse than that, Stella thought. If she and Cyrus had really fallen from the ship, no one would ever know what had happened to them. They'd just be . . . gone.

Misery clutched her heart. Trying to push it away, Stella focused all her attention on her hand joined to Cyrus's, their connection bathed in that strange golden light radiating from his skin.

Staring at his forearm, Stella realized abruptly that something was different. The gold light—somehow it had turned Cyrus's skin *translucent.* It was as if his arm were made of glass and she could see inside it, but what she saw made no sense at all.

Because what she saw was a collection of mechanical parts.

Gears, cogs, bolts, and metal plates took up the space where there should have been bones and muscle. Woven in and out of that strange menagerie were streams of golden light that reminded Stella of arteries and veins from the pictures she'd studied in her parents' medical books.

Disturbed by the sight, Stella tried to pull away, but she couldn't make her hand move. She and Cyrus might as well have been fused skin to skin. Panic made the blood pound in her ears, and it took her a moment to realize that through her shock, a voice echoed in her head. She didn't know where it came from or whose it was, but it repeated a single word. A word she'd never heard before, but somehow, she understood it was a word for what she was seeing beneath Cyrus's skin.

A name for what he truly was.

Olaran.

"Olaran," she whispered. When she said it, the vision before her flickered and faded, and Cyrus's arm returned to normal. Now she only saw a boy's forearm—smooth skin, tiny hairs, and freckles.

To look at it, she'd never know that, beneath the surface, Cyrus wasn't human at all.

He was a machine.

Olaran.

This isn't happening, Stella thought. *It has to be a dream.* Her stomach churned and heaved. She thought she might vomit. The darkness pressed in on her from all sides, trapping and suffocating. . . .

Stop! Make it stop!

As if the universe answered her cry, suddenly, the silence lifted, and the world came crashing in on Stella. She was back in the crow's nest on the *Iron Glory*, half frozen from the ice storm, holding on to Cyrus as he dangled below her. The gold light coming from his body had faded, but other than that, it was as if no time had passed at all.

But Stella's chest burned. She was crushed against the metal railing, pulled down by Cyrus's weight. How had she managed to keep hold of him during the vision? It didn't matter. She didn't think she had the strength to pull him up now.

Luckily, something else was happening around them that Stella hadn't noticed. The *Iron Glory* was fighting back against the storm. Its engines ground and groaned, and the smell of sulfur burned Stella's nose as the ship slowly righted itself. The world tilted, the crow's-nest floor coming back beneath her. Finally, she was able to shift her weight away from the railing, relieving the crushing pain.

Below her, Cyrus hooked his legs onto the crow's nest and pulled himself up and over the railing. He collapsed beside Stella. He'd lost his hat somehow, or the wind had blown it off. Ice crystals clung like beads in his dark hair.

"Are you all right?" he asked, looking over at Stella, his face colorless.

All right? When she'd just discovered there were people in the world who could change their faces and machines that could wear a human face? No, she wasn't all right, not by a long shot, but she nodded and pointed to the ladder. "Let's get off this thing," she said weakly.

He nodded. "My thoughts exactly."

Stella followed him as he crawled to the top of the ladder and began slowly climbing down from the crow's nest. Her body was present, the cold kiss of the wind stiffening her limbs, but in her mind, she was still seeing the vision of Cyrus's forearm, the machine parts, and the golden light.

She tried to analyze the science of it—if science was even involved. Touching him, touching that light, must have created some kind of connection between them that triggered the vision, allowed her to see what he truly was. That was why he'd insisted that she stay away. Did he know what she'd seen? Did he know that his secret had been exposed?

They made it down the ladder, and Stella almost wept in relief when her feet were back on solid ground. At least until she slid on the icy deck. But Cyrus was right behind her, grabbing her shoulder to keep her from falling.

Stella imagined five metal fingers digging into her skin. She yanked free of his grasp. "I'm fine!" she snapped.

"I was just trying to help." Cyrus came around to

stand in front of her, confusion swimming in his brown eyes. "What's wrong? You look like you've seen a ghost."

So he didn't realize what had happened.

Stella gritted her teeth in anger. The boy full of secrets. The boy who wouldn't tell his real name. What else was he hiding from her?

"Not a ghost," she said, and gave voice to the word that wouldn't stop churning in her thoughts. "An olaran."

Cyrus's eyes rounded, his breath fogging the air. "I see," he said after a minute. His voice was strained. "That's right. You touched me. I was so scared up there that I forgot."

"I'm such an idiot," Stella said, backing away from him. She held her hands out from her sides to keep her balance on the ice. The blister on her palm throbbed, a spot of painful heat in an icy wilderness. "All this time, I've been trying to guess your name—Connor, Olwin, Pierce, David—on and on like a game, and that was the last secret I should have been worrying about."

"I'm *sorry*, Stella," Cyrus said as the wind surged and howled around them. "I should have told you before, but I didn't think you'd believe me, and I didn't want to upset you any more than I already had."

Stella thought about that. She hated to admit it, but he had a point. She probably wouldn't have believed him if she hadn't seen what he was—what the Faceless man was—with her own eyes. What sane person would, in her place? She and her parents had often wondered about what the people in the uncharted lands would look like, how they would live, but in all her imaginings, she'd always believed the people of the uncharted lands would be, well, *alive*.

"Well, we're talking now—human to machine—so tell me what else you've been hiding!" Stella said. "Were you lying earlier? Do you actually know why the Faceless man is trying to kill us?"

Cyrus took a step toward her, closing the distance between them. She met his eyes, and then she wished she hadn't, for she wouldn't have seen the hurt shining there.

"I haven't lied to you about what I'm doing here," he said. "I stowed away because I got stranded in your part of the world, and I needed a way home. I don't know why the Faceless man wants to crash the ship, but if he does, it'll kill me too, and that's the *last* thing I want." He reached out a hand to her, a pleading look in his eyes. "Stella, the olarans—we're not machines, not the way you think of them. Our bodies are a combination of human and mechanical parts, but we're born; we have feelings, hopes, fears, dreams; and we can die, just like humans, sarnuns, and chamelins do."

"But how . . . how is that possible?" Stella asked.

He shrugged. "How do the sarnuns communicate mind to mind? How do the chamelins change their shape? Think about it. In their own way, they're just as different from humans as the olarans are."

But Stella shook her head. "It's not the same," she said. "You have machine parts under your skin. The same parts that make clocks tick and engines run, but that doesn't mean they're alive. You just . . . *Machines are not people.*"

The hurt in his eyes deepened, like the clouds darkening before the storm. "Do you really think that? That I'm less of a person than you are?"

"No! But I—I don't know! I just—" Stella couldn't finish. She didn't want to hurt him, except how could she hurt a machine? He'd been lying to her all this time about what he really was. Tears stung her eyes, freezing to her cheeks. Stella wiped them away furiously. Crying definitely wouldn't help her, and talking wasn't getting her anywhere either. She needed to get out of here, back to the cargo bay to tend to her wound. Go someplace where the hurt in Cyrus's eyes couldn't follow her.

She backed toward the hatch, but Cyrus stubbornly followed. "What are you doing?" he asked. "Stella, you have to say something!"

"Just leave me alone," she said. Seeing his stricken expression, she added, "Don't worry. I'm not going to turn you in to the crew. I just need to think. Don't try to stop me, all right?" Her throat tightened, and she knew if she stayed out here another minute, she'd start to sob.

Cyrus raised his hands in surrender. "Fine," he said. "I won't try to stop you. I learned my lesson the last time." His eyes narrowed. "But is that what explorers do where you're from—run away?"

"I'm not running!" Stella snapped, even though that was exactly what she wanted to do, turn and run back to the cargo bay as fast as she could.

"Your people *wanted* to go to the uncharted lands. To be a part of a bigger world." Cyrus's words cut like a knife. "But you didn't mean it, did you? You're afraid to see us the way we really are. You just want to see people who look like you."

"That's not fair!" Stella snapped. "I don't—"

But her words were lost when the hatch burst open and slammed against the deck. Stella slipped and fell to her knees on the ice just as a pair of crewmen came out the hatch and saw them.

⇒ FIFTEEN ⇐

For a split second, nobody spoke or moved. The crewmen stared at Stella and Cyrus, their mouths falling open in shock.

Then the tall one standing in the back said, "*Stella?*"

Stella blinked. She recognized the man. He was one of the deck crew her parents had introduced her to in the weeks leading up to the expedition. His name was Isaac, and he'd given her a tour of the main deck.

The other man's eyes narrowed in suspicion. "You know her?" he asked, his gravelly voice cutting through the dying storm.

"She's Martin and Eliza's girl," Isaac said, rubbing his face in disbelief. "Stella, what are you *doing* here?"

"I—" Stella had no idea what to say. The realization that they'd been caught—during a shouting match on the main deck, no less—broke over her like a bucket of ice water. How could she have been so stupid?

"Who's the boy?" the other crewman demanded, his gaze landing on Cyrus with the weight and chill of the storm. "And what were you two doing out here?"

Before either of them could reply, a man stepped out of the shadows from the direction of the stern. He hobbled over to them, clutching his ribs as if he was injured.

"Darin," Isaac said, rushing over to help support the man, whose face was twisted up in pain. "What happened to you? You're supposed to be at the security office."

"I was patrolling the deck, and I saw *him*," the man replied, jabbing a finger at Cyrus. "He was up in the crow's nest. I think he was going to slice through the support cables. He stopped when he saw me, came down, and attacked—he hit me in the gut with that." He nodded to the metal bar lying discarded on the deck— the same one Cyrus had used to brace the door shut earlier.

"What?" Stella burst out. "That's not true! Cyrus was trying to help, he—"

But she stopped as the man limped closer. She noticed that he was breathing unsteadily, his eyes were bloodshot, and he held his ribs as if he'd cracked or broken them in a fall.

Like a fall from the crow's nest ladder.

What was it Cyrus had said about the Faceless? They could change their appearance to blend in wherever they wanted. That was how the man had managed to remain undetected on board the ship. He could imitate any member of the crew, just as he was doing now.

To frame Cyrus as the saboteur.

Dread coiled in Stella's stomach as Isaac and the other crewmen closed in, forming a ring around her and Cyrus, their faces tightening with suspicion and anger.

Darin reached inside his coat and pulled out a metal chop saw, tossing it onto the deck with a loud clatter. "He dropped this on his way down the crow's nest ladder," he said.

Isaac picked up the saw. He examined it for a second, pricked his finger on the blade, and uttered a curse. He spat on the deck. "This could cut cable, all right," he said.

"Please," Stella said, panic growing inside her. She pointed to the Faceless man. "He's not what you think. He's lying! Cyrus, tell them!"

But Cyrus's shoulders were already slumping in defeat, as if he knew no one would believe him.

"We need some help up here!" Isaac shouted down the hatch. "Somebody get the security people on deck!"

"No!" Stella cried, but the other crewman surged forward, reaching for Cyrus. He didn't fight, only flinched as the bigger man grabbed his wrists and twisted his arms behind his back.

"Stella, come inside," Isaac said. "Step away from the boy."

He took her arm, pulling her toward the hatch. Stella resisted, but he was too strong, and the deck was too slick. The crewmen dragged her and Cyrus below.

The ship's security team met them in the hall.

≳ SIXTEEN ≋

The guards led them to the security office while Isaac went to get Stella's parents. One of the guards eyed her invisibility suit and wanted to know what it was. Stella smoothed the wrinkles in the black fabric and murmured that it was just cold-weather gear. It was the best lie she could think of in the moment. Fortunately, her hood was down from when she'd removed the veil up in the crow's nest; otherwise she would have had to explain the invisibility effect.

The Faceless man limped off with the other crewman, and Stella lost track of him when they turned a corner, disappearing into the bowels of the ship.

"I don't believe this," one of the guards said, shaking his head as he stared at Cyrus in disbelief. "He's just a boy. Kid, are you . . . Do you have any idea what kind of trouble you're in?"

Cyrus didn't answer, but Stella felt her whole world crashing down around her. All it had taken was the accusation of the Faceless man, and everyone was convinced that Cyrus was the saboteur. How could they be so blind?

But maybe she shouldn't be surprised. Maybe it was easier for them to believe a stranger was guilty, rather than one of their own turning out to be a traitor. If that wasn't bad enough, the real culprit was running around freely, and he could change his face to look like any member of the crew!

Lost in her worry and misery, Stella didn't resist when the guards sat her down in a chair in the corner by herself. She watched as they tied Cyrus's hands behind his back. Then they walked him over to the opposite corner and sat him down before surrounding him with guards. A flush of anger crept up his neck, but he didn't speak. He just stared at the floor, his jaw tight and eyes steely. But after a few minutes, even the anger drained away, until he just looked empty.

Defeated.

Stella would much rather have seen him enraged, fighting back, but at that moment, she felt as lost as he was.

The door opened. It was Drea, the first officer. She stepped into the security office, closed the door, and locked it behind her. Then she went straight to Cyrus, her feelers pressed against her back.

Drea projected her questions directly into Cyrus's mind, so Stella couldn't hear them, but he spoke his answers aloud, and the questions the guards occasionally interjected were just what she'd expected. *Who are you? Where are you from? How did you get on board the* Iron Glory?

Cyrus answered with as few words as possible. He told Drea he'd been a factory worker in Noveen and had snuck aboard the ship while the cargo was being loaded because he'd never been on an airship before and thought it sounded like an adventure. He claimed his parents were dead and that he lived with an uncle who worked and traveled on the 401 train out of Noveen. Cyrus said he was rarely around and probably hadn't even missed him yet.

As he spun his story, Stella realized that Cyrus had probably thought up all of those details beforehand in case he was ever captured. He might have told Stella the same story when they first met, if Stella hadn't seen him use his power outside the cargo bay. Maybe she would have believed him. He certainly sounded convincing and boldly looked Drea in the eyes when he spoke, never wavering in his speech.

Stella couldn't imagine what the first officer must have been thinking or if she believed any part of Cyrus's story. Though if she didn't, what was the alternative? If Cyrus told her he was from the uncharted lands and that he had magical powers to protect the ship from a saboteur who could put on a new face as easily as Stella cracked a smile, she'd probably think he was crazy.

The door to the security office opened again, and Stella's parents entered the room.

All the air left Stella's lungs. It hadn't been long since she'd visited her parents in the medical bay, but her heart still flip-flopped in her chest when she saw them. They were both more composed now than they had been the last time Stella had seen them, and as they entered the room, their gazes immediately found hers.

"Are you all right?" her mother asked. Without waiting for an answer, she knelt by Stella's chair and went straight into healer mode, checking her over for injuries. It took her all of ten seconds to find the angry blister on Stella's hand. "How did this happen?" she demanded.

"We found them outside during the ice storm," one of the guards said before Stella could answer. "It might have been the saboteur's doing."

"That's a lie!" Stella burst out angrily. She looked up when her father put his hand on her shoulder. "Cyrus isn't the one sabotaging the ship! We were trying to protect it!"

"Stella," Cyrus said sharply, looking up from the floor. "Don't. Don't say anything."

Stella read the plea in his eyes. He didn't want her to tell them about his powers, about what he was. Stella swallowed. But what if the truth convinced them that he wasn't the guilty one? That he wasn't even from either Merrow *or* Dragonfly?

But the truth might also make the crew even more afraid and suspicious of him. Hadn't she reacted with fear when she'd learned he was really a machine? He'd taken his cues from her and was trying to protect his secret.

Stella's mother looked at Cyrus, frowning. "Does he really need to be bound, Drea?" she asked. "The boy's surrounded by guards. He's obviously not going anywhere."

Drea glanced at Stella's mother, her feelers stirring around her shoulders, but one of the guards spoke up first.

"Considering that he managed to elude every crew member on this ship for the past week and tried to sabotage the *Iron Glory* at least twice, I'm not convinced we're being careful enough," the guard said.

Drea nodded in agreement, and suddenly, the sarnun woman's mental voice echoed inside Stella's head. She must have been projecting it through the room so everyone could hear her. "Doctors Glass, for the moment, I'm releasing your daughter into your care. I'll come to the medical bay soon to question her about her involvement in this, but right now I need to speak to the prisoner."

It was clearly a dismissal, but Stella didn't move. Instead, she glanced at Cyrus, willing him to look up at her, but he was staring at the floor again with that same look of defeat in his eyes.

Her father squeezed her shoulder. "Come on, Stella," he said quietly. "Time to go."

Reluctantly, Stella rose to follow her parents out the door. She looked back one more time to try to catch Cyrus's eye, but he didn't move. He seemed to have forgotten she was there at all.

SEVENTEEN

Stella walked with her parents to the medical bay in heavy silence. When she stepped inside, the room was a mess. Everything on the counters and exam tables had been knocked to the floor when the ship tilted in the storm. Broken glass, medicines, powders, and herbs were smeared all over.

"Watch your step," Stella's father said, getting the broom and dustpan, just as he'd done when Stella had come to see them before.

Stella's mother treated the wound on her hand, and afterward they spent a few minutes getting the room into a semblance of order so they had somewhere to sit. Stella picked up jars that were still intact and replaced them on the counters while her parents cleaned and swept the floor.

As they worked, a few of the crew came in with

minor injuries from the ship being tossed about during the storm. Stella took note, but the Faceless man wasn't among them, or at least he wasn't wearing the same crewman's form that she'd seen on deck. Stella's mother bandaged the men and women up and did her best to put off their questions and shocked glances in Stella's direction.

Stella ignored them, but seeing their injuries reminded her that fierce winds were no longer shaking and battering the ship. Whatever Cyrus had done to protect the *Iron Glory*, it had obviously worked. The ship had made it through the storm.

Cyrus had saved them all.

Now the crew had taken him prisoner, accusing him of sabotaging the ship.

Restless, Stella perched on the edge of the cot in the back of the room while her parents finished tending to the crew. When the last man had left the room with his arm in a sling, her mother and father pulled up chairs and sat down.

The way they'd gathered around her, quiet and expectant, Stella knew they were going to want an explanation. For everything. All those questions she saw swimming in their eyes were about to come.

How much should she tell them? She knew Cyrus didn't want his identity known, but Stella trusted her parents completely. If anyone was going to believe her story and support Cyrus, it was her mother and father.

Stella took a deep breath and launched into the story without waiting for them to ask. She started with the day she'd said goodbye to her parents on the palace grounds and then snuck onto the airship. She told them Cyrus's story about the olaran expeditions and how he'd stowed away on the *Iron Glory* after being stranded. For proof, she showed them the invisibility suit she was still wearing, demonstrating its power and how it worked, which prompted gasps and wide-eyed stares from them both.

She described the Faceless man and his abilities, how he planned to use them to blend in with the crew, sabotage the ship, and frame Cyrus for it.

Her parents interrupted with questions now and then, but mostly the room was silent while they let her talk. When she was finished, Stella's voice was hoarse. Her mother handed her a glass of water.

Now that the story was finally out there, Stella felt exhausted, as if a weight had been lifted from her shoulders. No matter how much trouble she was in with her parents, no matter how angry they might be at her, she was glad to have told the story to someone else, to share the burden she'd been carrying ever since she learned about the Faceless man and discovered what Cyrus really was.

"Well," her father said, clearing his throat. He shot a quick glance at the door, making sure there was no one passing by who might overhear them. "I think you were right not to tell the crew about Cyrus, at least not yet.

Tensions are very high right now, and as long as they believe Cyrus is the saboteur, the revelation that he's also a . . . machine . . . or part machine is just going to make things worse."

"They already are worse," Stella's mother countered, inspiring hope inside Stella. "The crew thinks they've captured the person who set the fire and sawed through the support cables, but he's still out there. Don't we owe it to the crew to warn them?"

"Even if they accept what Cyrus is, they've seen no sign of this Faceless man," Stella's father said, "and if he can look like any member of the crew, they're not likely to be able to find him."

"It also means we don't know who to trust," Stella said quietly.

Silence fell over the room at that grim truth. If the Faceless man could imitate any of them, he could use that power to influence the other crew members, turn them against one another, or stoke their fear and suspicion of Cyrus. He could cause all kinds of strife.

Her mother was right. Things were bad enough when they knew there was a saboteur on board, but now they were so much worse.

"We'll just have to find a way to convince the captain and first officer that the real saboteur is still out there," Stella's mother said. "Maybe wait a couple of days for everyone to calm down and clear their heads."

"With any luck, by that time we may have cleared the

mountains and be able to land," her father agreed. "But we'll need to be watchful until then, look for any crew member acting strangely or doing anything out of the ordinary. It's also possible that the Faceless man is hiding somewhere on the ship, nursing his injuries and not in any position to attack again soon."

"He did take a hard fall to the deck," Stella said, shuddering at the memory of their encounter at the top of the crow's nest.

"So we also need to watch for crew members coming in with injuries from a fall," Stella's mother noted. "Good to know."

With that much sorted out, Stella felt a little bit better. But as the minutes ticked past, her parents grew very quiet, and new worries gnawed at her. She desperately wanted to know what they were thinking, yet she was afraid to ask. She'd told them almost everything that had happened since she snuck aboard the ship, but she'd left out one important part.

She left out *why* she'd done it.

As she sat there, Stella realized her parents were waiting for her to tell that part of her story. She felt it in the weight of their silence. They were giving her a chance to gather her thoughts, but if she didn't say something soon, she knew they would demand an explanation.

"I'm sorry," she said. Unable to meet their eyes, she stared at the floor instead. "I wasn't expecting any of this to happen. If I had known . . ." What would she have done differently? Nothing. She would do anything to protect her parents from the saboteur. And now that she'd had the chance to calm down and think, she realized that she didn't regret meeting Cyrus. If they'd never met, she'd never have been able to help him protect the ship. They'd accomplished more together than they could have done alone.

Even if he'd lied to her about who—what—he really was.

Her father cleared his throat. "If Cyrus and the Faceless man had never come on board the ship and everything had gone according to your plan, when would you have come out of hiding?" he asked. "When we reached the uncharted lands?" Stella couldn't tell by his tone what he was feeling. Her father was always the hardest person in the family to read.

She nodded. "I didn't want to take the chance that the ship might turn around to take me back," she said.

"What if the ship had landed in an area with bandits or slavers?" her father continued, his voice rising slightly. "What if the ship had been captured and the crew taken captive?"

Stella didn't have answers, and worse, she knew all three of them were thinking the same thing—that it might still happen, and with the Faceless man on board waiting to strike, the journey was already much more dangerous than any of them had expected. "At least we would be together," Stella said, "and I would know what had happened to you. I couldn't stand it if you . . . if you both just didn't come home."

Out of the corner of her eye, Stella caught her mother bowing her head, rubbing her temple with two fingers. "Mom, please say something," she begged.

But it was a long moment of painful silence before Stella got an answer. "I was so sure," her mother said, shaking her head. "The day we left, I was certain you were going to be all right. You were sad and worried, of course—we all were. But you seemed so strong too, so brave, and it made me feel better than I had in weeks. I told myself that everything would be fine. It never once crossed my mind that you might have been planning something like this."

Stella wanted to sink into the floor, to fall onto a cloud and float away. "I was only brave because I knew it wasn't really goodbye," she whispered.

"You were worried for our safety?" her father asked, leaning forward so Stella would turn to look at him.

"Yes . . . I mean I was, but there's more." What was she trying to say? Stella felt lost. Why couldn't they just yell at her? Why did they have to try so hard to *understand*? She didn't want to explain it, to look inside herself. All she wanted to do was shut her eyes and hide.

"Please, just be angry," she said, reaching out to her

mother. She stopped shy of touching her arm and drew back. "You deserve to be angry, to shout and throw things and tell me how stupidly I've acted."

But her pleas didn't do any good. Both her parents remained stubbornly calm. "You've been many things, Stella," her father said. "You've lied, behaved recklessly and irresponsibly—but you're not stupid. And you've also been courageous and resourceful, and proved more than capable of handling yourself in a crisis. Yours and Cyrus's actions saved the *Iron Glory* and everyone on board, even if we're the only ones who realize it." He glanced at his wife. "We haven't forgotten that, have we?"

"No, we haven't," her mother agreed. "When we get home, we'll need to have a long talk about all this, the lies you told, and the worry and hurt you've put us—not to mention your grandparents—through, but for now . . . I wish I could be angry with you, Stella. Anger would be so much easier, but I'm just too afraid of what's going to happen next." She looked at Stella's injured hand as she spoke. "I'm terrified that I'll be so wrapped up worrying about your safety that I won't be able to do my duty to this ship and the people on it. I wanted to drop everything when I saw you in that security office. I forgot all about the crew and their needs after the storm, because all I could think about was that you were here, and you were in danger. That Faceless man might have killed you, and it would have destroyed me."

Shouting was nothing compared to this. If her mother had slapped her, it wouldn't have hurt as much.

"I'm sorry," Stella said, knowing it wasn't enough. "I was just so afraid." Her voice dropped to a whisper.

"There was always the risk that something might happen to us," her father said. "But you—"

"No, that wasn't all," Stella interrupted, digging her fingernails into her palms. She had to tell them. She owed them this. "Part of me was afraid that everything would work out fine, that it would be an amazing expedition, the trip of a lifetime."

That stunned them silent for a moment, but her mother recovered first. "So you wanted the expedition to fail?" she asked, bewildered. "Why, Stella?"

"Because the expedition means that things are changing," Stella said. "The world is so much bigger than I thought it was, and that's exciting and wonderful, but . . . maybe I don't want *everything* to change. What if the people and places you find in the uncharted lands are more exciting than our life back home?"

Stella knew how important her parents' work was to them, their passion for making new discoveries. No matter how much they loved Noveen, it couldn't compete with the wonders of the uncharted lands. If, despite everything, this mission succeeded, King Aron would likely send many more expeditions over the mountains, and of course, he'd order her parents to be a part of them. He had to have the best. They'd be gone weeks, then months, at a time. Longer and longer periods of them slipping away, until one day her parents wouldn't be a part of her life anymore. Then where would she be?

"Oh, honey." Her mother reached out and cupped Stella's face in her hands. "Listen to me. There is *nothing* in the uncharted lands that would make us want to give up the life we've built with you," she said.

"You're our whole world, Stella," her father said, his voice rough. He leaned over and laid a hand on her arm. "Don't you know that?"

Stella wanted to believe them. She really did. With her parents here beside her, she felt safe, as if all the crucial pieces of herself were in place. But the doubt lingered, a voice in her head whispering that the uncharted lands would lure them away, take them places she couldn't follow.

"How can you be sure?" Stella asked. "What if, once you've seen—"

"Nothing we see is as important as you are to us, Stella," her father said. "Yes, the world is changing, and we can't ignore that. But just because we can't go back to the way things were doesn't mean that we'll lose what we've built as a family."

"Your father's right." Her mother leaned forward, brushing strands of hair out of Stella's eyes. "And it's not just the geography of the world that's different now.

We've all been changed—by the Iron War, by the peace we're trying to forge between Merrow and Dragonfly, and by these new adventures, and that can be frightening, not knowing what the future holds. There are so many new people to meet and to try to understand. The way you're trying to understand Cyrus."

Cyrus.

It was as if her mother's words were a spell, or maybe they broke the spell, but suddenly all of Stella's confused, painful feelings came rushing in at her. The threat of death, the fear of losing her family, and the discovery of what Cyrus was—it was all too much. She reached out, and her mother enfolded her in a hug just as Stella burst into tears.

She let it all out. All the worry and fear that had been knotted in her chest ever since she found out her parents would be going on the expedition without her. Harder to manage was the regret over what had happened between her and Cyrus. Yes, he had lied to her, but Stella had hurt him in return.

Cyrus's face flashed in Stella's mind, followed immediately by the image of the machine parts under his skin. Were his parents like him—a hybrid of human and machine? She supposed they must be. Either way, they were waiting for him right now, in the uncharted lands. Or did they believe he was dead, since he didn't return with the rest of his people when he was supposed to?

We have feelings, hopes, fears, dreams.
And we can die.

That was what Cyrus had told her.

No matter what lies beneath their skin, if they felt even half what Stella did as she sat there with her parents, then she could only imagine the pain and panic Cyrus's family were going through, thinking their son was lost forever. She and Cyrus were so much more alike than Stella had ever realized.

Stella lifted her head from her mother's shoulder. She'd been shocked before, her mind reeling over the idea that Cyrus could be both a person and a machine, but she should have thought it through. He was right. Stella's people had come on this expedition hoping to make new discoveries in the uncharted lands. Well, Cyrus was without a doubt the biggest discovery of her life, and what had she done? She'd run away, unable to accept him, let alone allow that they might become friends.

She had to make things right. Even if he didn't want to be her friend now, she owed Cyrus her life, her parents' lives, and the rest of the crew's. The *Iron Glory* would be lost without his protection. She had to do whatever she could to help him get home.

She wiped her tears. "Cyrus is . . ." How could she explain it to her parents? "When I first met him," she said, remembering that day in the cargo bay, "I thought he was the most arrogant, annoying boy, only thinking about himself. Oh, I just wanted to toss him out into the clouds."

"Sounds like a promising start," her father said with a chuckle, while her mother just smiled knowingly.

"But that's just what he wants you to think," Stella went on. "When he thinks no one's looking, he changes. He's . . . sad and lost." She reached out to squeeze her mother's hand. "He just wants to get home to his family, but now he's a prisoner, and there's no way for me to help him."

"We'll find a way," her mother said firmly. "Give it some time, and we'll talk to the captain. For now, I think you need rest." She added, "In a real bed, for a change."

But they stayed in the medical bay for a while longer, talking and just being in one another's presence. Stella had missed them so much. Eventually, though, her eyelids drooped, and her head got so heavy she could barely hold it up.

Her father took her to their quarters and brought in another cot for her to sleep on. When Stella lay down, she still found herself fighting sleep, worrying about Cyrus and the Faceless man. She also thought of her and Cyrus's belongings, abandoned down in the cargo bay. Would she have a chance to retrieve them before one of the crew—or worse, the Faceless man—found the hiding place?

Her father seemed to sense her restlessness. "We'll

wake you if anything happens," he promised her. His voice was warm and soothing and brought with it all the comfort and meaning of home.

His words were the last thing Stella heard before she fell into an exhausted slumber.

EIGHTEEN

The next day, Stella kept busy helping her parents in the medical bay and keeping watch for the Faceless man around every corner. She wasn't allowed to see Cyrus, but Captain Keeler and First Officer Drea came by to question her about her activities on the ship and her time with him. Stella answered them as honestly as she could without betraying Cyrus's secrets or revealing his identity.

They never rebuked her for stowing away on board the ship, although Stella suspected there might have been conversations with her parents about it in private. This brought on a fresh wave of guilt at the idea of her mother and father being reprimanded on her behalf.

Stella tried to convince the captain that Cyrus was innocent, that the real threat was still out there, but she could see by the look in his eyes that he didn't believe her.

"The boy is a very good liar," the captain said at one point. "Maybe you saw a shadow in the storm, and he convinced you that someone was coming after you."

Sure, Stella thought, biting her tongue. A shadow carrying a glowing rod that shot sparks at the tip. That must have been it. But she couldn't say that out loud. Wherever the Faceless man had gone, he'd taken the weapon with him, so she had no proof of its existence. The blister on her hand could have been explained by any number of things, considering she'd been up in the crow's nest all through the storm.

"We've searched the ship thoroughly," the captain went on. "We even found your camp in the cargo bay. If there were someone else hiding on board, we would have found him by now."

He spoke to her as if she were a small child. Stella had to grit her teeth to keep from screaming in frustration. They would *never* find the real culprit, not when he could change his face to look like whomever he wanted. If only she could tell them that. But she knew they would never believe such a far-fetched story.

As if sensing Stella's frustration, Drea spoke, her voice a soothing echo in Stella's mind. "Don't fret, my dear," she said. "It's not just you the boy's deceived. He's hiding secrets, but I promise you, we'll do everything in our power to keep the ship safe."

So Stella could do nothing but wait as the *Iron Glory*

drew closer and closer to the uncharted lands. The navigator predicted that soon they would leave the mountains behind completely and could start looking for a place to land and begin exploring.

That night, Stella lay in her cot in her parents' room, alone. Her mother and father were staying late in the medical bay, preparing for when the ship landed and the expedition moved outdoors. Shifting onto her side, she leaned over and shoved her hand beneath the mattress, where she'd hidden the invisibility suit. She kept it near her at all times and was determined to keep it out of the Faceless man's reach.

Their journey was getting closer and closer to being over, yet there'd been no more signs of the Faceless man, no more instances of sabotage. Had he given up trying to crash the ship? That seemed too much to hope for. Maybe he really had hurt himself too badly in the fall from the crow's nest to do any more damage.

As she lay in the dark, brooding, a strange, faint sound reached Stella's ears. If the room hadn't been empty and quiet, she might not have heard it at all. It was soft and repetitive, a *click-whir-click* noise . . . like some small machine running nearby, or maybe an echo coming up from the engine room.

Click . . . whir . . . click.

Closer now.

Stella sat up, her eyes drawn to the crack of light

shining beneath the door. But the sound wasn't coming from the hallway, it was . . .

Inside the room.

Above her.

She jerked her head up, and there it was, barely visible in the dim light—a small insect flying unsteadily toward her, bumping against the ceiling as it went.

Now, that was odd. Stella got out of bed and moved to stand underneath the thing to get a better look at it. She hadn't seen any insects on board the ship. It was too cold and the ship was flying too high, but she supposed that didn't mean there weren't any. This little one could have stowed away at the same time she did.

You're far away from home now, Stella thought with a pang of sympathy.

Suddenly, the insect stopped bumping the ceiling, hovered in the air for a moment, and then zipped down, swooping right in front of Stella's face.

Stella jumped back in surprise, but the insect followed her, hovering persistently near the bridge of her nose. She turned her head from side to side, bobbed up and down, but every time she moved, so did the little bug.

Click . . . whir . . . click.

Surely it couldn't . . . see her?

She squinted at the insect and realized it was a beetle. Its wings were coppery red, just like the little figure she'd seen in Cyrus's knapsack that day she'd knocked him out with the powder.

Stella's mouth fell open in shock. It wasn't *like* the beetle—it was the *same* beetle! But that hadn't been a real insect. She could have sworn it was just a statue or a toy or . . . something.

Or a machine, a little voice inside Stella's head whispered.

The hairs on her neck and arms prickled. Cautiously, Stella raised her hands and cupped them beneath the hovering beetle. Swiftly, it folded its wings up and dropped onto her palm. The whirring sound cut off, and the antennae jutting from its tiny head quivered as if to say, *Well, it's about time.*

Stella stared at the thing. Was it an insect-machine hybrid, like Cyrus? Could it communicate? She leaned in close to whisper to the beetle.

"Can you understand me?" she asked, her warm breath making the beetle's antennae dance.

The beetle shifted in her palm, rotating until its head was facing away from Stella. Then it lifted and spread its wings as if it was going to fly off.

"Oh, please don't go," Stella said.

But the beetle wasn't taking off. Instead, it broke the silence by emitting a high-pitched whine from its abdomen. After a second or two, the sound faded, replaced by a voice.

"Stella?" the voice asked. It was low and scratchy, echoing in the quiet room.

Stella gasped. That was *Cyrus's* voice, coming from inside the beetle.

"Stella, I don't know if you'll get this message—this is the first time they've left me alone long enough to record it—but you have to listen to me." He sounded upset. "I know you're mad at me, and you've got reason to be, but you have to forget about that and do something about the Faceless man.

"I heard from the other security officers that the ship is almost out of the mountains. I don't know why the Faceless man is trying to crash the ship, but it's obvious he doesn't want the expedition to reach the uncharted lands. He's going to try again, Stella, and I can't do anything to stop it or protect the ship while I'm locked up in here. It's up to you, but there's something you need to know. It's true the Faceless man can make himself look like anyone he wants, but there are limits to his powers. I met a few of the Faceless ones during the expedition, and no matter how hard they try, there's always something, some detail about their appearance they can't alter. Now, think back. You've seen the Faceless man change. You might have seen that detail without realizing it. You can use that to catch him, Stella."

Stella tried to remember her encounter on the crow's nest. She remembered the Faceless man had gone from an older man to a younger man in the blink of an eye. She'd been so shocked she hadn't noted any other details, except how dead and empty his eyes had seemed.

Stella caught her breath.

His bloodshot eyes. That was it. The detail the man couldn't change. He'd had terribly red eyes in both faces, as if he hadn't slept in days. It might not be enough to catch him, but it was a place to start.

Static crackled from the beetle. The message wasn't finished. "If you want to send me back a message, you can use the tictan—the beetle," Cyrus said. "Press the little button beneath its wings, and you'll have a minute or so of recording time. Once you're done, let the beetle go and it'll find me. I've programmed it to go back and forth between us." His voice dropped. "Don't worry. This one's just a machine. It's not alive, so you don't have to be afraid of it."

Stella's heart squeezed in her chest.

"Anyway, if you can send a message back . . . just . . . please do it," Cyrus said. "I need to know what you're thinking."

With that, the beetle tucked its copper wings back against its body and settled into her palm, where it lay, unmoving, like the statue that she'd once believed it to be. Obviously, that was the end of the message.

Stella sat down on the edge of her cot, a jumble of feelings coursing through her. The scientist part of her marveled at the tiny contraption in her hand. A machine that could hold a voice and carry messages! And somehow, the beetle had known to come straight to her. Was there no end to the wonders in Cyrus's land?

It all felt like magic.

Stella shook her head. Another part of her couldn't afford to think about that now. The important thing was that Cyrus had reached out to her, despite the risk that someone might discover he was sending secret messages. He was trying to warn her, but more than that, he was upset.

And trapped.

She needed to make things right between them, and then together they could come up with a plan for catching the Faceless man. But she wasn't going to accomplish any of that by sending one-minute messages through the beetle, no matter how amazing a machine it was. She needed to be able to look Cyrus in the eyes when she spoke to him.

Stella got up and dressed, slipping quickly into the invisibility suit. With the exception of her parents, no one among the crew knew of its existence. She could use the suit to sneak into the security office and get to Cyrus. Maybe even free him. Then they could go hunt for the Faceless man together.

When she was ready, Stella put the inert beetle into the suit's pocket and made her way out into the hallway, checking first to make sure it was deserted.

The stairs at the end of the hall would take her all

the way up to the hatch to the outside deck or down to where the security office was. Stella headed down. She had to take extra care on the metal risers so that her footsteps didn't echo and give her away.

When she got to the next landing, she glanced down the hallway. A guard was standing in front of the security office door as usual. Undeterred, Stella crept along the hallway, pressing her body against the wall opposite the guard. She slowly closed the distance between them, her eyes scanning the floor as she went.

There. A small rusted screw lay on the floor near the wall. Crouching, Stella picked it up and flicked it down the hallway. It clattered to the floor, and the guard's attention snapped in that direction. He pushed off the wall and walked down the hall to follow the sound.

"Who's down there?" he called.

Quickly, Stella went to the door and eased it open a crack. Thankfully, it didn't squeak.

Inside the security office, there were two rooms. The main office had two more guards in it, but Stella got lucky. There was a woman sitting at a desk in the corner opposite the door, her back to Stella, and a chamelin sleeping on a cot nearby. There was a ring of keys on his belt.

Opposite the cot was a door on the right-hand wall. Stella would have bet all the coin she had that Cyrus was locked in the room behind the door.

Her resolve wavered as she spied on the guards. Counting the man in the hall, there were three of them assigned to watch Cyrus. She hadn't expected there to be so many, not for one boy. Even with the invisibility suit, she wasn't going to be able to distract all the guards long enough to get Cyrus out of here, not by herself. In fact, it would take every bit of skill she'd accumulated with the suit just to get past these two.

Moving ever so slowly, Stella stepped into the room and closed the door behind her. Maybe she couldn't bust Cyrus out of here, but she'd come too far not to at least try to sneak in to see him. And they still had to come up with a plan for catching the Faceless man.

Sweat dripped down her back, and Stella's hands trembled as she made her way over to the cot, her eyes never leaving the keys on the chamelin's belt. She hoped that he was a deep sleeper, because in his lizard-like form, all his senses were enhanced. The slightest noise and she risked waking him.

Carefully, she knelt down beside the cot until she was at eye level with the keys. The woman at the desk was writing something in a journal. The only sound in the room was her pen scratching the paper's surface and the steady, quiet breathing of the chamelin.

Swallowing her fear, Stella reached out a shaking hand and closed her fingers around the key ring, pressing them together in a bunch as slowly and as quietly as possible so they wouldn't jingle. Then, using her other hand, she started to unhook the key ring from the belt.

The chamelin snorted and rolled over, tugging on the keys.

Panicked, Stella moved with him, frantically working to unhook the ring as she went. The chamelin was about to roll over onto her hand, trapping her and probably waking him. At the last second, Stella loosed the ring from the belt and pulled the keys free.

She'd done it. Letting out a quiet sigh of relief and casting a glance at the woman still writing, Stella stood up and went to the door. A gentle test told her it was locked. Keeping an eye on the woman at the desk, Stella tried each of the keys until she found one that slid into the lock.

Now the final test. All the woman's attention was on the journal in front of her, but if she looked up just once, she'd see the door to Cyrus's room opening by itself.

Stella counted to ten in her head, dredged up her courage, and turned the knob on the door. She eased it open slowly . . . so slowly.

The woman didn't move, didn't look up.

Stella opened the door just wide enough to slip into the room.

≈ NINETEEN ≈

There wasn't much in the room, just a small cot in the corner with a table and a lantern. Cyrus lay on the cot on his side, facing away from her. He looked like he was asleep, but Stella knew better. Having slept just a few feet away from him in the cargo bay for several days, she knew that when Cyrus truly fell asleep, he flopped onto his back, flung his right arm over his eyes, and snored. Not loud, obnoxious snoring, but more like quiet snuffling sounds that went on all night.

Using the flickering lantern light on the table to guide her, Stella made her way quietly over to the side of Cyrus's cot and crouched down. She laid her left hand on the boy's shoulder, at the same time putting her right hand over his mouth.

Cyrus jumped and immediately jerked forward, trying to free himself from her hold. He let out an involuntary yelp, but luckily, Stella's hand muffled the sound. "It's all right," she whispered in his ear. "It's me."

She'd meant to reassure him, but instead of relaxing, Cyrus just pulled harder to escape her, squirming and twisting on the cot until Stella removed her hand from his mouth. She kept hold of his shoulder so he'd know where she was.

"Are you crazy?" Cyrus hissed angrily when he could speak. He scowled at the empty air. "You scared me half to death. What are you doing here?"

"I got your message," Stella said impatiently. She came around the side of the cot and sat down on the edge so she could keep one eye on the door. "I think it's safe to talk. One of the guards is asleep and the other's occupied."

She took off her veil and hood, deactivating the suit so Cyrus could see her. The suit had been a lifesaver in an ice storm, but, indoors, it was like baking in an oven. She raked sweaty bangs away from her forehead.

"That's better," she said, keeping her voice low. She reached into her pocket and pulled out the beetle, handing it to him.

Cyrus looked at the object, confusion joining the scowl on his face. "Why did you risk coming here?" he asked. "Why didn't you just send the beetle back with a message?"

Suddenly self-conscious, Stella looked down at the

floor. It was harder to talk to Cyrus now that she was visible. When he was able to look at her, she couldn't hide anything. There was so much she wanted to say, but the words caught in her throat.

The silence stretched, and finally Cyrus sighed, rubbing the back of his neck. "Aw, this is such a mess," he said. "Listen, is there any way we . . . I mean . . . Stella, can we start over?"

He wanted a fresh start. Stella felt her nervousness slipping away. This was what she'd hoped for, wasn't it? She couldn't mess things up now. "Yes!" she said, letting the words tumble out before she lost her courage. "Cyrus, I'm so sorry. About everything. I'm sorry you're locked up here, and I'm sorry for what happened the day of the storm."

She folded her hands tightly in her lap. "You were right about what you said—about me. I've been trying to be this great explorer off to see the world, but I had no idea what I was getting into. I'm terrified of tight spaces, so I obviously wasn't meant to travel on an airship. I have the chance to see the uncharted lands, yet every night I lie awake wishing I were home in my own bed, where I'm safe and everything makes sense! And there are all these possibilities for new discoveries, but at the first sight of one, I ran away and I . . . hurt you. I'm the worst explorer ever."

"Now, wait a minute. Slow down. I didn't mean

you were a bad explorer," Cyrus said. The light from the bedside lamp illuminated the distress in his eyes. "I shouldn't have said it like that."

"It doesn't matter." Stella shook her head. "I didn't mean what I said either. But the Faceless man had just come after us, and then I saw that vision of your arm, and I was just so shocked and scared it made all those terrible things come out." She'd accused him of not being a *person*. Who would say a thing like that?

But Cyrus nodded as if he understood. "I should have told you the truth before the storm. The way you found out my secret—it would scare anyone to pieces." Stella opened her mouth to protest, but he held up a hand to stop her. "No, I mean it. Any other human in Solace would have taken one look inside my mind, screamed his head off, and dropped me from that crow's nest like a sack of salt. But not you," he said, looking at her now in wonder and admiration. "Your hand never even slipped."

Stella didn't want to think about what might have happened if she'd let go. "Is that what caused the vision?" she asked, shifting the conversation to a less frightening subject. "Was I really looking inside your mind?"

Cyrus nodded. "I don't completely understand how that part of my power works, but when I touch someone while I'm using it, it's like there are all these doors around my mind and heart that open up, and whoever

I'm touching can just step through. I can't hide anything from them. I think maybe it's because while I'm creating a barrier, all my own shields are down, if that makes any sense. My power's handy, but that's a really inconvenient side effect, let me tell you." He sighed. "Although, in this case, I'm glad you know. I'm so tired of keeping secrets." He shook his head, and unexpectedly, a grin tugged at his lips. "You make it impossible anyway, with your eyes."

"My eyes?" Stella was suddenly wary. "What do you mean? What's wrong with my eyes?"

"There's nothing *wrong* with them," Cyrus said quickly. "I'm not saying they're magical or anything. It's just when I look into them, I don't want to lie to you." He ran his hand through his hair. "And the more it seemed like we were becoming friends, the worse it got. Talk about inconvenient. Here I was with all these secrets, and you're asking questions and staring at me with those earnest, *please tell me the truth* eyes. I didn't stand a chance."

For a minute, Stella was speechless. *Wait.* Was he complimenting her eyes or not? She couldn't decide. But if he really couldn't lie to her . . .

"All right, then. If you're so powerless against me—what's your real name?" she asked, leaning forward so he got the full effect of her truth stare, or whatever it was.

He slumped back onto the cot, raising his hands in defeat. "It's *Cyrus*," he said with a groan.

"Ha!" Stella said, keeping her voice low but triumphant. "See, you're not helpless after all. You're just—wait. Wait. One. Minute." Slowly, the truth dawned on her, and she pulled a death glare instead of a truth stare. "Your name really *is* Cyrus, isn't it? You just tried to make me think it wasn't!"

He nodded sheepishly. "When we met and you asked me my name, I blurted it out without thinking. I couldn't believe I was such an idiot! Seriously, those eyes of yours are dangerous. You should be careful where you point them."

Stella didn't know whether to laugh at him or strangle him. All this time, she'd been trying to guess Cyrus's name, when she'd been using it all along. She decided she might as well laugh. "Good," she said. "I'm glad Cyrus is your real name."

"Because it means you won't have to memorize a new one?"

"Excellent point, but no." She grinned at him. "I'm glad because I like it," she said. "It's a nice name."

He grinned back, and hope sprang in Stella. Maybe they really could start over, even after everything that had happened. Maybe they could be friends. There was still so much she wanted to know about him. "Are all the people in the uncharted lands human-machine like you?" she asked tentatively. "Olarans?"

"That's right," Cyrus said. "No humans, sarnuns, or chamelins. In fact, when we first saw your people—

humans, I mean—we thought you were olarans too. It was only by studying some medical books that we found out your physiology is different."

"And do they all have . . . powers . . . like you and the Faceless man?" Stella asked. "Putting up barriers and changing their appearances?"

"Some of us do, but not everyone," Cyrus said. "Those who have powers are usually employed in some way by the alagant—sorry, that's our word for 'queen'—when they come of age, because we're unique. I'm not sure if that's what I'll do or not. My parents don't have any special powers, but they know several people in the royal district of Kovall who do." He added, "That's where most of the olarans live—the city-state of Kovall. It's huge, bigger than any city on your side of Solace, and so beautiful." There was a thread of longing in his voice. "A high stone wall encircles it, and the wall's covered in murals done by famous artists. If the *Iron Glory* stays on course, we'll reach the city not long after we've crossed the mountains." He smiled. "It's my home."

Kovall. All this time Stella had wanted to know where Cyrus lived. It sounded like an amazing city.

"How did you get stranded on your expedition?" she pressed. Before, when she'd asked him this question, he hadn't answered, but now that they were beginning to trust each other, Stella hoped he would confide in her. "What happened?"

Cyrus didn't immediately reply. He reached in his

pocket and pulled out the piece of paper she'd found while he was unconscious the first day they'd met. He must have hidden it and the beetle somehow when the guards had taken him. "I assume you were able to read this, since it's written in your language?" he asked.

Stella nodded, her cheeks burning in embarrassment. He must have guessed she'd gone through his belongings while he slept, but if he was upset that she'd rummaged around in his things, he didn't say it. "Why is it written in one of our languages instead of yours?" she asked, and then another thought struck her. "How do you even know our Trader's Speech?"

"The expedition I came over on was the last of five, remember," Cyrus explained. "By that point, we'd picked up enough of your language from studying books and listening to your people. It's not so different from our own. As for the note, the person who left it didn't want to leave any traces of our people behind, including our language." Cyrus unfolded the note and read it aloud. "'I hope you find this because it means you got away. I'm so sorry. We couldn't wait. I'll tell them everything. It's my fault. I'm so sorry.'" He spoke the words with no inflection. When he'd finished, Cyrus crumpled the note into a tight ball and bounced it off the wall. "My teacher wrote that," he said in a dull voice.

"Your teacher?" she asked, surprised. Cyrus had never mentioned having one.

"It's actually an exciting story," he said. He smiled, but it was a bitter, malicious expression, and not like Cyrus at all. "It just doesn't have a happy ending."

"Will you tell me anyway?" Stella asked. She desperately wanted to understand Cyrus, to know what was causing him so much anger and pain.

"The expedition I joined was divided into several groups once we crossed the mountains," he began, his eyes taking on a faraway gleam. "Each group traveled to a different part of your lands. The idea was to cover as much ground as possible in a short amount of time. I told you we came in airships, right? Well, we hid them all over—in caves, deep inside forests, places we hoped they'd never be found. Our ships have the ability to cloak themselves, like an invisibility suit, but it was still no guarantee that someone wouldn't discover them accidentally."

"Invisible ships." A memory jolted Stella, and she leaned forward excitedly. "During the Iron War, there were stories that came out of the Independent Nation of Archivists claiming that they had an airship long before the *Iron Glory* was built. There were witnesses who swore they'd seen it flying over the mountains, but after that, it was never seen again, so I always thought the stories were made up. Could the ship have been one of yours?"

Cyrus nodded. "It was, though it wasn't part of our

expeditions. It was sent alone over the mountains as an advanced scout. Our people thought it had been lost—it had been gone for years—until one day, it turned up again in Kovall.

"As for my group's ship," he went on, "we hid it in a cave in the foothills of the Hiterian Mountains, not far from the scrap towns and meteor fields."

Where the strange objects fall from other worlds, Stella thought. The objects the archivists studied. She wondered if Cyrus had ever seen a meteor storm. She and her parents had talked about taking a trip north to study the phenomenon, but when they got the opportunity to travel to the uncharted lands, they'd pretty much abandoned the idea.

The *Iron Glory* shuddered under a sudden wind gust, and Stella's stomach lurched. So far, she'd managed to forget about being in the small room, the tight space, but the ship had just reminded her. She took deep breaths until the flash of panic had passed.

"Are you all right?" Cyrus asked, reaching over to touch her shoulder. "You look pale."

"I'm fine," Stella said. She wondered, not for the first time, why the pitching ship didn't bother Cyrus. Could machines, or hybrid machines, get airsickness? "Keep talking," she told him. "How many people were on the ship with you?"

"There were ten of us," Cyrus said, resting his hands

in his lap. "Mostly scientists, along with some soldiers for security."

"Were there other people your age?" Stella asked. She couldn't imagine it, but then again, maybe Cyrus was older than he looked. Maybe the olarans aged differently than humans.

"Not on that expedition," Cyrus said. "On previous ones, yes. But I was only allowed to go because my teacher had requested it. He's a scientist and a high-ranking official in Kovall. I'd been apprenticed with him for over a year, so he thought I was the best person to help him with his research." His hands clenched into fists. "And I *wanted* to go on the expedition. I wanted it more than anything, even though my parents said no."

That sounded familiar. Stella knew what her own parents would have said—*No, no, no way, never in a million years*, or something along those lines.

Cyrus's face was shadowed, his eyes full of unhappy memories. "They were furious when I told them that my teacher had arranged everything. My father is a diplomat, so he petitioned the alagant to intervene and keep me home, but like I said, my teacher is very powerful in the royal court, and he has more influence than my father, so the alagant sided with him." His voice dropped. "I remember being so happy. I felt like I'd won a battle against my parents. I wanted to *gloat*."

Stella understood that feeling all too well. If King

Aron had intervened and declared that she could join her parents on the expedition to the uncharted lands, she would have been overjoyed, ecstatic.

"What happened?" she asked.

"Oh, we fought over it for weeks." Cyrus stared at the floor as he spoke, his shoulders tense. "I said awful things. Told them they were just jealous because I was getting to do something they never could have dreamed. In the end, I said goodbye and went on the expedition.

"Once we arrived, the plan was to explore our designated lands for two weeks, collect as much information about your people as we could, then meet back at the ship and go home." He looked up at her and shrugged. "Easy, right? And mostly, it was. My teacher and I covered the area around the scrap towns. We even got to see a meteor storm from a safe distance. Watching objects from other worlds streak from the sky in clouds of green dust—I'd never seen anything like it. Afterward, we headed south toward the archivists' nation. Everything was going great." His expression hardened. "And then the slavers found us."

A chill went through Stella. She had heard stories of slavers, of course, but King Aron's soldiers kept most of them out of Noveen, so they weren't something that she feared the way other people living in less protected cities did. "Were you captured?" she asked, though she feared she already knew the answer.

Cyrus nodded, eyes wide and jaw tight with anger. "They're the only thing about your people I *hate*," he said. "When slavers hit you with their dust, you're just . . . *caught*, and helpless, and all of a sudden, home's so far away it might as well be another world. . . ." His voice trembled, chest heaving, and by the dim light, Stella realized there were tears standing in his eyes. Lost in that terrible memory, Cyrus was terrified.

Stella finally understood. That was why he'd been so angry when she'd used the knockout powder on him. He'd been a victim of slaver's dust. In that moment, he wasn't at all like the person he'd been when they first met, so sure of himself, not shaken by anything. Now he was just a boy who was alone, far away from home, and terribly afraid.

She shifted and scooted closer to him. Without a word, she put her arm across his shoulders and tugged him toward her until their foreheads touched. He took her other hand and held it in a tight grip, and for a while, neither of them spoke. She listened to his ragged breathing; felt his cold, clammy skin against hers; and willed some of her strength and warmth into him. She didn't know if she was helping or not, but eventually, his breathing quieted, and he lifted his head to look at her. He still clutched her hand, making Stella's fingers tingle with numbness. She didn't complain or try to pull away.

"It's all right," she whispered. "We don't have to talk about this anymore."

But Cyrus shook his head and wiped his eyes. "I need to tell someone," he said. "I've never told the story before. It's been inside me all this time like a knot that just keeps getting bigger, tighter, and it *hurts*." His voice cracked. "He left me, Stella," Cyrus whispered.

"Who left you?" Stella asked, wanting to comfort him. "Your teacher? I thought you were both captured?"

"We were," Cyrus said. "They raided our camp one night and took us both, but my teacher managed to escape the next morning. I was sure everything was going to be all right then. We were supposed to leave for home in four days. I thought he'd go meet up with the others at the ship and they'd form a rescue party to come after me. We weren't that far from where we'd hidden the ship. I thought *surely* they'd come back to get me. They wouldn't just abandon me." He shook his head as if he still couldn't believe it. "I was wrong. No one . . . no one ever came."

"What?" Horrified, Stella thought of the message written on the crumpled paper. *I'm so sorry.* "They didn't even *try* to rescue you?"

"For all I know, my teacher told them I was dead," Cyrus said, and the anger was back in his voice, a rage so intense it made his brown eyes look black. "Whatever the reason, I was on my own. I got lucky, though. After a week, the slavers camped near a railroad water station. The 401 train made a stop there during the night, and someone from the crew, a chamelin, was flying around, scouting the area, and saw the camp. He swooped in like a storm, sent the slavers running, so I ran too. Eventually, the slavers regrouped and chased me. I ran for miles, dodging their paralyzing dust and the bolas they use to trip and catch their victims. I hid when I could, and somehow, I lost them. I was exhausted, but I kept going. Finally, I made it back to the cave where we'd hidden the ship." Cyrus's gaze flicked to the crumpled note on the floor. "All I found was the message my teacher left me. They were gone, and that was it. I sat on the cave floor, reading the note over and over, realizing that I had no way home."

"Oh, Cyrus, I'm so sorry." Stella knew the words could never be enough. She laid a hand on his shoulder, but he was absorbed in his memories and didn't seem to notice.

"The worst part was when I started thinking about my parents," Cyrus said. He slumped, his expression crumpling. "All that time I'd spent being angry at them for trying to keep me off the expedition because I thought they didn't trust me. But it wasn't that at all. They didn't trust my teacher to take care of me. My parents must have known what kind of person he was, that he'd sacrifice me in a heartbeat if it meant saving his own skin.

They knew, but I didn't believe them. I was just so sure I was right about everything."

"It doesn't matter now," Stella insisted, giving his shoulder a gentle shake. "You made a mistake, but you were so brave, Cyrus. You found another way home. We're getting closer every day, and when we finally make it, you can tell your parents you missed them and didn't realize what you were getting yourself into." She smiled, hoping to coax one from him in return. "They won't care about all the awful things you said. They'll just be glad you're safe."

To Stella's relief, Cyrus did smile back. It was a small, tremulous thing, but it took some of the pain from his eyes. "You're right," he said. "They'll be . . . so happy." His expression quickly turned serious again. "But the Faceless man is still out there," he said. "Now that the *Iron Glory*'s made it through the storm, he'll come up with another way to sabotage the ship. It's only a matter of time."

"We have an advantage thanks to you," Stella said. "I know what detail the Faceless man can't hide. It's his eyes. Both times that I've seen him, his eyes were bloodshot. It means we'll have to get up close to spot him, but it's a start."

"Hmmm, that is something," Cyrus said thoughtfully. "But I think if you're going to mount a search, you should focus on the lower decks."

"Why? You think he's hiding there?"

"He might be, but it's more that I think he'll go after the *Iron Glory*'s engines," Cyrus said. "It's the best way to cripple the ship. If he tampers with the steam gauges, creates a pressure buildup, it could cause an explosion. But I've been in the engine room, and sabotaging things in there won't be easy. There's a large crew monitoring the engines at all times."

"What about a fire?" Stella asked. "He might try that again. There are plenty of things around that'll burn."

"That's true," Cyrus said. "If he tries that, he'll want to make sure the blaze spreads fast, too fast for the crew to put it out. However he does it, he'll have to be careful, because if he tries again and fails, the crew will know I'm not the saboteur."

Stella considered that. "Maybe that explains why he hasn't done anything *yet*," she said. "He's planning, biding his time while you're a captive and—" She stopped. A thought occurred to her that sent a chill through her entire body. "He may come after us first. Come after *you*, Cyrus. You were protecting the ship during the storm, and the Faceless man knew it. That's why he was coming up the crow's nest after us. He was trying to stop you. As long as he knows you're able to protect the ship, he won't want to act unless he's taken care of you first." Her stomach twisted at the thought. It meant Cyrus really wasn't safe anywhere, even locked up in the security office.

She looked at Cyrus, but he appeared to be lost in thought, tapping a finger against his knee. "If that's true, maybe we shouldn't do anything," he said slowly. "Rather than hunt the Faceless man down, we could try to draw him to us."

"You mean set a trap?" Stella asked.

He nodded. "With me as the bait. The Faceless man knows exactly where I am, so we just wait for him to come here."

Stella frowned. She didn't like the word "bait." Not one bit. "He's almost gotten to you once already," she said, "and I've had a taste of what that rod can do to a person. I can't even imagine what effect it would have on someone who's part mechanical."

"It's called a Lazuril rod," Cyrus said. "In our language, it means 'living light.' And you're right—it's nasty enough on humans, but it can do different things to an olaran. On its lowest setting, it knocks us out by disrupting our mechanical processes. On its highest settings, a Lazuril rod can kill us. I've never been hit with one on any setting, and believe me, I never want to be."

He smiled weakly at her. Stella suddenly became aware that he was still holding her hand. He hadn't let go during their conversation, and she hadn't noticed until that moment. It had just felt . . . right. Now that she was aware of it, though, a blush streaked across Stella's cheeks. She ducked her head so he wouldn't see her burning face.

What was she going to do? She couldn't be the one to pull away first. He might think—what would he think? What did *she* think? And why was her heart beating so fast?

Just as she was starting to panic, Cyrus turned to her and said quietly, "By the way—thanks," before gently squeezing her hand.

That made Stella look up, though her cheeks were still hot. "For what?"

"For coming here, for listening," he said. "The truth is, Stella, you're not like anyone I've ever met." Now his face was the one turning bright red. "I just . . . I wanted you to know that."

Stella was speechless. There were so many things she needed to say, but she knew she would have to get out of the cell soon and get the chamelin's keys back before he missed them. Yet she hated the thought of leaving Cyrus here alone, just waiting for the Faceless man to show up. He needed protection, *some* kind of advantage against the enemy.

Impulsively, she stood up and started to undo the clasps on the invisibility suit. "If you're going to insist on making yourself bait for the Faceless man, you need to take back this suit," she said. "I can't keep a lookout every hour of the day, so you should at least have a way to hide from the Faceless man if it comes to that."

But Cyrus shook his head. "You need the suit to get out of here, remember? You can't let them see you."

"Well, maybe I can sneak the suit back in here to you somehow and then—"

"Stella," Cyrus interrupted gently, "I'll be all right—I promise. Besides, you can keep a better watch if you're invisible."

Stella was out of ideas. She knew he was right, but still she hesitated, not wanting to abandon him. "Are you sure about this?"

He nodded, and his expression clouded. "To tell you the truth, I don't really like being invisible."

"Really?" She was surprised. Wearing the suit around the ship made her feel safe and free. She could go anywhere she wanted.

"I don't know why, but whenever I would put on the suit and disappear, I'd have this weird feeling that even when I took it off again, people still wouldn't be able to see me," Cyrus said. "I'd just be gone forever." He glanced at her sheepishly. "I know what you're thinking. It's a stupid fear, right?"

"It's not stupid," she said softly. He had been lost for so long. Of course he was afraid. "But I see you, Cyrus, and I won't let you disappear. No matter what happens, I'll make sure you get home to your family. I promise."

He smiled sadly. "Don't make promises you—"

"I *promise*," Stella said, cutting him off. She refastened the invisibility suit. "I'll look for the Faceless man, and I'll keep you updated on the search through the beetle."

She tried to sound confident, for Cyrus's sake, but she couldn't shake the feeling that they were running out of time. They had to catch the Faceless man before he did something that the ship couldn't come back from.

≈ TWENTY ≈

The next day, in between spending time with her parents, Stella slipped away and patrolled the ship in the invisibility suit, searching for crew members with bloodshot eyes and sweeping the area around the security office for any suspicious activity.

So far, there had been no sign of the Faceless man. The captain planned to land the ship as soon as they cleared the mountains and there was an area that looked inhabited. Stella knew that their first contact with the people of the uncharted lands would most likely be the city of Kovall from what Cyrus had told her, and the crew of the *Iron Glory* was in for a surprise, if the city was as big and grand as he'd described.

That was, if they even made it that far.

Stella tried not to think about that. She paused in her search at midday because her mother had asked that they eat lunch together while her father ran the medi-cal bay. Stella had a sneaking suspicion that meant her mother wanted to talk to her about something.

They met in the ship's cafeteria, but once they'd stacked their trays with food and sat down at a table, Stella's mother said, her voice deceptively casual, "So, Cyrus is cute."

That was all it took. Stella's face was on fire in an instant. "*Mom*," she said, hoping that her mother would recognize the *please be quiet and let us never speak of this again* tone in her voice.

But she didn't, of course. "Just an observation," Eliza said, holding up her hands. "Purely scientific analysis." She raised an eyebrow. "Why? You don't agree?"

Oh, she was good. Stella had forgotten for a moment how well her mother knew her. It was a wonderful, warm feeling, like a tiny sun inside her, to be known so well, but it was also extremely inconvenient.

"Boy, this sandwich is really good," Stella said quickly. "And the tea. The tea on this ship is great." Then she remembered that she hadn't taken a sip yet.

Her mother chewed her bottom lip, as if she was get-ting rid of a smile, but she didn't comment on the change in topic. "All right, then, maybe you can tell me about your adventures camping in the cargo bay." Her brow furrowed. "How *did* you manage sleeping down there in the small space? Didn't it bother you?"

Stella shuddered at the memory of those early nights. "It was awful at first," she said. "But Cyrus helped me get through it. He taught me to use the invisibility suit so I could go outside on the upper deck. It helped to be out in the open air, and what an amazing view. I wished he could have been there with me to see the sunset that night."

Her mother listened as she chattered on, until Stella realized abruptly that her mother had gotten her to talk about Cyrus after all. Sneaky. She'd forgotten that about her mother too. Or maybe it was just that Cyrus was the only thing on her mind. She sighed, giving into the inevitable, and mumbled, "Yes, he's cute. From a purely scientific perspective," she added hastily. "And he's . . . tall."

"Hmmm," her mother said, as if they were discussing a research paper instead of a boy. "Tall. Yes, I believe he is." Her expression abruptly turned serious. "He must miss his family very much."

"He does, but it's not just that," Stella said, wanting her mother to understand. "I think for a while he lost hope that he was ever going to make it home again. Or he buried his hope so deep that it was hard for him to find it again. That's why I promised to help him." She hadn't thought about it this way before, but as she spoke, she knew the words were true. "If he can't find hope, then I'll feel it for him."

It sounded silly when she said it aloud, but her mother didn't laugh. She reached across the table and put her hand over Stella's. "I'm glad that Cyrus found you," she said. "He couldn't have asked for a better friend. I'm proud of you, Stella."

"Thank you." Unable to meet her mother's eyes, Stella smiled down at her sandwich.

They ate in silence for a while, until Stella realized she had questions of her own. The cafeteria was empty except for the two of them, but Stella leaned forward and dropped her voice. "What's going to happen when we land and meet the olarans?" she asked. "And what about Merrow and Dragonfly? Will they be able to get along with each other?"

Even though the crew believed they'd captured the saboteur, there was still tension between the two sides. Stella had sensed it in the short time she'd spent among them. What if that affected their meeting with the olarans? What if Kovall didn't welcome them? Everything the expedition was about to do felt so big yet so fragile, as if one wrong move would bring it all crashing down.

Her mother hesitated before replying, and her gaze seemed to turn inward, as if she were a hundred miles away in her memory. "I wish I had answers for you, Stella, but I just don't know," she said. "None of us—humans, sarnuns, chamelins, or olarans—are perfect. But at some point, we're going to have to *want* to coexist. If we spend all our time fighting change and fighting each other, eventually we'll lose ourselves, lose the future we want for our children. But I promise you, your father and I will do everything we can to make sure that doesn't happen."

Stella nodded, unexpected tears welling up in her eyes. *King Aron was right*, she thought. Her parents really were the best people for this mission. They were explorers, talented healers, but they cared about people too. No matter what, they wouldn't lose themselves, and they wouldn't forget about their home. How could she have ever doubted that?

Her mother reached across the table to pick up Stella's empty tray, but Stella threw her arms around her mother and hugged her tight.

"Whoa, what's that for?" her mother asked, hugging her back.

"I just . . . I love you, that's all," Stella whispered.

"I love you too," her mother said, her voice thick.

They left the cafeteria a few minutes later and headed back to the medical bay. One of the engineers had come in with steam burns on his leg, which required the attention of both of Stella's parents, so Stella took the opportunity to slip away, using the excuse that she was going up on deck for some fresh air.

What she actually did was go put on the invisibility suit for more scouting.

She started at the security office, as usual. She recognized the guard and passed in front of him slowly, looking at his eyes. They were normal, not bloodshot at all.

Stella covered the other decks, staying out of the way of the crew, and ended up topside. She scoured the deck around the crow's nest and then headed to the back of the ship, knowing she would have it to herself at this time of day.

She glanced over the railing and, as usual, found herself overwhelmed by the dizzying view straight down.

But today something was different.

The mountains were gone.

They were passing over a thick evergreen forest. Tall green spikes reached toward the sky, and Stella imagined she could smell the pine scent even from this height. The air blew warmer on her face than she'd ever felt it. It wouldn't be long—it might even happen today— until they'd passed over the forest and found some open ground to land on.

She couldn't wait to tell Cyrus. He was almost home.

Stella turned from the railing and jumped back in surprise.

One of the crew was leaning over the railing a few feet away from her. At first, Stella thought he was airsick and throwing up over the side, but when he straightened, Stella saw he was holding a spyglass. He'd also been enjoying the view.

He turned toward her, slipping the spyglass inside his long coat.

His eyes were red and bloodshot.

The Faceless man was standing right in front of her.

Stella sucked in a breath, and that was what gave her away.

⤜ TWENTY-ONE ⤝

The Faceless man reacted instantly. Plunging a hand into his pocket, he pulled out a fistful of white powder, which he threw into the air all around him.

Stella tried to dodge the powder, but it hit her square in the chest, leaving a white stain and effectively giving away exactly where she was.

Time to run.

Stella spun and took off, but the Faceless man was fast. He bounded after her and caught up in three strides. He grabbed her by the hook of her suit and pulled her back, hauling her over to the railing. Stella's back hit the metal bar, the breath whooshing from her lungs, but she was more worried about the dizzying drop thousands of feet to the ground.

The Faceless man planted himself in front of her and grabbed the collar of her suit, tearing off her hood and undoing the invisibility power. "If you scream, I'll throw you off this ship," he warned her.

Stella didn't scream, but she did look around frantically for one of the deckhands, for *anyone* to help her, but the few people moving around on deck were all at the bow, and she and the Faceless man were hidden behind a large bin of parachutes stored at the back of the ship.

"I know you've been looking for me," the Faceless man said, his bloodshot eyes hot with anger. He shook her once, hard. "I knew you were out there somewhere, hiding in the suit, but it doesn't matter. Nothing you do now can stop me."

His stale breath was hot on her face. Stella tried not to gag. "Tell me why you're doing this," she demanded. "We don't want a fight with the olarans. We're coming to your lands in peace."

"*Peace*," the Faceless man said, turning the word to acid. "I've spent more time on your side of the world than any other olaran. I was there during the Iron War. Your people fight over every scrap of resources and your kind of 'peace' would doom our people and strip us of everything we have."

"What *you're* doing will kill Cyrus!" Stella countered, her voice rising. "He's one of your own people!"

The Faceless man's eyes blazed a warning, and he pushed her against the railing. Stella choked back her fear and fell silent.

"You should have stayed on your side of the world," he said. "I will protect my people from you, no matter the price. Once the boy is taken care of, this ship will fall from the sky."

With those words, he pushed her.

Stella toppled backward over the railing, her arms flailing toward the empty sky.

≈ TWENTY-TWO ≈

The world turned upside down. With her remaining shreds of concentration, Stella caught the last rail rung with one hand. Her whole body jerked, but she held on, stopping herself from plunging thousands of feet to her death.

Don't look down, she told herself, her legs swinging wildly beneath her. *Whatever you do, Stella, don't look down.*

She also tried not to think about the fact that she didn't have a very good grip on the rung and her fingers were slipping.

"Help!" she screamed. "Somebody help me!"

There had been chamelins patrolling the deck earlier. Surely one of them would hear her. Mustering up as much strength as she could, Stella reached up with her other hand and grabbed hold of the rail, but in doing so, she looked down.

Clouds swirled below her, the distant trees waving, their points spearing the sky like knives. Stella went light-headed and squeezed her eyes shut.

Footsteps pounded across the deck in response to her cries. Stella looked up at the face of one of the deckhands who appeared over the railing. When the young man saw her, his eyes widened.

Stella sighed with relief. It was one of the chamelin guards. He stepped back and transformed, wings exploding from his back as he changed to his lizard-like form and leaped over the rail, gliding on the air currents. He circled and came up beneath her, grabbing her around the waist.

Stella let go, and he flew her up and over the railing again, depositing her back on the deck in one smooth motion. "Thank you," she told the chamelin. He put a hand on her arm to steady her, but Stella waved him away. Scanning the deck for any sign of the Faceless man, she sighed. He was nowhere in sight.

It didn't matter. She knew where he was going and took off running across the deck.

"Wait!" the chamelin cried after her, in the middle of shifting back to his human form. "What's going on? What happened?"

But Stella didn't stop. The _Iron Glory_ was in terrible danger, and she had to warn everyone.

TWENTY-THREE

Stella burst into the medical bay, startling her parents, who were crushing herbs in a mortar and pestle.

"What is it, Stella?" her father asked immediately, dropping the tools and taking her by the shoulders.

"Cyrus," Stella said, panting. "The Faceless man. He's coming. He's going to try to crash the ship. I don't know how, but he's done something. I . . . I saw him."

Voice shaking, she told them everything that had just happened. Her father's face was a mask of fury when she'd finished.

"We're going to the captain this instant," he said. "He's going to listen to us."

"No!" Stella said, tugging on his arm. "Mom, Dad— the Faceless man can imitate any of the crew. He could imitate the captain, and the crew will never believe us if we question the captain! We can't trust anyone, and

Cyrus is the only one who can protect the ship. The Faceless man will go after him first. We have to break him out of the security office!"

"Stella, he's surrounded by guards," her mother said. "If we can warn them—"

"By the time we get them to listen, it might be too late!" she insisted. "Cyrus got the *Iron Glory* through the storm. He's the only one who can help us."

Stella hadn't planned to come running to them like this, but she needed them on her side. She didn't think she could break Cyrus out on her own. Sneak in, yes, but getting him out was another thing entirely. If only she had more time, she might have been able to come up with a different plan, but this was all she had.

Stella's parents looked at each other, fear and uncertainty written all over their faces.

Finally, Stella's mother said, "I'll go to the captain and tell him everything about Cyrus and the Faceless man. It's a risk, but I think it's one we have to take. In the meantime, Stella, you and your father go get Cyrus. Do whatever you can to protect the ship."

Stella's father nodded, but worry was etched in every line of his face. "You realize if we do this, there will be repercussions," he said. "If the captain doesn't believe you, he might arrest us for setting Cyrus free. We're not soldiers, but we're still under his command for the duration of the expedition. He could bring us before the king when we get home, claim we committed treason by defying his authority and putting the ship in danger."

"I know," Stella's mother said, her voice dropping, but there was a layer of iron beneath it. "I don't like to think about what could happen and what it would mean for our daughter, but we can't turn away from this, Martin. The ship is in danger, and so is Cyrus. That boy's parents aren't here to look out for him. Imagine if it were Stella, captured and far from home. Wouldn't we want someone to protect her?"

Her father glanced at Stella, and the look on his face was full of love, sadness, and fear, all at once. She was seeing sides of her parents she'd never glimpsed before, and part of her didn't want to. She didn't want to see her father afraid. She wanted him to tell her everything was going to be all right.

And the thought of her parents going to prison for treason . . . she couldn't let that happen. "I don't want you to get in trouble because of me," she said. "Maybe it would be better if I just—"

But she didn't get any further than that before her mother interrupted. She was wearing her *over my dead body* expression. "Don't even think about arguing with me, Stella. We'll do this together or not at all. And we're not doing this because you asked us to; we're doing it because we have a responsibility to protect this ship and crew from harm."

Stella opened her mouth to argue, but the determined expression in her mother's eyes stopped her. "All right," she said, fighting back her fear. She pushed all thoughts of the future out of her mind and began gathering her supplies for what they were about to do.

She opened her alchemy case and began passing out smoke bombs to her father while she haltingly explained her idea. She'd been working on a way to bust Cyrus out since she'd visited him the night before. She'd just hoped she wouldn't have to use it.

Twenty minutes later, Stella was heading up the stairs. When she reached the landing, she peeked down the hall in the direction of the security office. The usual guard was standing in front of the door, looking bored.

Stella consulted her mental map of the ship, going over which rooms were on this deck. Besides the security office and the small room where Cyrus was being held, there was a supply closet at the far end of the hallway, a washroom on the opposite side of the hall, and, directly next to the security quarters, a conference room where the captain took meetings with the rest of the crew. It was a long, narrow hall, just like all the others on every deck of the ship.

Her father had come down a few minutes ago and was supposed to have taken up a position in the washroom, waiting for her signal. Stella hesitated a minute to make sure the guard wasn't going to look her way. Then she reached in her alchemy case and pulled out one of her smoke bombs and some matches. Lighting the fuse as quietly as she could, Stella crouched down and placed the smoke bomb on the floor by the stair rail.

She didn't have long to wait. Smoke quickly filled the small area and began pouring down the hallway. Stella ran and hid around the corner, before reaching back into her alchemy case for her knockout powder.

"Fire!" cried the guard. "We've got a fire up here! Somebody help!"

Stella heard a door burst open, and footsteps pounded down the hall. Two guards, including the one who'd been standing at the door, burst into the stairwell. Quickly, Stella raised the compact and blew a cloud of the knockout dust into their faces.

Unlike when she'd used the dust on Cyrus, the guards succumbed immediately, crumpling to the floor in a heap. Stella crouched between their prone bodies and unhooked a ring of keys from one guard's belt. She kept the compact ready in her other hand.

She stepped out into the hall just in time to see another cloud of smoke pouring from the washroom where her father was hiding. A third guard had just come out of the security office, shouting for his fellows, but the cloud of smoke was too thick for him to see they were unconscious in the stairwell. He ran for the washroom, yanking open the door to search for the source of the fire. A pair of hands—Stella's father's—grabbed the guard by the shirt collar and pulled him inside.

Less than a minute later, her father slipped out of the washroom, looking pleased, and shut the door behind him. Stella ran down the hall to meet him.

"Any trouble?" she asked.

Her father batted smoke away and shook his head, holding up the small container of knockout powder Stella had given him. "It worked perfectly. Let's go," he said, motioning toward the security office. "I'll distract whatever guards are inside. You use the invisibility suit and go get Cyrus."

"Got it," Stella said. She knew they didn't have much time. The smoke from the bombs would draw out the rest of the crew, who'd sound the alarm while looking for a fire.

She raised the hood of the invisibility suit and activated it before her father opened the door, and together they went inside.

The woman Stella had seen the other night was guarding Cyrus's door. She looked up in surprise when Stella and her father walked in. "What's going on out there?" she demanded.

"It's a fire," Stella's father said. "I need your help right now. There are men down."

The woman's eyes widened. She shot a quick glance at the door, hesitated, then said, "All right, let's go."

They ran out of the office, leaving Stella alone. Her plan was working perfectly! She took the guard's keys and tried them in the lock one at a time. Her fingers trembled as she thought about Cyrus waiting on the other side of the door. On her fourth try, the key slid into the lock.

Stella pushed the door open and saw Cyrus standing in the middle of the room, his body tense as if expecting an attack. When Stella shut the door behind her and pulled off her hood, he relaxed.

"What's going on?" he asked, hurrying over to her. "Is it the Faceless man?"

She nodded. "We have to get out of here and go somewhere safe."

Cyrus's eyes widened. "But, Stella, where can we go? They're going to know you broke me out of here. There's nowhere we can hide."

"I made you a promise, remember," Stella said. "Once we stop the Faceless man and the ship is on the ground, you're going back to your family. Now, come on. We don't have time to waste!"

She turned to the door, but it opened before she could get close enough to put her hand on the knob. Stella's father burst into the room, slamming the door shut behind him and leaning against it.

"What's wrong, Dad?" Stella asked. "Where are the guards?"

She searched his expression, wondering what was wrong, but she found it was impossible to read his eyes.

His very bloodshot eyes.

≈ TWENTY-FOUR ≈

As quick as Stella's brain was at solving problems, it took her some time—a whole five seconds, to be exact—to understand what those bloodshot eyes meant. Part of her tried to explain them away logically. She'd said herself her parents liked to work late. And they probably hadn't gotten much sleep on this expedition with the excitement and stress, so of course they were exhausted, and their faces would show it. *See?* Such an easy explanation, it was silly.

Her heart wasn't much help either, because it was too busy screaming in denial at everything her eyes were telling her.

The Faceless man would never disguise himself as her father, because no one would believe it. Her father was a gentle, kind person who would never raise his hand to hurt anyone. He'd rather die. The Faceless man wasn't capable of that kind of compassion. The crew would see through him in an instant.

Yet Stella hadn't.

Her mind quickly cycled back to the conversation with her parents in the medical bay. Her father's eyes hadn't been bloodshot then—she was sure of it. But they *had* been in the hallway outside the security office, and it wasn't because of the smoke, she realized now. So the Faceless man had probably switched places with her father while he was hiding in the washroom, waiting to ambush the guards. Which meant her father was still there, unconscious or worse.

Helpless, trembling with rage and fear, Stella could only hope he was all right.

The Faceless man twitched his right arm. A familiar metal rod slid from his sleeve into his hand. For the first time, Stella noticed that there was a small hilt of sorts at one end, which the Faceless man gripped. It must be what protected his hand from the burning touch of the metal when the weapon was active.

Flicking his wrist, the Faceless man brought the Lazuril rod up and squeezed the hilt, and in response, a familiar sparking blue light blossomed from the prongs. He brandished it in front of him, staring them down. "If either of you scream, I'll use the rod," he said calmly, even politely, but his eyes were hard and cold as granite. A chill crawled along Stella's spine.

Then we'll both scream, she thought defiantly, *both of us at once. We'll bring the guards, and the crew will come running. They'll stop you before you can even think about using that weapon on us.*

Except the guards were unconscious, and the crew were distracted in the hall by the false fire.

Stella opened her mouth, but no sound emerged. The Faceless man had trapped them both, and worst of all, he was still wearing her father's face. She couldn't look at it, that mask that was both exactly like her father and not at all like him, its beloved expression twisted into a sneer.

"You led me on a chase, boy," the Faceless man said to Cyrus, then turned to glare at Stella. "And you . . . you almost killed me."

Stella flinched, her elbow bumping the wall of the small room. Nowhere to run. She could try activating the invisibility suit, but it would be at least ten seconds or so before she vanished, more than enough time for the Faceless man to strike her with the rod. "I d-didn't mean to hurt you," she stammered, though she doubted the man believed her.

"Just like the rest of your kind," the Faceless man said. "Violent, unthinking brutes. I was disgusted by what I saw in your city."

"That's a funny thing to hear from someone threatening us with a Lazuril rod," Cyrus said, his eyes narrowed.

The Faceless man chuckled, but it sounded more like a growl. "You made it necessary," he said. "When I first saw you, it was in the factory where the *Iron Glory* was being built. I stayed to spy on the builders' progress and you looked familiar, but I didn't recognize you, at first. The last expedition team was long gone by that time, and I didn't know anyone had been left behind. But when the airship was finished and I saw aletheum gleaming in its envelope, I knew you had to be olaran—that you were responsible for it." The man's eyes glittered with malice. "Do you have any idea what you've done, boy? How could you give the Dragonfly territories that precious material?"

"I had to." Cyrus's face flushed with anger. "The *Iron Glory* was my only way home. I needed to protect the ship."

The Faceless man shook his head. "You *doomed* the ship," he said. "No matter the cost, her people"—he jerked his chin at Stella—"can't be allowed to possess aletheum. You forced me to destroy them."

Cyrus's face lost all color. His mouth opened and closed, and his shoulders slumped. Stella wasn't so steady herself.

Could it be true? Was the Faceless man trying to bring down the ship because Cyrus had strengthened it with aletheum? Was it really so precious that he would kill everyone just to keep it from her side of Solace?

The Faceless man held up the Lazuril rod, still addressing Cyrus. "The day of the storm, I only meant to incapacitate you, prevent you from using your power to protect the ship. On my honor, I wouldn't have killed another of my kind."

"Your honor?" Stella said incredulously. "You weren't going to kill him, but he'd die with the rest of us when the ship crashed!"

"*No,*" the Faceless man countered swiftly. "I have no intention of dying on this ship. I have parachutes and supplies hidden on the main deck. No matter where I land, I know how to survive and navigate my way back to Kovall. A minor modification to my plan allowed for me to take the incapacitated boy with me when I escaped." He lowered his arm, letting the Lazuril rod's tip rest near the floor. "I'll take you with me now, boy, if you'll go. I swear I'll return you to Kovall safely."

Silence fell in the room, but the blood thundered in Stella's ears. Rather than killing Cyrus, as she'd been sure he'd come to do, the Faceless man was actually offering to take him home.

Stella searched his face and those bloodshot eyes for a trace of deception, but she found none. His gaze was direct and open, and for once, the emptiness in his eyes was gone. In fact, in that moment, more than any other, he most resembled Stella's father, who often expressed the same honesty. The similarity was repulsive to Stella, but it made it easier for her to believe him.

"Well, boy?" the Faceless man asked. "What's it going to be?"

Cyrus looked him in the eye and shook his head. "I'm not going with you," he said hoarsely. "It's true—for a long time the only thing I cared about was getting home, no matter what I had to do to get there. I wasn't thinking about anything but myself. I'd seen the worst of this side of Solace, and I wanted to escape." He looked at Stella, and she saw the determination and sorrow in his eyes. "But things are different now."

Stella understood. Cyrus meant the words for her. She gave him a reassuring smile, but the Faceless man sniffed in derision. "It doesn't matter," he said. "Their people are a threat to our lands. I must act to protect my homeland from invasion."

"Wait a minute," Stella said, her brow furrowing in confusion. "You said you stayed behind when the last expedition left. That means you're all alone here and making decisions for your people?"

"That's right," Cyrus said, catching on. "Before the last expedition, you knew our alagant was getting close to formally reaching out to the humans, sarnuns, and chamelins on the other side of the mountains. But you don't want that, so you're acting on your own, aren't you?"

"You're only children," the Faceless man spat. "You look at the world in wonder, and you think that every adventure and risk will yield something great. And like the alagant, you can't see that there are darker forces at work. The alagant has sent manned expeditions to study the Merrow Kingdom and the Dragonfly territories, but she hasn't seen your nature as I have. She hasn't seen you fight over resources or your eagerness to conquer. She must be protected from herself as much as from your people."

Cyrus's fists clenched. "You'd destroy everything the olarans have worked for," he growled. "You'd twist everything they're trying to do."

Yes, he would, Stella thought. Because that was what fear could do to someone. Fear so extreme that it became madness. All the Faceless man saw when he looked at Stella's people was war, two greedy kingdoms fighting over precious resources. And it was true. They *had* been guilty of those things, but now they were trying to move forward, to create a future together, and the expedition was crucial to that.

"You don't have to do this," Stella said, daring to take a step forward to make her appeal. "Trust your alagant. Let her meet us and let her decide if we're a threat or, better still, let us *prove* to you that we aren't. That man whose face you stole would never hurt anyone, and the people on this ship don't deserve to die because you're scared of what we *might* do!"

"Stay where you are," the Faceless man warned, pointing the Lazuril rod at Stella. At its nearness, she felt the hairs on her arms stand up. "What you say might be true," he allowed. "You helped this boy, which is more than I expected from one of your kind, but I can't trust that there are enough people like you. And even if you could convince me, it's much too late now to change things."

Dread clenched Stella's gut and her eyes widened. "What do you mean?"

"What did you do?" Cyrus demanded.

"Did you really think I'd come after you here and risk getting captured if I hadn't already put my plan into motion?" The Faceless man flicked the rod back and forth now, almost playfully. "You're just the last detail that needs tying up, the last layer of the ship's protection that must be stripped. The *Iron Glory* was doomed ten minutes ago. In another ten," he added, "it will explode."

TWENTY-FIVE

This has to be a dream, Stella told herself. She must have fallen asleep, and her anxious mind had conjured up this sick nightmare of the Faceless man. Wearing her *father's* face, no less. Her father, coming to tell her the *Iron Glory* was going to explode.

She waited and waited to wake up, but nothing changed.

"Stella," Cyrus said. "Stella!" He waved his arm to get her attention, which made Stella wonder how many times he'd called her name before she heard him. She looked at him, saw the panic and sorrow in his eyes. Well, what good would those do? Those were just feelings, and they didn't matter. Not when the ship was doomed and her parents were going to die and neither she nor Cyrus would ever see home again. It was too much. Stella breathed deeply, sucking in gulps of air, to keep from throwing up.

"Stella, I'm so sorry," Cyrus was saying while Stella struggled not to vomit. Why was he apologizing? It wasn't as if any of this was his fault. The ship would already have crashed if it weren't for him.

At least she and her parents would be together if this was the end. If she'd stayed in Noveen, where it was safe, she would have spent her life waiting, wondering why they never came home to her.

"I'll give you one last chance to come with me, boy," the Faceless man said. He'd stopped paying attention to Stella. It was as if she weren't even in the room. All the man's focus was on Cyrus, waiting to see if he would change his mind.

"You should go," Stella finally told Cyrus, her mouth bone-dry and voice raspy. "Escape if you can." The Faceless man was offering him a way off the ship. Why should he have to die if there was a way to save him?

"You can't be serious," Cyrus said, staring at Stella as if she'd just suggested he sprout wings and fly. "I'm not leaving."

"Then I'm sorry," the Faceless man said. He raised the Lazuril rod and took a step forward. "I didn't want it to come to this."

"Me neither," Cyrus said, and before Stella could open her mouth to scream, he launched himself at the Faceless man. "Run, Stella!" he cried.

The Faceless man swung the Lazuril rod, but Cyrus was already too close. He hit the man around the waist, his momentum driving them both into the wall. The impact must have disrupted the Faceless man's power because suddenly, his features blurred, re-forming into the older face he'd worn the day of the storm.

Stella ran to help Cyrus, but the boy shouted, "No!" He wrestled the man against the wall and turned to her, face red and straining. "You can save the ship. It has to be the engine room. Warn them!"

The Faceless man grunted and tried to shove Cyrus off him, but the boy stubbornly hung on. He twisted the Lazuril rod, but Cyrus slammed his elbow into the Faceless man's arm, pinning it above his head.

Cyrus's mad charge had also cleared a path to the door. The very last thing Stella wanted to do was leave Cyrus here, fighting the Faceless man alone, but he was right. If she didn't at least try to warn the crew, they would all be dead in minutes.

She made a break for the door. Yanking it open, she cast one last glance at Cyrus struggling with the Faceless man and ran from the room.

She made it to the hallway and almost collided with Drea. The captain, Stella's mother, and a handful of other crew members were there too, crouching by the unconscious guards. When the first officer saw Stella, her feelers stirred and pointed at her.

"What happened?" Drea demanded, her mind voice echoing in Stella's head. "Your mother came to see the captain and me, claiming that Cyrus—"

"Help him!" Stella interrupted, grabbing Drea's arm and all but shoving her toward the security office. "Cyrus is being attacked!"

"Attacked?" the captain said, getting to his feet. Stella's mother and the other crew members looked up in alarm. "By whom?" he demanded.

"The traitor! It's all true—everything my mother told you!" Stella had no time to try to convince them. She had to get to the engine room.

"Stella, are *you* all right?" her mother said, coming up to embrace her daughter. "You're shaking!"

"I'm fine," Stella said, pulling away, "but you have to find Dad! I think he's in the washroom, unconscious."

Her mother's eyes widened. *"What?"*

"Please, just help them!" she cried. "I have to get to the engine room, or the ship's going to crash!" Without another word, she took off running.

"Hold on!" The captain reached out to grab her as she flew past, but Stella dodged him and made it to the stairwell before he could catch up. He shouted again for her to stop, but Stella just ran faster.

Luck was with her in that no one was on the stairs. Unhindered, Stella jumped down them, skipping two and three steps, almost tripping and sprawling on the metal risers.

But what was she looking for once she got to the engine room? Cyrus might have guessed what the Faceless man had done to the ship, but he hadn't had time to share the details. All Stella knew was that there was going to be an explosion.

If that was true, the Faceless man must have found a way to tamper with the boilers, like making the pressure build up in such a way that the crew wouldn't notice, at least not until it was too late. So she had to find out which of the boilers he'd sabotaged and get the engineers to bring down the pressure before it exploded.

Finally, Stella reached the second deck. She charged down the hallway, boots clanging on the metal floor, and threw open the door to the engine room. A blast of heat and sulfur-ridden steam hit her in the face. She coughed and waved her hand in front of her.

The room was hot, lit with the bright orange glows of the fires that fed the engines and kept the *Iron Glory*'s propellers turning. A dozen or so men and women moved about the room, some of them shoveling fuel into the fires, others checking the steam gauges or talking in small groups. None of them looked upset or panicked. They had no idea that one of their boilers was about to blow.

Just beyond the doorway, a metal catwalk encircled the room, allowing Stella to see all the activity from her position above. Two sets of stairs, one on each side of the room, led down to the engine pit. Stella stopped at the top of the stairs, put two fingers in her mouth, and let out the loudest, shrillest whistle she could manage to get the engineers' attention.

A dozen heads turned and looked up at her simultaneously. All over the room, eyes widened and brows furrowed as the engineers saw Stella. Maybe some of them even recognized her from when she'd been introduced to the crew with her parents.

"Listen to me!" she yelled down at them. "I know this is going to sound crazy, but one of the boilers is about to explode. We have to stop it!"

For a second, nobody moved or said a word. Then a few of the engineers looked at one another in confusion, murmuring something Stella couldn't hear.

"Where did you come from, girl?" one of the men standing near the base of the stairs shouted up to her. "You're not supposed to be in here."

"She's one of those stowaways—Martin and Eliza's girl," another engineer said, wiping sweat from his forehead.

"She must be lost," said a woman with dark hair tied back with a green handkerchief. "You need to turn around, girl. It isn't safe to be here."

As they talked, Stella's panic spiked. They were all going to die just standing around talking. She had to make them listen.

Stella ran across the catwalk and down the stairs, charging into the engineers' midst. She grabbed the man closest to her by the arm and shook him. "Please," she begged. "One of these boilers is going to explode! If we don't find which one, everyone on board the ship is going to die when the *Iron Glory* crashes!"

"Stop telling stories," said the man she was shaking. He wore stained overalls and had only a small patch of gray hair on the top of his head. He scowled at Stella. "You want to cause a panic?"

But the woman wearing the green handkerchief was looking at Stella, concern filling her brown eyes. "What makes you say that?" she asked. "The saboteur's been caught, and the engines are all working fine. We just ran a check on the water levels and safety valves about twenty minutes ago."

"That's not it," Stella said, shaking her head. She let go of the man in the overalls and turned to the woman. The other engineers closed in, forming a semicircle around them. "The captain caught the wrong person. The real saboteur did something to one of the boilers. It's going to explode if we don't fix it fast!"

"That's impossible," said a young man with long, shaggy blond hair pulled back in a horsetail. "I checked each of the boilers myself. If one of them had been damaged, I'd have seen it or there would have been a change in the pressure."

"Unless someone tampered with the inside of the boiler shell somehow," the woman with the green handkerchief said thoughtfully. "If they weakened it enough, the pressure would do the rest, eventually cause it to rupture." She looked at her colleagues. "The force of the explosion would blow the whole thing out the side of the ship."

"You're not seriously listening to this, are you, Laura?" said the blond man. "The girl's out of her head."

Stella didn't bother getting angry at him, but she was aware that time was slipping by and needed them to stay with her. The woman, Laura, *was* listening to her. That was all she cared about it. "Think back," Stella said. "Do you remember anyone working on any of the engines in the past few days?"

Laura nodded and pointed behind Stella at one of the massive boilers. "We had the number two engine down for maintenance this past evening," she said. "Ellis said the gauges weren't reading right."

"I didn't say that." The man in the overalls crossed his arms over his chest and looked at Laura indignantly. "I wasn't even on duty in the evening. I was down with airsickness in my bunk."

Despite the heat of the engine room, a chill passed over Stella.

Laura pursed her lips and shook her head vehemently. "Yes, you were sick in the morning, but then you came in to work later, said you were feeling fine. You recommended we wait several hours before firing up number two. So that's what we did."

The other engineers nodded, confirming Laura's

story. Ellis, the man in the overalls, threw up his hands. "I'm telling you that never happened! What is wrong with you people?"

"You are both right," Stella cut in. She grabbed Laura's arm and dragged her over to the number two engine. "I'll explain, but you have to shut it down right now."

"Here, let me check it again," the blond man said, and moved toward the gauges.

No, Stella wanted to scream. There was *no time!*

Several pairs of footsteps clanged on the catwalk above them. Stella looked up. It was Cyrus, trailed by a pair of guards and the captain himself.

"Stella!" Cyrus shouted. "Did you find it?"

"Hey now," said the blond man, pointing at Cyrus. "Isn't *that* the saboteur?"

The captain held up a hand for silence. "Check the engines," he ordered. "They may have been tampered with."

Laura nodded and turned to her team. "You heard the captain. Let's shut down the number two engine, just to be safe. Afterward, we'll inspect it and sort all this out." She glanced at Stella. "You keep back—go stand near the stairs." Then she turned all her attention to the engine and began shouting orders to the rest of the assembled crew.

Stella ran up the stairs to the catwalk to join Cyrus and the captain. Only then did she notice that he held the Lazuril rod in his hand. It had been deactivated, its metal tip no longer glowing. "What happened to the Faceless man?" she asked.

"Drea and the captain got him," Cyrus said. "He tried to change his face to one of the guards, but they saw him use his power."

"We've finally apprehended the right man," the captain said, his face tense. "But he wouldn't tell us what he did to the ship."

Cyrus watched the crew running to tend to the engines, checking gauges and pressure. "Maybe I can buy them some more time," he said.

He handed Stella the Lazuril rod, which she tucked into the waistband of her trousers. Cyrus raised his hands. Gold light outlined his fingertips as his power surged. "I'll put a barrier around the engines, something to keep them—"

But those were the last words he got out before the explosion.

TWENTY-SIX

The shriek of tearing metal pierced Stella's ears, a second before she was blown completely off her feet. There was an instant of weightlessness, of floating terror, and then she crashed down on the catwalk.

Pain shot up her side. She might have screamed, but her voice was lost beneath the awful sound of grinding metal.

The air filled with smoke. From her position on the ground, Stella caught a glimpse of some of the engineering team—the blond man's horsetail, Laura's green handkerchief—all lying flat, sprawled across the room. Some of them began to move, but most lay still where they had fallen. There was a chorus of low, painful moans, and neither Cyrus nor the captain were anywhere in sight.

"Cyrus!" Stella cried. Smoke filled her lungs, and she

coughed, the movement sending ripples of pain across her rib cage.

A flash of light pierced the haze like a sunbeam through a storm cloud. Pulling herself to her knees, Stella crawled toward the glow and found Cyrus. He was on his back a few feet away from her on the floor of the catwalk.

Gold light poured from his hands and eyes and streamed downward, covering the lower level of the engine room in a bright shimmer like a soap bubble. Inside the bubble, a deadly haze of metal and fire churned.

Somehow Cyrus had managed to wall off the engines at the moment of the explosion. Swirling inside the barrier was a hailstorm of debris, shards of twisted, burning metal that would have torn them all apart if it had been allowed to break free. If he hadn't already been in the process of calling on his power when the boiler blew, they would all have been killed instantly. That much Stella knew.

Stella leaned down to whisper in Cyrus's ear. "Are you all right?" she asked, her voice quavering. She couldn't tell if he was injured. The light pouring off his body was so bright it hurt to look at him.

He reached out a trembling hand to her. "Help me up," he said weakly. "I have to . . . see what happened . . . to the engines."

Stella took his hand and pulled them both up off the

floor. She gasped at the sudden flood of heat up her arm. This was beyond a fever and much hotter than he'd felt when she touched him that day up in the crow's nest.

Are you all right? she wanted to ask again, but the words died in her throat as his thoughts opened to her. She closed her eyes, but the images tore through her mind, too fast for her to see them all clearly. There were a man and a woman Stella had never seen, standing in front of a house with a birch tree growing in the yard. Another man walked up to the couple, a man with dark, graying hair, wearing a long lab coat. Before he could reach them, Stella's view turned and soared upward, and there were airships streaking through the sky, dozens of them, flying over a city so shining and vast it dizzied her. Then Cyrus let go of her hand, and the pictures vanished, leaving nothing but brief, glowing afterimages.

The world tilted under Stella's feet. For a second, she thought it was dizziness, a side effect of being connected to Cyrus's mind, but he was staggering too. The whole room was shifting. It was the ship. Stella reached out and snagged Cyrus by the belt, grabbing the catwalk railing with her other hand to keep them both on their feet.

"Oh *no!*" Cyrus choked.

"What's wrong?" Stella had never heard such terror in his voice.

"The boiler," Cyrus said, pointing with a hand that still radiated golden light. "I wasn't fast enough."

Stella looked down. Below them, the smoke was clearing, allowing them to see the extent of the damage through Cyrus's bubble.

What she saw nearly made her lose her grip on Cyrus and the catwalk railing.

A broken cage of twisted metal bars was all that remained of the boiler. Whatever device the Faceless man had used had ruptured the shell, causing the pressurized steam trapped inside to escape through the opening all at once, with a catastrophic amount of force.

In the explosion, the boiler had ripped free of its moorings and went in the only direction Cyrus's barrier hadn't been able to reach in time.

It had blown a hole out the side of the *Iron Glory*.

Stella had a surreal view of hills and trees wheeling past the gaping tear as the ship spiraled toward the ground. A gust of wind blew through the engine room, stealing the rest of the smoke. The ship listed sharply, turning the level catwalk into a steep, slick ramp. Stella braced her feet and yanked on Cyrus's belt to keep him from sliding off.

"The *Iron Glory*'s going down!" she hollered. "Cyrus, grab the railing! Everyone, hold on to something!"

The few engineers who could move scrambled to find something sturdy. The rest were unconscious, bleeding from wounds or pinned by debris that had escaped Cyrus's barrier. He looked around at all the helpless people, his gaze coming to rest on Stella last. The gold light filled his eyes, and his skin was deathly pale. Grief and guilt twisted his face.

Stella could see that he blamed himself for this, for being too late.

She wanted to wrap her arms around him and tell him that it wasn't his fault. But that wasn't what he needed. Not now. Instead, she stared at him in defiance, the blood thundering in her ears.

"I'm *not* giving up!" she shouted. "And neither are you!"

The golden light flickered, as if a tremor had passed through his body. But then the radiance surged back, and Cyrus's hands clenched into fists on the railing.

"You're right—we're not going to die," he said, "not like this!" He turned toward the hole in the ship and said over his shoulder, "Can you anchor me?"

Stella pulled Cyrus to her and positioned him between her and the catwalk railing. She wrapped her arms around him from behind and gripped the metal bar, trapping him securely. They were as close as they'd been since she was comforting him in his cell. "What are you going to do?" she asked.

"I'm going to extend the barrier to the whole ship," he said. "We'll still crash, but if it stays up, the *Iron Glory* won't be destroyed. Hold tight, though, because we're in for a bumpy ride." As he spoke, the golden bubble that had contained the explosion grew, and Cyrus swayed on his feet. Stella tightened her grip as the bubble passed through the engine room walls and out of sight.

"What will this do to you?" Stella said into his ear. "You can barely stand as it is. You're exhausted from using your power to contain the engines."

"I'll be fine," he replied, struggling to focus.

But he wasn't. With her arms around him, Stella could feel his body trembling, his muscles balled tight under the fabric of his shirt. "Cyrus, you're too weak. You can't—"

He turned and let his head rest briefly against her shoulder. "If I don't, we're all going to die," he said.

Stella's insides knotted. She wanted to deny it, but deep down she knew he was right. For herself, her parents, and the rest of the crew, Cyrus's barrier was their only hope.

She tightened her grip on the railing. "I've got you," she said in a choked voice. "Do what you have to do. I won't let you fall."

"I know you won't." He lifted his head and flashed her one last lopsided grin, and then the golden light exploded in a brilliant nimbus around his body.

Stella kept a tight grip on Cyrus's waist, but the light now completely obscured him. It was like holding on to a star. She squeezed her eyes shut against the painful glow. The heat built and built, until Stella's arms and neck were slick with sweat, the light searing her skin even through the thick fabric of the invisibility suit.

His mind opened to her again, but this time Stella saw no fleeting images, nothing but a single word Cyrus repeated over and over in his head.

Please.

Please.

Please.

The ship rocked beneath them. The engineers' screams tore through the room, and Cyrus's body convulsed. Stella dug her heels in and pressed her body against his back to hold him steady. The wind blasting through the hole in the ship built to a roar as the *Iron Glory* picked up speed, gravity pulling them down, spinning them toward the earth.

Stella didn't know when she started screaming. Her lungs burned with it, the sound buried in Cyrus's back. Images flashed in her mind, her own thoughts this time. She saw her parents, smiling and laughing in the lab, her mother hugging her before she boarded the ship. She saw Cyrus rolling his eyes as she tried to guess his real name.

The catwalk rattled and shook beneath them, as if it was tearing away from its moorings. Stella felt herself slipping to her knees, her strength giving out as the weight of the falling ship pressed her down. She clamped her teeth together and forced herself upright. A thunderous *boom* split the air, and suddenly the railing tore from

Stella's hands. She opened her eyes and flailed, reaching for Cyrus, letting the light blind her, but her hands grasped only empty air.

She was floating again.

This was what it felt like to fall out of the sky.

TWENTY-SEVEN

But this time, when she hit the ground, the world shattered. Awareness returned in pieces. Stella was lying on her back, with something sharp poking her in the side. She opened her eyes to bright spots of yellow and orange. While she waited for them to clear, she moved her right arm, reaching for whatever was jammed into her side.

It was the Lazuril rod, still tucked into her waistband beneath the invisibility suit, and thankfully, still deactivated. Stella readjusted it and then tried pushing herself up to a sitting position.

That was a mistake.

Pain roared through her left arm, so hot and bright that Stella ground her teeth. The room spun, the spots in her vision turning streaky. Panting, Stella lay still, hoping the pain would pass.

After several minutes, her vision finally cleared enough for Stella to see that she had landed on the bottom level of the engine room, not far away from the wrecked boiler casing. She lifted her head to see how badly she was hurt.

Her left wrist was pinched beneath a section of the catwalk. The whole structure had collapsed and broken into three pieces. The smallest of these had trapped her. If it had been one of the bigger sections, it likely would have killed her.

Careful not to move her arm this time, Stella reached forward with her other hand and pushed the ruined catwalk off her. It gave way and clattered to the floor.

With the pressure removed, the pain was significantly less, but Stella knew her wrist was badly sprained, if not broken.

She was lucky, but she wasn't so sure the same could be said about Cyrus. She had to get to her feet, had to go and find him.

Sunlight filtered in through the hole in the side of the ship, giving her enough light to see the wreckage around her. The engine room had been torn apart, with debris strewn everywhere. The other engine's boiler had ruptured sometime during the crash, though its metal cage or Cyrus's barrier—or both—had managed to keep it inside the engine room. That must have been the last loud boom that had torn up the catwalk, Stella thought.

Cries echoed through the ship, making her briefly forget her own pain. She stood up, cradling her injured wrist against her stomach as she carefully made her way around the engine room, searching for the others. Three of the crew lay unconscious near the cracked boiler. They might have been trying to stabilize the pressure before the crash, to keep it from rupturing as long as they could. Stella bent down to check for their pulses. A wave of relief left her dizzy again.

They were alive.

But where was Cyrus?

"Cyrus?" Stella moved on and found three more engineers, two of them conscious and with only minor scrapes and cuts on their faces.

"Laura's trying to get to the medical bay," one of them said. "The captain went to answer the calls for help from the rest of the ship."

For all Stella knew, her parents could be among the wounded. What if the medical bay had been as badly damaged as the engine room in the explosion? They could be . . . could be . . .

Stella forced herself to swallow her panic. She could only focus on one thing at a time, and right now she had to find her friend.

"Did you see Cyrus?" she asked the engineers. "Does anyone know what happened to him?"

The blond man had been wiping his face with a rag.

He looked up at her. "I saw him," he said, his voice hushed. "He was standing in the middle of that gold light. I've never seen anything like it. When that first boiler blew, he had his arms up like this." The young man lifted his hands as if he were pushing against a wall. "And this wave of light came out. It passed right through me, and when the boiler went, it threw metal everywhere like a hailstorm. The shards were flying right at me, and I thought for sure I was dead. But that light—it swallowed them all up, slowed them down like they were moving through water. And then they just . . . stopped. I don't know how, but that boy saved my life."

He saved all our lives, Stella thought.

And might have traded his own to do it.

She moved on, her search becoming more frantic as the minutes passed. She hurled debris aside with her good hand, banging and clattering her way through the engine room. Her left wrist throbbed, making her bite the inside of her cheek.

"Cyrus!" she called desperately. "Cyrus, where are you?"

And then, in the back corner of the engine room, she heard a soft moan.

Cyrus was propped up with his back against the wall, eyes half open, head lolling to one side.

Stella scrambled over to him and dropped to her knees, immediately checking him over for injuries. His head, neck, and torso were all unmarked. Falling in the back corner of the room, he'd escaped the worst of the debris shower.

He was barely conscious but otherwise unhurt.

At least on the outside.

Stella laid her head against Cyrus's chest and listened to his heartbeat. It was sluggish, as if it were taking everything inside him to keep it beating.

Stella braced her good hand on the wall for a moment to control her trembling, and then she reached for him. "Cyrus, can you hear me?" she asked, gently tipping his chin toward her. "Do you know where you are?"

His skin was still hot to the touch, but not painfully so. It was impossible to tell if he really was running a fever or if it was just the aftereffects of his power.

Slowly, Cyrus opened his eyes and focused on her. "Stella," he croaked. "Are you all right? The catwalk . . . fell."

"Lots of things fell," she agreed, and made herself smile for him, both so he would know she was all right and so she wouldn't betray the panic welling up inside her like a scream. She couldn't wait for Laura to bring back help. She had to get him out of here now, had to find her parents. "Do you think you can stand?" she asked. "We need to get to the medical bay."

"Pretty tired," he said, his eyes fluttering closed. "Maybe I'll just rest for a minute."

"No, you don't," Stella said, taking him by the shoulder. She hated to move him without knowing the extent of his injuries, but she felt a terrible certainty that if he fell unconscious now, he wouldn't wake up again. "On your feet, Cyrus. We can't stay here."

He lifted his head and opened his eyes. "All right . . . I'll try," he said. He took a moment to gather his strength and then pushed himself away from the wall.

Stella bent forward, letting Cyrus hold on to her shoulders. With only one good hand to brace against the floor, she struggled awkwardly to get them to their feet. Luckily, she'd dragged Cyrus around the cargo bay twice before when he was unconscious, so she knew she could lift his weight. Once they were standing, they leaned on each other for support.

It was the longest and slowest journey through the ship that Stella had ever taken. Only one of the stairways out of the engine room remained, crooked and covered with debris. They had to crawl up it on all fours to reach the door. Once they'd navigated past that and out into the hall, Stella stopped to get her bearings.

The whole ship looked different now, changed into a nightmarish mess. Piles of debris had buried the doors to some rooms and blocked certain passages to the upper decks. Stella could hear muffled voices and banging behind these obstructions. She tried to lever aside some of the debris, but most of it was too heavy. Whoever was back there would have to find another way out or wait to be rescued by the crew.

Most of the gaslights had been taken out by the crash, torn from their moorings and strewn on the floor in piles of glass shards. The only light came from the windows letting in sparse sunlight from outside.

Worst of all, the *Iron Glory* had crashed on its side, turning some of the walls into floors and ceilings into walls. The contents of rooms had spilled out into the hallway. A supply closet had emptied buckets, crates, and tools all over the floor. There was even a stray boot lying in one corner, missing its mate. Stella and Cyrus were forced to crawl or climb over the uneven surfaces, and Stella's wrist screamed in protest every step of the way.

Finally, just when Stella thought she wasn't going to be able to hold them upright any longer, they reached the medical bay. Or what was left of it. The examination tables had been overturned, and cabinets dangled from the walls, their contents spilled all over the floor. Broken glass crunched under Stella's boots as she and Cyrus limped inside.

Her mother was on her knees at the back of the room, wrapping bandages around a crew member's head. There was a whole row of patients already laid out on blankets beside him.

Stella's father was nowhere in sight.

"*Mom,*" Stella said, her voice breaking with a mixture of fear and relief.

Her mother's head jerked up, and when she saw Stella, for an instant her face crumpled, eyes shining with tears. Then she took a visible breath and composed herself.

"Stella," she said, her voice steady and calm, a healer at work. "Are you two all right? Bring Cyrus over here." She pointed to a blanket near the wall and finished the wrap on her patient before crossing over to the pair. Cyrus didn't greet her mother. His eyes were glassy, and he moaned softly, turning his face to the wall once he was on his back.

"He used up all his strength," Stella said as her mother listened to his heartbeat with her scope. "I mean all of it. He's never done anything like that before, but he was protecting the ship. We would have died if he hadn't put up a barrier with his power."

The words tumbled out of her. Stella cradled her injured wrist against her body. Pushing up her sleeves, she noticed for the first time that the skin of both her arms was unnaturally red and tender where she'd been holding on to Cyrus. His power had been so intense it had left behind light burns on her skin.

She could only imagine what it must have done to Cyrus inside.

"His heartbeat," her mother started before pausing and pulling the scope's ends out of her ears. "Well, there's a deep mechanical sound beneath the beat. It would be hidden if you didn't use an instrument to listen for it. But even taking that into consideration, I don't think his heart is functioning normally. What I don't have is knowledge of how his mechanics work in harmony with the organic parts of him." She smoothed a hand over Cyrus's forehead, her eyes soft and sorrowful. "I don't even know his anatomy."

"So there's nothing you can do?" Stella's throat was raw, and there was a weight pressing down on her chest.

Her mother slowly shook her head. "He needs one of his own doctors. I can make him comfortable, but if he's going to recover, he'll have to do it on his own." She turned to examine Stella's wrist. "I'll need to wrap this," she said.

Stella pulled away from her mother's grasp, wincing. "What does a sprained wrist matter if Cyrus is *dying*?" Her voice was high and strained. She looked around the medical bay. All of her mother's patients were hurt worse than she was. They needed her attention more. And her father . . . he . . .

"Where's Dad?" Stella asked, her voice dropping to a whisper.

Her mother's calm facade cracked, but she recovered. "We found him unconscious in the washroom, just like you'd said, and I revived him with some spirits of hartshorn. But we were separated just before the explosion.

The last time I saw him, he was headed to the engine room to check on you. Knowing your father, he's out caring for other survivors now."

She left the rest unsaid, but Stella could fill in the blanks. He was out looking for others, assuming he hadn't been hurt or trapped somewhere in the ship. And she and Cyrus hadn't encountered him on their journey from the engine room.

Overwhelmed, Stella leaned over to take Cyrus's hand for comfort. His skin wasn't hot anymore. In fact, it was cold, so cold that she pressed her fingers to his neck to check his pulse. Holding steady, but how much longer would that last? Stella felt herself coming apart, piece by piece, just like the *Iron Glory* had as it fell out of the sky.

TWENTY-EIGHT

Stella peeled off the invisibility suit while her mother brought her an ice pack, draping it over her swollen wrist. Then she joined Stella in watching Cyrus's chest rise and fall. A noise in the hallway alerted them to someone coming, and they both looked up anxiously.

A moment later, Drea stumbled into the medical bay. She was bleeding from a deep cut to one of her feelers, which Stella's mother insisted on stitching up. Drea reported that most of the crew, including Stella's father, were still missing and assumed trapped in various parts of the ship. Captain Keeler was already organizing rescue efforts. As soon as Stella's mother could get enough of the remaining men and women functional again, they would need to join the search for survivors.

"I've sent two men outside to scout the crash site," the

sarnun woman said, her voice reaching out to everyone's minds in the medical bay, including Stella's. "There are no cities or settlements anywhere in sight. The terrain is rocky, and trees are sparse. There's a stream nearby that looks clear. Once we test it to confirm, we'll have a plentiful source of water. There's also an east-west road a few miles away that's lightly traveled, but so far we haven't encountered any locals."

"We're on our own, then," Stella's mother said. She'd been in the process of treating a chamelin engineer with a dislocated shoulder.

The chamelin looked over at Cyrus. "How's the boy?" he asked, coughing and wincing at the pain the movement caused him. "I heard he put on quite a show in the engine room. Saved all our skins, guiding the ship down the way he did."

Drea's feelers snapped toward him. "Did you see it?"

The chamelin nodded at Stella. "Not me, but Codi was going on and on about seeing the two of them up on the catwalk in the engine room. She protected him, and he protected the ship. I don't know how they did it, but Codi said it looked like some kind of magic."

Drea came over and crouched next to Cyrus, her feelers settling around her shoulders like living vines. "Is he going to be all right?" she asked.

Stella shook her head. She wanted to tell Drea what her mother had said, that maybe Cyrus would recover on his own, but she was too much of a healer herself to ignore the signs. Cyrus was slipping away.

"I'm sorry," Drea said with a pang in her voice. "We'll make him as comfortable as possible." The sarnun woman laid her hand on Cyrus's forehead. "If he wakes again, I'd like to know. I want to thank him myself for saving us."

Stella nodded. "I will." She took Drea's arm when the sarnun started to rise. "What happened to the Faceless man?" she asked. "Did he escape?"

Drea sighed. "The guards had him in custody right before the explosion, but after that, I don't know. Wherever he ended up, it's likely he's injured or trapped, just like the rest of the crew. I'll put together a search team as soon as we've accounted for everyone else. We'll find him."

Her promise didn't make Stella feel any better. If he was free, the Faceless man could go back to imitating any of the crew to avoid capture. "Look for bloodshot eyes," she told the sarnun. "No matter what face he's wearing, it's the one detail he can't change." If they were lucky, maybe the Faceless man had simply left, now that he'd gotten what he wanted in crashing the ship.

Drea left the medical bay soon after and another wave of wounded crew members made their way in from other parts of the ship. Stella and her mother flitted about, but Stella kept an eye on Cyrus. An hour later, he finally did open his eyes, and Stella didn't bother to call Drea back. She had too many things to say to him, questions to ask.

The moment Drea had mentioned a road near the crash site, Stella had started to make plans.

If there was a road nearby, that meant the city of Kovall, Cyrus's home, was close. He'd told her it was just on the other side of the mountains.

Kovall would have supplies. Kovall would have food. And doctors.

"Hey," Cyrus said, his voice coming out in a whisper. But his eyes were clearer than they had been in the engine room, as if the short rest had restored a little of his strength. A smile pulled at his lips. "You look terrible."

"Well, you can't expect me to get dressed up to come to your sickbed," Stella said, grateful for his smile and teasing. It was easier to keep things light. "I only get cleaned up for special occasions."

"Too bad," Cyrus said. "We could have gotten dressed up for Kovall. Would have shown you the city. Taken you to the river and the Baluway Bridge. They light lanterns along the riverfront at night."

"Sounds beautiful," Stella said. *Keep him talking,* she thought. He needed to stay conscious. "But I don't speak your language, remember? How would I get by in the city?"

"I'd . . . teach you," Cyrus said. "It's not so hard."

"Really?" Stella asked, keeping her voice neutral. "What are the olaran words for 'hello' and 'goodbye'?"

"'Antya,' for 'hello' or 'good day,'" Cyrus murmured. "'Sinhave,' for 'goodbye.'"

Stella repeated the words, testing the clicks of the consonants on her tongue. When his attention drifted, she reached into her pocket where she'd kept the beetle. To her relief, it hadn't been damaged, despite her fall from the catwalk. She activated its recording device, hoping the words wouldn't be muffled with the beetle still in her pocket.

"How would I say 'yes' or 'no' in your language?" she asked, drawing his gaze back to her.

He gave her the words, and she repeated them loudly and clearly. She asked him for more, smiling, making a game of it. He played along. And then, trying her best to sound casual and hoping that his injuries had clouded his thoughts enough that he wouldn't think too deeply about the question, she asked. "What about 'doctor'?"

It didn't work. His eyes, half closed, flew open and pinned her. A spark of life came back, as if he was calling on all the reserves of strength left in his failing body. "What are you doing, Stella?" he demanded.

"Learning your language," she said, pretending to adjust his blanket. "I don't want to feel like an outsider when I go to Kovall."

He took hold of her uninjured wrist, not hard, but

enough to drag her gaze to his face. "How soon were you planning on going there?" he asked quietly.

She hesitated, but there was no fooling him. He knew her too well. "As soon as possible," she said. "I'm going to get help."

"You are *not* doing that."

She smiled down at him, but she ached inside. "You aren't even close to being able to argue with me," she said.

His eyes filled with sorrow. "Stella, it's too late," he said. "I can feel it." He put his hand against his chest. "I can hold on for now, but I'll be gone in a day or two."

The words were like punches. "Then I'll have to hurry, won't I?"

Now Cyrus was getting angry. He was also the most lucid he'd been since the crash. Spots of color bloomed in his cheeks, and he pushed himself upright, bracing one hand on the wall next to him. If Stella had known that anger was all it took to make him improve, she would have tried to irritate him an hour ago.

"We're at least a day out of Kovall, and you want to travel with that injury?" Cyrus said, pointing to her wrist.

"It's not as bad as it looks," Stella lied. "By tomorrow I won't even feel it."

He went on as if she hadn't spoken. "You don't know the city and you don't speak our language."

"You gave me the words I need," Stella said. She pulled the beetle out of her pocket and held it up, its red wings shimmering. She clicked off its recording device. "I'll send the beetle back to you with updates on my progress toward the city. If I get lost, I'll just describe where I am, and you'll get me back on track. Once I get to the city, all I have to do is find a doctor and bring him back here."

Cyrus's eyes lit up when he saw the communication device. "No, you don't need to go anywhere. Just send the beetle. We'll record our location and send it to the city for help."

Stella waved a hand impatiently. "You said yourself the beetle is best at short range. Have you ever tested it over the kinds of distances we're talking about?"

"No," Cyrus said through clenched teeth. "But it's a better option than sending you out alone. What about the rest of the crew? Surely someone can go with you. One of the chamelins can probably fly you there in half the time."

"The chamelins are either too injured to fly or trapped somewhere in the ship with the rest of the crew," Stella said. "Anyone else who isn't too injured to stand is helping with the rescue before it's too late. None of them can be spared, but I can. I've thought this over, Cyrus. The best option is that I go to the city as fast as I can."

Cyrus opened his mouth and closed it again without speaking. He was running out of arguments—and his brief spurt of energy was fading. "This is crazy," he muttered, his head falling back onto his pillow. "We just survived a terrible crash, and now you want to run out into the unknown again. Where is the girl who was so afraid of the olarans? I want her back."

That brought a smile to Stella's face. "Too late," she said. "That girl's gone for good. You're stuck with me now." It had been a wild, sometimes frightening journey, but somewhere along the way, it had turned Stella into a true explorer.

Cyrus stared at her, slowly shaking his head. "Will you at least tell your parents what you're up to?" he begged.

"I'll tell my mom," Stella said. Her gaze went automatically to the door of the medical bay. "Dad is missing somewhere on the ship."

Cyrus's face blanched. "Oh, Stella, I'm sorry." He reached for her, but his hand trembled with weakness. "I don't want you to get hurt," he said.

"I know," Stella said, squeezing his hand. "And I don't want you—or anyone else—to die."

Cyrus licked his dry lips and reached for the beetle. "If you're going to do this, you'll need directions to get around in the city. I'll give you a bunch more olaran words to learn, but the most important one is 'Akeata.' It means 'Tinker.'"

He said it again in his language, and Stella repeated it, her brow furrowed. "What's a Tinker?" she asked.

"He's the best doctor in Kovall," Cyrus explained. "But more than that, he's . . . important to the olaran people, especially to the alagant and the royal family. He's a scientist, like your parents, and an inventor. He was the one who organized our expeditions across the mountains and did the most detailed studies of your people. If you can get to him, convince him what you are, he'll come running to help."

Stella's heart leaped. "Are you sure?"

Cyrus nodded. "Oh, yeah. He's a brilliant man, but he never actually got the chance to go on the expeditions. The alagant thought he was too important to risk, so he stayed behind. If he got the chance to meet a group of human explorers, he'd jump at it."

He sounded like just the person Stella needed—and someone whom Cyrus admired. "Do you know him well?" she asked.

"He and my father are friends," Cyrus said, "and he taught me all kinds of different ways to use aletheum. That's how I was able to put it in the *Iron Glory*'s gasbag during construction. I'll give you directions to get to his house in the city. I can even draw you a map if you can get your hands on some paper."

Stella brought him some stiff bandages and a pencil and they started to plan. Cyrus sketched the map as well as he could, but his hands were still shaking, the light in his eyes fading as he struggled to stay conscious and alert.

Stella vowed she would bring back help for her father and the crew. She would save Cyrus, the way he had saved them all.

Stella Glass, alchemist, healer-in-training, and professional stowaway, was going to be the first human to explore the olaran city of Kovall in the uncharted lands of Solace.

⪻ TWENTY-NINE ⪼

When Cyrus finished the map, he wrote a brief note on the back of the bandage in his own language for Stella to give to the Tinker so that he would know she could be trusted. Stella took it and then gathered up all the supplies she thought the crew could spare from the medical bay. If she could scrounge some more food from somewhere before she left the ship, that would be wonderful, but she wasn't counting on it.

She put on the invisibility suit but paused at Cyrus's bedside, impulsively leaning down to kiss him on the forehead. He'd been asleep, but his eyes fluttered open and slowly focused on her.

"I'll be back soon," she whispered, her throat tight. "Wait for me, all right?"

His eyes softened, and he reached out and weakly squeezed her good hand. "I'll try," he said. "But there's something I want to tell you, Stella, just in case . . . well, you know."

Cyrus's face blurred as Stella's eyes filled with tears. "Go ahead," she said, fighting to keep her voice steady as she laced her fingers with his.

"I just want you to know that I don't regret anything," Cyrus said. "For a long time, I was so mad at myself for joining the expedition to your lands. After the slavers captured me, I didn't want anything to do with your part of the world. Then I met you, and everything changed. *You* changed me. I can't ever thank you enough for that, Stella. For giving me hope."

Stella squeezed his hand tight. "Hold on to that hope, Cyrus," she begged. "I haven't forgotten my promise. I *will* get you home."

Reluctantly, she let go of his hand. If she didn't make herself leave now, she knew she wouldn't be able to.

She turned away, going to her mother next. As much as she hated to say goodbye to Cyrus, she'd been dreading this conversation with her mother even more and was fully prepared for an argument. In fact, she half expected her mother to tell Drea, who might try to force her to stay. But she had to take that risk. She couldn't leave without an explanation. She'd failed to confide in her parents once, and she wouldn't do it again.

When she explained what she was about to do, for a

moment her mother said nothing at all. Then she stepped forward and drew Stella into her arms.

"I don't want you to go, Stella," her mother said. "I think it's dangerous, and too many things could go wrong."

Stella nodded, burying her face in her mother's shoulder. "But if I don't go . . . if I don't try . . ." She couldn't finish the sentence.

"I know," her mother murmured, stroking Stella's hair with trembling hands. "I want you to stay here, to be safe . . . but . . . I'm not going to tell you that you can't try to save your friend."

Stella pulled back in surprise, looking into her mother's eyes. They were full of sorrow, fear, and pride. In that moment, Stella had the feeling that saying those words had been more painful for her mother than saying goodbye to Stella in Noveen, harder to endure than the crash. This time she was the one sending Stella into an unknown land, and neither of them knew what the consequences might be.

"I'll be careful, Mom," Stella said as tears spilled down her cheeks. "And . . . thank you. I promise I'll come back soon. I'll bring help—we'll find Dad, and everything will be all right."

Oh, how she hoped that was true.

Her mother nodded, wiping away the moisture from Stella's cheeks. "You should go now, while everyone's distracted searching the ship for survivors. I'll cover for you as long as I can."

Then she pulled Stella in for one last, bone-crushing hug. Stella inhaled the scent of her mother's perfume and drew all the strength she could from the embrace. It was a hug that said so many things between mother and daughter yet needed no words at all.

Stella pulled away and left the medical bay without a backward glance. She activated the invisibility suit and made her way cautiously through the ship, managing to avoid the search parties moving among the wreckage.

When she stepped outside the remains of the *Iron Glory*, she paused to get her bearings and examine the wrapping on her injured wrist. The swelling had gone down, but it was still painful and tender. It wouldn't be good for much on this trip. She carried her sack of supplies in her good hand and set out for the road that Drea's scouts had found.

The area around the crash site was an open, rocky field. In the distance, far to the east, was the expanse of pine forest they'd flown over on the last day of their journey. Somewhere beyond that lay the mountains.

When she was far enough away from the crash site that the *Iron Glory*'s scouts wouldn't see her, Stella stopped, deactivated the invisibility suit, and took it off so she was wearing her regular clothes. Then she looked back at the airship wreckage.

She'd known it would be bad, but knowing that hadn't prepared her for the twisted ruin before her. Shattered propellers dug furrows into the grass, a punctured hull lay like an open wound, and even the mast and crow's nest had been torn down and thrown dozens of feet away from the crash site. The ship's gasbag was intact, thanks to Cyrus's aletheum, but tangled in a mass of cables and half draped over the bow of the ship.

Tears blurred Stella's vision, and for once, she was grateful for them. She didn't want to see the *Iron Glory* like this. The beautiful ship, her rising star, had fallen for good.

It would never be able to carry them home.

Don't think about that now, Stella told herself. It didn't matter anyway. Her home was with the people who were most precious to her. They came from both sides of the mountains, but they were all right here.

They counted on her for help.

She turned away from the ruin of the *Iron Glory* and headed west, walking for a few miles with only Cyrus's words running through her head. "Stay on the road and you won't get lost," he had told her. "All roads lead to Kovall eventually. It's the biggest city for miles."

The road she traveled cut a path through vast fields of swaying grasses and wildflowers, some she didn't recognize at all. Foxes and rabbits occasionally poked their heads out of hiding, but there were strange creatures too.

A brown snake with green spots lifted its head from the grass. Stella froze and backed away slowly, hoping the thing wasn't poisonous, when she realized the snake was covered in *fur*. It wasn't a reptile at all, but something new. She made a mental note to ask Cyrus about it later.

She walked on, keeping an eye out for more strange new species. So far, there were no houses or signs of people for miles in every direction. She'd asked Cyrus a little about the area, and he guessed they were in the Beldt Grasslands. He'd explained that it was a large tract of land to the east of Kovall that was owned by the city and that would eventually be turned into a public park or held for new construction as the city continued to grow and expand.

Seeing it firsthand, Stella stared out at the vastness, shielding her eyes against the sun. She'd grown up in a crowded city, but even the land outside Noveen didn't feel as wide open, nor as endless, as this.

It was Stella's first inkling that the land she found herself in now was very different from her own. Empty, yet full of beauty and possibilities.

Still, after several hours of walking, despite her wariness, a part of her wanted to encounter someone. A person. A voice that wasn't the cry and flutter of birds stirring the tall grasses. It was so quiet out here, and the road scrolling away in front of her for miles was daunting and lonely.

She stopped for a few minutes to eat some food late in the day. She hadn't managed to scrounge much, but it would get her through the journey to Kovall. Part of her had been hoping she'd reach the city in a day, but her wrist ached and her ribs and body were still sore from her ordeal in the engine room, all of which slowed her progress.

When she finally stopped to sleep for the night, Stella took a moment to watch the horizon deepen from rich orange to a glorious, burning red. It wasn't the same red she'd seen while soaring the skies over the Hiterian Mountains, but the open fields allowed the riot of color to touch every blade of grass and turn it copper before fading to a cool twilight blue.

Before the light vanished, Stella looked down the road one last time. A surge of excitement tickled her scalp. In the distance, almost hidden by the gathering dark, were the outlines of dozens of tall buildings. They blurred together, tiny with distance, but it was unmistakably a city. A very large city.

All roads lead to Kovall.

Stella made a rough camp in the tall grass. In addition to the meager food she'd scrounged, she'd packed a couple of blankets, and of course, the invisibility suit and the messenger beetle. She'd also brought the Lazuril rod, which she kept close by, just in case. She nibbled on some cheese before curling up in her blanket.

Sleep turned out to be impossible. Stella's mind wandered to what it would be like in the city full of olarans and decided that since she couldn't sleep, she might as well do something useful. She took the beetle out of her pocket and listened to Cyrus's language lesson. A small part of her thought it would make her nod off, but it didn't. She already knew by heart all the words he'd given her. Now they just made her think about the day to come. Her stomach clenched with apprehension.

She wished Cyrus could be with her when she stepped through the city gates. What if she didn't make it back in time or the olarans thought she was an enemy? What if the Tinker didn't believe her when she told her story?

To distract herself from her worries, she decided to record a message for Cyrus, to let her know how much progress she'd made.

"Cyrus, it's nighttime now, and I can see Kovall in the distance. I should be there early tomorrow. The grasslands are beautiful, and even the smell of the wildflowers is different here, or maybe I just want it to be. Please send me a message back as soon as you get this so that I know you're with me. Then I won't feel so alone."

Stella ended the message, raised her hands above her head, and released the beetle. It spiraled into the sky, moonlight glinting off its copper carapace.

Travel fast, she thought. *Fly straight.*

She lay back down to sleep again. She must have been more tired than she'd thought, because the next time she opened her eyes, it was morning.

A few hours after she started out on the road, the beetle *click-whir-click*ed its way up behind her and then dipped into her line of vision, circling her head once before it landed in her outstretched hand. Stella's hands shook as she activated it to play back the message.

"Stella, I'm still here. No better, no worse. I'm glad you told me how close you are to the city. It almost makes me feel like I'm there with you, like I'm going home."

Cyrus's voice dropped to a faint whisper, and Stella had to press the beetle against her ear to hear the word "home." A long silence followed, and Stella thought the message might be over. But Cyrus's voice came back, softer, weaker, but still with her.

"Stella, would you do something for me? Would you send the beetle back one more time before you get to the city? I want to record a message for my parents, just in case . . . in case I don't make it. I want them to hear my voice, so that they know I was all right, in the end. Do that for me. Please."

The message ended, and Stella stared at the beetle, as if she could see through its eyes, all the way back to the ship and to Cyrus. She activated it for another recording.

"Cyrus, don't you dare give up on me! You're not going to die. I can see Kovall clearly now. So much metal!

You didn't tell me it would shine like that in the sun. It's beautiful.

"Record your message for your parents, but I'll never have to deliver it. Please hold on a little longer, Cyrus. I'm coming."

She sent the beetle flying and doubled her pace, not caring about the pain in her wrist or her fatigue.

She was close now. So close.

The path Stella traveled gradually began to widen, intersecting other, larger roads. One minute, there were no signs of civilization, and the next, the grasslands gave way to farms surrounded by stone walls and fences. Smoke curled from chimneys, and for the first time on her journey, Stella saw some olarans, men and women who worked the fields with tools and machinery that she had a hard time identifying.

Tall, spherical tanks sloshed with water as they wheeled up and down the corn rows, stretching out eight metal arms, four on each side, connected to hoses that jetted clean, cold water to irrigate the land. The machines were impressive, but even more amazing was that they appeared to be operating by themselves, with no direction from the farmers.

Stella tried not to stare, and as she passed by, she nodded to the farmers. A man tipped his hat to her and shouted a greeting, which Stella returned, remembering Cyrus's language lesson. Then she hurried on, not wanting to seem rude but also not wanting to reveal that she couldn't understand anything beyond the basics of the olaran language.

As she continued on the road, Stella crossed a series of railroad tracks and sometimes even found herself traveling alongside a passenger train. The locomotives were similar in design to those in her part of the world, but they were sleeker, lighter, and nearly silent as they cut across the land like the edge of a knife.

Stella blended in easily with the traffic that had now joined her on the road, moving steadily toward the city. There were enough people traveling on foot—likely walking in from nearby farms—that she didn't stand out. The olarans all appeared to be human, just like Cyrus and her, and except for her clothing, which differed a little in style from the people she passed, she might have been any other citizen of Kovall.

Eventually, a set of metal gates came into view ahead of her, similar to the gates protecting Noveen. However, the sheer size of these, and the city beyond, was overwhelming.

Cyrus was right. Kovall was so much bigger than her city, bigger than any city she'd ever seen. As she passed through the gates, she was swallowed by the immensity of it all. The streets were narrow and jammed with people, and the buildings soared so high they blocked the sun. Stella had to crane her neck to look up at them.

Many of the largest ones were made of metal, and they glittered brightly in the sun like the gasbag of the *Iron Glory*.

They're made of aletheum, Stella realized, or a similar material. They also looked much newer than the stone houses and buildings she walked past, as if the metal structures were slowly taking over.

Dozens of smaller railroad tracks crisscrossed the streets and even rose up several stories in the air. Rumbling along the tracks, not nearly as silent as the locomotives, were miniature trains carrying even more people. These were open to the air and more primitive than the passenger trains traveling outside the city, more like steam-powered carts. But they moved with a speed that made Stella jump whenever they zoomed past. The whole city seemed to move faster, was more mechanical, than she'd ever expected.

Again, she wished that Cyrus were here to explain it all to her, but she didn't have time to stop and take in the sights. She needed to find the Tinker's house. She moved onto a sidewalk, out of the way of both the street traffic and the people hurrying past, and pulled out the map Cyrus had drawn for her.

As she was trying to get her bearings, the beetle drifted down and settled on her shoulder, its clicking and whirring sounds drowned out by the city traffic. Startled, Stella scooped the beetle off into her hand.

Relief flooded her. She'd begun to worry that the distance from the ship to Kovall was too great for it to travel, and she knew how important it was to Cyrus that she get his message to his parents.

In case. Just in case.

She activated the message and raised the beetle to her ear. There was some static and scratching sounds, as if the beetle's mechanics had been strained by the long journey.

"Hello again," a man's voice hissed in her ear, unfamiliar at first, but then Stella realized who was speaking and nearly flung the beetle away in shock. "Did you miss me?"

It was the Faceless man.

≈ THIRTY ≈

The Faceless man was back, and he had the beetle, which meant he'd somehow gotten to Cyrus. Stella leaned against a building, afraid her legs wouldn't support her, while she played the message.

"I know that you're on your way to Kovall to bring back help for your friend, but it won't matter. Cyrus is dying. You can't save him. But you *can* save your parents, if you do exactly what I say."

Stella felt the ground heave beneath her. Had the Faceless man also gotten to her mother and father? She stared at the beetle, at her distorted expression in its copper shell. How could this be happening? The Faceless man had become a nightmare she couldn't wake up from.

"I'm willing to let them go unharmed if you abandon this mission and come back to the ship alone," the

Faceless man's message went on. "Tell no one who you are. Ask no one for help. If you disobey me, your parents will be the first ones to pay the price."

The beetle finished its message, but Stella stood frozen in the cool shade of the building, trying to form any coherent thought.

It wasn't enough that the Faceless man had brought down the *Iron Glory*. Now he was targeting her parents. If she brought back help, if she brought the olarans to her people, he'd kill them.

And he *would* do it—of that, Stella had no doubt. The thought made her light-headed with terror.

But why? What did the Faceless man hope to gain now? He'd already crashed the ship. Why didn't he just escape and disappear among his own people?

Because the crew is still alive, Stella realized with a shudder. Her people could still make contact with the olarans. In the Faceless man's mind, there was no victory unless he kept that from happening. If Stella brought back help, his plan would be thwarted, but her parents were in danger.

And if she came back alone, Cyrus would die.

Stella slid down the wall of the building until she was sitting on the ground. Her body had gone cold all over, yet she was sweating, fighting the tight ball of panic and fear expanding in her chest.

The Faceless man was offering her a choice. Except

he wasn't, because it was two impossible things, a situation she could never live with, no matter what she did. She'd survived the storm and the airship crash, but this was a choice that would break her in a way nothing else ever could.

Her parents or her best friend.

Stella drew her knees up to her chest and rocked back and forth as she fought to center her thoughts, to come up with any plan that would save all the people she loved most.

She tried to pull together everything she knew about the Faceless man. It all came back to what he was after. If she obeyed him and came back alone, he claimed he would spare her parents, but he must also realize that, eventually, the crew would seek out the olarans anyway. The only way he could stop them was to kill everyone else on board the *Iron Glory*.

And if that was his plan, would he truly let her parents live?

There was no way she could trust his word. Stella lifted her head and, using the wall for support, pushed herself unsteadily to her feet. She had to stop the Faceless man once and for all. No matter the risk, it's what her parents would want her to do. They wouldn't want her to break her promise to Cyrus.

She needed help if she was going to have a chance to save everyone.

Mom, Dad, please hold on, Stella thought. *Cyrus, I'm coming.*

Gathering her courage and slipping the beetle into her pocket, Stella checked Cyrus's map one last time to confirm where she was and then started off. She walked quickly down wide, twisting avenues, dodging the miniature trains and keeping to the shadows of the looming buildings.

Soon she found herself in a residential neighborhood, quieter streets lined with trees that bore yellow fruit the size of grapes. Stella passed a public park and in between the houses, she caught a glimpse of a shining ribbon of water.

That must be the Baluway River, she thought. Cyrus had said the Tinker lived not far from there. She was on the right track. All the houses on the street were numbered, and the Tinker lived in 1721.

The farther she walked, searching for the number, the larger the houses got, and the farther back from the street, until they became estates with sprawling, sculpted lawns and formal gardens. The noisy vehicle traffic faded away. Instead, people strolled along the sidewalk, dressed in beautiful, tailored clothing. Expensive clothing. Stella suddenly felt terribly out of place in her plain trousers and dirty, wrinkled shirt.

Just when she was starting to think she was in the wrong neighborhood, she found it, 1721 in big bronze numbers on a white stone column. There was another column to her right, both of them flanking a tall wrought-iron gate, the bars filed to sharp points seven feet up at their tips.

Stella swallowed. Obviously, the Tinker wasn't thrilled at the idea of uninvited guests.

She walked up to the gate to get a better look at the property. The Tinker's estate lacked the grand gardens and lush flowers of the other houses she'd passed, but it more than made up for it with the variety of trees. Willow and oak, birch, and more of the yellow fruit trees dotted the wide lawn. Beyond them was a large stone house, easily three stories tall. Besides its size, there was nothing remarkable about the house itself, but rising up beside it was the strangest tower Stella had ever seen.

It was all made of metal except at the very top, which was composed of sheets of glass. The structure reminded Stella of a lighthouse, but there was no ocean nearby, not according to Cyrus's map, anyway.

Well, standing out here staring at the house wasn't getting her anywhere. Stella grabbed hold of the gate and pulled on the bars, but it was locked tight. "Antya?" she called out in the olaran language, hoping to attract someone's attention, even a groundskeeper or a servant. Strangely, there were no guards around, at least not that she could see. She'd expected a house with such an intimidating and unwelcoming atmosphere to have security patrolling the property.

"Antya?" she tried again, but there was no answer.

Frustration swelled in her. She hadn't come all this way just to be thwarted by a fence. Stella walked along the barrier, determined to circle the place until she either found another entrance or located someone who would listen to her.

She'd made it around the side of the house closest to the tower when she saw her first chance. Two of the metal spikes on the fence had rusted off, creating a tiny gap just large enough for someone like her to climb over.

Heart in her throat, Stella glanced toward the street to make sure no one was looking her way. Then she quickly pulled the invisibility suit out of her pack, crouched down behind some bushes, and slipped it on. She brought the veil down over her face and waited a second for the suit to cloak her.

Then she grabbed hold of the iron bars and began to climb. Her injured wrist throbbed in protest, but Stella bit her lip and tried to ignore the pain. The metal was slick against her gloves, and twice she slipped to the ground and had to start all over again. Finally, she grabbed hold of the horizontal bar running across the top of the fence near the spikes. Gritting her teeth, she pulled herself up and partway through the gap.

It was narrower than she'd thought. The back of her suit snagged on a spike, trapping her. Twisting, Stella reached over her shoulder to try to pry it loose, but she couldn't get hold of it. She was stuck with her torso on one side of the fence and her legs swinging free on the other.

Graceful, Stella. Very graceful. At least no one could see her.

She braced herself on the horizontal bar, shimmying and twisting to try to free herself. The pain in her wrist spiked, making it harder to concentrate. Sweat rolled down her neck inside the suit.

A soft tearing sound reached her ears.

To her horror, the air in front of Stella shimmered, and the outline of her hands and arms became visible, as if she'd been running down a corridor and the suit could no longer match the background.

She'd pulled herself free of the spike, but the suit had been compromised. She wasn't fully visible, but anyone walking by on the street or looking out from the house would see the distortion around the fence. They'd know something wasn't right.

Frantic, Stella pushed herself up on the bar and swung one leg over the fence, then the other. She dropped to the ground and stumbled, coming to rest on her hands and knees. Slowly, she stood up and looked down at herself.

The suit was still partially functioning. If she didn't move, she blended into the background. But as soon as she walked forward a few steps, no matter how carefully she moved, there was a ripple in the air, and the outline of her body became visible.

She didn't have time to stop to try to repair the suit. All she had to do was get to the house before someone stopped her. At least now she didn't have to worry about moving slowly.

Casting one last glance around her, Stella broke into a run, ducking behind trees when she could, and headed straight for the front door.

Passing through a grove of birch trees, Stella entered a small sculpture garden. Rows of statues perched atop tall stone plinths flanked a gravel pathway that led up to the front door. But instead of being made of stone, the statues were constructed of the same glimmering metal as some of the buildings she'd seen when she'd first arrived in Kovall.

An *aletheum garden*, Stella thought.

There were six of the statues, all of them giant wolves in various poses. Some curled up as if sleeping, others tense and ready to pounce, their sculpted chests gleaming in the sunlight. Those poses were beautiful yet frightening at the same time, which seemed out of place in the otherwise peaceful surroundings.

Stella passed the sculptures and found herself at the base of a set of stone steps leading to the front door. She reached up and took off the hood of her invisibility suit to deactivate it. She went over in her head—for possibly the hundredth time—what she might say to the Tinker.

Everything sounded terrible.

Hello, my name is Stella Glass, and I come from across the mountains. No, really, I do. Stop looking at me like that.

Hello, my name is Stella Glass, and I'm human. Yes, I said "hu-man." Pleased to meet you.

Maybe she should keep things as simple as possible.

Hello, my name is Stella Glass, and I desperately need your help.

From behind her came a sharp metallic creaking sound, and then a low growl rumbled across the garden like thunder.

The hairs on the back of Stella's neck shot up, and she whirled, choking on a scream.

One of the giant metal wolves was no longer seated on its stone plinth. It was standing behind her, staring down at her with glowing crimson eyes.

THIRTY-ONE

Instinctively, Stella backed away from the huge wolf, but she forgot about the steps behind her. Her foot caught on the stone and she fell, landing on her tailbone. Pain shot up her back, but Stella barely noticed. Terror had a firm grip on her.

One by one, the other five statues came to life. Metal joints creaked as the wolves rose up, stretched, and turned their heads toward Stella. Crimson fire ignited in their eyes, and with a graceful leap, they were on the ground and slowly stalking toward her. The closest wolf opened its mouth to reveal teeth that were actual razors.

Stella forced herself to breathe, trying to get her brain back to functioning while every muscle in her body seized with the need to escape. Were these wolves like the olarans? Half animal and half machine? But that couldn't be right—they didn't have a wolf's thick pelt; their skins were clearly metal. What about their brains or their hearts? Could they be reasoned with like Cyrus?

Or were they simply hungry?

The last thought broke her. Stella launched herself from the steps and took off running around the side of the house as fast as she could.

Hollow metallic howls filled the air, paws pounding the ground as the wolves gave chase. Stella imagined she felt the vibrations beneath her feet.

She didn't have the first clue where she was going. Even if she made it back to the fence, with her injured wrist, she'd never be able to climb over before the wolves got to her. The same went for climbing a tree. So she stayed as close to the house as possible, dodging around willow branches and leaping over bushes as she ran. Her best hope was either to find a door into the house or find someone—*anyone*—patrolling the grounds who might call off the wolves.

"Help!" she screamed. "Somebody, help me!"

As she rounded the corner of the house, the metal and glass tower loomed ahead of her. At its base was an old wooden door. Stella put on a last burst of speed, trying to reach the door before the wolves overtook her.

She hit the door at a full run, her shoulder banging

into the wood. Ignoring the fresh burst of agony, Stella grabbed the knob and twisted it.

Locked.

A sound that was half scream and half sob burst from Stella's throat. She turned, ready to run again, but the wolves had cut off any hope of escape. They surrounded the base of the tower, their great metal bodies throwing long shadows across the beautifully sculpted lawn.

They had cornered their prey, but Stella realized she had a weapon of her own. She wasn't about to go down without a fight. She wrenched open her sack of supplies and pulled out the Lazuril rod. Activating the weapon and holding it in her good hand, she began waving it from side to side.

"Go ahead!" she yelled, defiant as one of the wolves crept toward her, its metallic belly brushing against the ground and emitting a spark. "If you want to eat me, I'm going to make sure you get the shock of your life!"

"Well, they don't actually eat people, my dear," said a voice from behind her.

Stella jerked in surprise and nearly dropped the Lazuril rod. The door to the tower was now open, and a man stood at the threshold, regarding her with some amusement.

"Good thing too, since they have no digestive processes to speak of," the man went on, gesturing to the air as he spoke. "It would just be a lot of teeth gnashing and crunching and . . . well, general *messiness.*"

"Messiness?" Stella squeaked. Her gaze went from the man to the pack of wolves and back again. He had thick, curly dark hair with gray wisps starting at the temples, and he wore a brown lab coat and apron bulging with tools. *Could he be the Tinker?* Stella wondered while maintaining a firm grasp on the Lazuril rod. She was no longer certain where to point it: at the wolves or the man who kept them. "Listen, can you please call them off? I'm not a trespasser. I swear!"

"You're not?" the man said curiously. He adjusted a pair of wire-framed glasses. The lenses were covered in fingerprint smudges. "That's good to know. The way you were climbing over that fence looked a little suspicious at first, I must admit, but then again, I'm not one to discourage such an eager guest."

Stella's mouth dropped open, and she lowered the Lazuril rod a fraction. "You saw me? But I was barely visible!"

The man flashed a crooked smile that made him look younger than he'd first appeared. If this was the Tinker, he wasn't at all what Stella was expecting. She'd pictured an old, serious scientist. "Well, I don't want to brag," he said in a tone that made it clear that was exactly what he wanted, "but when you've worked on chameleon net technology in trial phases for as long as I have, you learn to watch for the signs." He hesitated. "I mean, *literally*, watch for signs of the invisibility effect wavering—it's a critical component of the testing phase."

Stella's head was spinning. A tiny part of her thought she might even be dreaming. Or maybe she'd fallen and hit her head trying to get over the fence and her stressed mind had conjured up half a dozen giant metal wolves plus a babbling scientist.

Or maybe these were just the sort of common occurrences she would have to get used to in the uncharted lands.

At the appearance of the man in doorway, the mechanical wolves had indeed backed down and were now sitting placidly in the grass. Stella allowed herself to relax just a bit. "Are . . . are you *the* Tinker?" she asked. She tried to remember the word in Cyrus's language.

And then she froze.

She was speaking in her own language, Trader's Speech from her side of Solace. She'd been speaking it when she cried out for help earlier.

But the man in the doorway was also using Trader's Speech. He'd been speaking it right along with her this whole time. She just hadn't realized it until now because she'd been so terrified of the wolves.

He offered her that crooked smile again, eyes gleaming behind his glasses. "I am indeed the Tinker, and you, if I'm not mistaken, are a flesh and blood human. No machinery required." He held the tower door open wider. "Come inside, my dear. We have a great deal to discuss."

Her mouth hanging open, Stella looked from the man to the yawning doorway before her feet began to work, and she cautiously stepped inside.

⪢ THIRTY-TWO ⪡

The inside of the tower was a disaster. Stella knew
her parents were occasionally messy in the lab, but
their space was immaculate compared to the Tinker's.

A rusty metal staircase led to upper floors, but on
the ground level, there were papers, lab equipment, and
a multitude of oddities crammed onto every available
surface, along with dozens of plates of half-eaten, moldy
food. The room couldn't have been dusted in at least a
decade. Engines and their components littered the floor,
causing Stella to tiptoe gingerly across the room in an
effort to avoid harming them or herself. But once inside,
the Tinker buzzed around the room as if nothing were
amiss, checking dials and switches on machines that
Stella had no name for. He shoved a helmet covered in
wires off a stool and onto the floor before rubbing his
sleeve over the stool in a futile attempt to clean it. After

wiping his brow, he presented the seat to Stella for her to sit down, in what she assumed to be a rather gracious manner.

"Tell me everything," he said, flitting off to another table lined with a row of spotted ferns in tin can pots. Four of the five were shriveled and brown, but the Tinker didn't seem to notice. He grabbed a book with a cracked leather cover and selected a pencil from the hand of a fully articulated hamster skeleton. "Start with your name. I want to know everything about where you came from and how you got here. Spare me no details!"

"I'm afraid it's a long story, and we really don't have time for it," Stella said, reaching into her bag to retrieve Cyrus's note for the Tinker. "I came here because I need your help to—"

"All in good time!" the Tinker interrupted. "Your name, please."

"My name . . . my name is Stella," she stammered, trying to gather her scattered thoughts. She sat down on the stool and placed the Lazuril rod awkwardly across her lap. She'd been prepared for the Tinker to scoff at her story, not take notes on it. "And you're right, I'm human, but—"

"Aha! I knew it!" The Tinker swept a stack of papers off another stool, creating a chain reaction that knocked over several glass jars, one of which popped open, releasing a cloud of moths. Stella was pretty sure they were made of metal, wings clinking and glittering in the dim light as they flew haphazardly toward the top of the tower. The Tinker ignored these too.

He sat down and hooked his feet on the stool's bottom rung. "Your language was the first hint," he said, sounding out of breath. "All our expedition members learned it, of course, but you speak with such ease and clarity that you can't be anything but a native speaker."

Stella tried again. "That's fascinating, but listen—"

"No, there's more to it," the Tinker interrupted again as if she hadn't spoken. He scratched his chin, staring at her as if she were a specimen preserved in a case. "I suppose it's something in the way you move. You can really see it when you're running. We olarans are not so . . . fluid . . . when we run. Maybe I'm the only one who would ever notice. You see, I've been studying humans for a very long time." He pointed to the wall behind her.

Stella swiveled on her stool. On the wall was a map of Solace. She'd caught a glimpse of it when they first entered the tower. Now that she looked closer, though, she saw that it was a map of the uncharted lands *and* her side of Solace, with the Hiterian Mountains splitting them down the middle. It was the most complete map of the world she'd ever seen.

"Did you draw that?" she asked, turning back to the Tinker, her curiosity getting the better of her.

"I did—as well as these." He opened the cracked leather book to a certain spot and handed it to her.

Stella had expected a page full of notes, so she was surprised to see a pencil sketch of a young boy and girl. The boy was small and thin, and the girl had wild, tangled hair and a wide smile.

"Who are they?" she asked. "Are they human?"

The Tinker nodded. "Our earliest expeditions didn't have a crew," he explained. "We sent our ships to your side of the world to map your geography. One of them was gone a very long time. So long we thought it was lost. It eventually returned, and I pulled this image from its memories. There was quite a bit of affection associated with these two individuals."

Stella stared at the sketch. Cyrus had told her about the olarans' airships, but she still had a hard time imagining being able to tap into a machine's memories to create a picture.

"You remind me of them," the Tinker said thoughtfully. "I think it's your eyes."

Stella flipped to the next page. More sketches covered the paper. She ran her fingers over the faces, pausing at the image of a familiar boy.

Her heart lurched.

Cyrus.

He shared a page with a sketch of a young girl with dark hair and an open, inquisitive face.

"Those are olarans," the Tinker said, eyeing the page that she'd stopped on. "Members of our expeditions to your lands." His eyes clouded. "There are about a dozen of them in all—the ones we lost track of."

Lost track of. Stella heard the sadness and regret in the Tinker's voice. "You mean the ones who were left behind," she said.

"Yes. I hope we may find them someday." A wistful smile creased the Tinker's face. "Ah, Stella, I had so many hopes for our expeditions to your lands. I've been pestering the alagant for over a year, begging her to make contact with your people. It's long past due, I said! There's *so much* we can learn from each other!"

His eyes sparkled with excitement and determination. Stella understood then why Cyrus had sent her here. Of all the people on his side of the world, the Tinker was definitely the one who would want to help her the most.

"Well, you'll be happy to hear that at least one of your lost explorers has been found," she said. If that didn't get his attention, nothing would. "That's why I'm here. Cyrus needs you."

The Tinker gasped at the news and rose from his stool, but Stella held up a hand before he could interrupt her again. "Please, I want to tell you everything, but we just don't have time. The heart of it is, this boy," she said, tapping Cyrus's portrait, "is my best friend, and I need your help or he is going to die."

The Tinker's eyes widened. Slowly, he sat back down. "By all means," he said. "Tell me how I can help."

☰ THIRTY-THREE ☰

Stella gave Cyrus's note to the Tinker. After he read it, she told him the story of what had happened with Cyrus, of the Faceless man and the crash of the *Iron Glory*, as fast as she could get it out. She even played the Faceless man's message back on the beetle. She finished and sucked in a breath just as the Tinker could no longer sit still. He sprang up from his stool and paced the room, stopping only long enough to make more adjustments to his strange machines. Then he snatched a tattered knapsack from a hook on the wall and began stuffing it full of things from around the lab. Stella hoped that meant he was packing his things, prepared to come with her. Every so often, he'd pick something up—a machine part or a tool—scowl at it, then toss it aside. An expression of fury spread across his face.

"Are you all right?" Stella ventured. She hadn't gotten up from her seat, half afraid that the Tinker would bowl her over in his haste to pack.

"The situation is much worse than I thought," he said, walking toward the map of Solace and tearing it down, leaving remnants of the ripped corners stuck to the wall. He folded it up to a manageable size, and it too went into the knapsack. "I never dreamed that one of our own—a Faceless, a member of the expedition, no less!—would betray us like this." His voice rose until he was almost shouting. "The aletheum is a rare resource, to be sure, but to murder for it is madness! Peace and communication between our peoples is the key to the future. We can do so much more together than we can apart."

Like the Merrow Kingdom and the Dragonfly territories, Stella agreed. Working together, moving forward, was their best hope.

But Stella had her own share of hopes, and right now, they all rested on the man in front of her.

"Can you help me save Cyrus and the others?" she asked. "We aren't too late, are we?"

"Too late?" He stopped pacing and shook his head, eyes blazing with determination. "No, I don't believe that. But you're right, we don't have time to waste either. Cyrus had to have used an enormous amount of power to save your airship—more than his body can regenerate on its own. Right now all of his vital systems are straining just to keep him alive. He needs an artificial boost to his regenerative capacitor or he won't make it."

Stella tried to make sense of what the Tinker had just said but gave up after a few seconds. "Can you give him that—the capacitor boost?"

"I've already packed the tools," the Tinker said, gesturing to the knapsack, which was overflowing now. He stripped off his apron but kept on his lab coat, then grabbed two pairs of goggles and threw one of those to Stella. "Come upstairs," he told her, "and get that beetle ready to record. We don't have time to make a full report to the alagant, but I'll send a message to let the palace know where your ship is. With any luck, the guards of the royal house will be right behind us, ready to provide support."

"What about the Faceless man?" Stella asked, hurrying up the stairs behind him. They climbed all the way to the top floor of the tower, to the room with glass walls that had reminded her of a lighthouse. More piles of junk littered the room, but in the center, a space had been cleared for a large object covered in a white sheet.

The Tinker's face darkened. "He doesn't stand a chance," he promised.

"But I told you he has my parents!" Stella grabbed the Tinker's arm. He looked down at her distractedly. "If we just show up with an army in tow, he'll kill them!"

"We'll have a head start on the guards," the Tinker

assured her. "We can go in quietly, with our own smaller force. The wolves will be waiting for us outside the city."

The mechanical statues—Stella shuddered involuntarily at the memory of being chased by the giant terrors. "But you said they weren't alive, that they don't eat people."

"Yes, well, in the strictest sense of the word, they aren't alive," the Tinker said as he picked up the edge of the white sheet. "But they are made of a rarer form of aletheum, which, without getting into too much detail, means they are very close to sentience. And they do *bite*, but only if I command them to attack."

Stella tried to digest this. "But how is that sentience possible?" she asked, bewildered. "The aletheum is just metal—it's in the invisibility suit and the *Iron Glory*'s gasbag."

"A diluted form of it is," the Tinker corrected. "You'll find diluted aletheum all over Kovall. It's quite plentiful, in fact. But in its purest form—which only I and a handful of others are authorized to work with— aletheum is a living material."

That stopped Stella in her tracks. "Wait a minute. The metal is *alive*? And you used it to try to bring the wolves to life?"

The Tinker shook his head. "It's more accurate to say I tried to give the aletheum a form in which we could establish a rapport. We've had success in the past with a handful of our airships, living vessels with enormous capacities for memory and communication. Like the airship I told you about earlier. The wolves are a poor imitation of that, but I'm working on them. Until then, they can be programmed individually or as a group, and I can also control them with the instruments on this."

The Tinker snapped the sheet and yanked it off the object in the center of the room, flapping his arms with a grand flourish and an explosion of dust.

"Behold, our rescue vehicle—the ornithopter *Irregulum!*" he said.

Stella coughed and blinked at the small craft. It was essentially two seats surrounded by a metal cage, with a pair of folded-up wings, which the Tinker proceeded to unfold and lock into place as Stella watched. The last words she would have used to describe the ship were "sturdy" and "safe."

"Hold on," she said as her overwhelmed mind slowly comprehended what the Tinker intended, "you mean this thing actually flies? We're going to fly in it?"

"Of course it *flies.*" The Tinker looked a little hurt. "I built it myself. It's not sentient, mind you, though it *is* a little temperamental in high winds," he said with a chuckle. "Lean over the side if you feel sick. But not too far," he added helpfully, "or you'll tip the craft and fall out."

"I'll . . . try to remember that," Stella said, already feeling queasy.

One thing was certain: if she survived this flight, she was going to have an incredible story to tell Cyrus.

But remembering Cyrus made her think of the Faceless man, what he might do to her parents, and what he'd said about her people being the doom of the olarans.

"Is that why the Faceless man is doing all this?" she asked, feeling the truth of it all dawning on her as she spoke. "He's not just afraid of us because we went to war over resources. He wants to protect the living aletheum, doesn't he?"

The Tinker nodded sadly. "I'm afraid so. The aletheum's secrets are closely kept by our people. The Faceless man likely fears that even a little knowledge of it will be too much for your people to resist."

"But you just told me the secret," Stella pointed out, eyes widening. "Are you supposed to do that?"

"No," the Tinker said, smiling at her, "but Cyrus said in his message that he trusts you, and I also consider myself an excellent judge of character. You've brought Cyrus back to us and risked your life to protect him. I'm confident you'll be able to protect the secret of aletheum as well."

He clapped his hands together. "Now, we have no time to waste! We need to send our message to the palace, and then we can be on our way."

Stella handed Cyrus's beetle over to the Tinker, and he recorded a quick message for the alagant. He spoke in the olaran language, so she didn't understand what he was saying, but she assumed he was explaining the situation and requesting immediate assistance for the *Iron Glory.*

While she waited for him to finish, Stella put on her goggles and pushed her hair back out of her eyes. Climbing into one of the ornithopter's seats, she strapped herself in with a flimsy safety harness that didn't do any more to quell her fear of falling out of the ship. The Tinker strode to the wall of windows, which Stella realized were actually glass doors with several folding panels. He unlatched and peeled them back, opening the whole front of the tower up to the sky. Then he sent the beetle flying off to deliver its message.

"Why is it named the *Irregulum?*" Stella asked as the Tinker returned to the craft and strapped in next to her, his knapsack clutched in his lap and his hands flying over the controls.

"Irregular flight patterns," the Tinker said absently, "and sometimes it handles like a lump in the sky. I've been working on its engine—experimenting with internal combustion and its effects on aletheum, the usual testing." He shrugged. "It's quick, but it doesn't always fly straight. The key, for our purposes, is its size makes it fast. We'll make the journey back to your *Iron Glory* in a fraction of the time it took you to walk."

That was what Stella wanted to hear. She sat back in her seat as the ornithopter's engine roared to life, its vibrations rattling every bone in her body through the seat. Sputtering and clunking, it inched forward on its landing gear, wings extended and prepared for takeoff.

She hoped, anyway.

"One thing," the Tinker said as they neared the edge of the tower, which offered Stella a stomach-churning view to the lawn below. "It takes a second or two for the engine to kick in, so prepare yourself for a bit of a drop."

"What do you mean by—"

But that was all Stella managed to get out before the ornithopter ran out of floor. Instead of soaring into the sky, the craft dropped off the edge of the tower like a stone and plummeted toward the ground.

≋ THIRTY-FOUR ≋

A scream ripped from Stella's throat. The lawn was coming up to meet them . . . so close . . .

With a deafening roar, the ornithopter's engine caught and surged, its wings straining against gravity. An instant before they would have hit the earth, the craft leveled off, dipped once more, and then launched into the sky.

Suddenly, they were flying so fast and so high that Stella was dizzy. All she could do was hold on tight to the craft's metal cage as the Tinker's estate fell away beneath them. They flew over the city, and when Stella worked up the courage to look down, she was treated to a breathtaking view of the Baluway River, busy with steamboat traffic and divided by bridges with more mini trains running back and forth across it. These moving metal wonders got smaller and smaller with distance, and all too soon, Stella and the Tinker had left the city behind them.

"All right now?" the Tinker asked, grinning at her. "I can't promise a smooth ride, but the view is unbeatable."

Stella couldn't argue with that. Feeling bolder, she leaned over the side of the craft to get a look at the ground. She drew back in surprise and tugged on the Tinker's sleeve. "Look," she said, pointing.

Directly below them, the pack of six mechanical wolves fought to keep pace with the ornithopter.

"Excellent!" the Tinker shouted. "They'll be incredibly fast over the open fields once we're out of the city. We're on our way, Stella! We're on our way!"

Stella sat back in her seat, wishing she shared the Tinker's excitement and confidence. But her mind drifted to Cyrus, and her worry about his health returned. The Tinker said he could heal him, but what about the Faceless man? He had her parents prisoner, and even with the army of metal wolves charging to the rescue, she still didn't know what they would find when they reached the *Iron Glory*.

Rummaging in her sack of supplies, Stella took stock of her own resources. The beetle was gone, and the only weapon she had was the Lazuril rod. She still wore the invisibility suit, of course, but with the tear in the fabric, it no longer worked properly.

But maybe the suit wasn't what was important, Stella

thought, running her hands over the shimmering fabric. If it was as powerful as the Tinker claimed, the aletheum could be put to other, more specialized uses that she might be able to take advantage of.

She tugged the Tinker's sleeve again to get his attention. "Tell me more about this suit," she said.

"Happy to!" the Tinker said, and immediately launched into a lecture. While he talked, Stella planned, and they flew on through the late afternoon and into the evening. By the time night had fallen, Stella could tell they were going to reach the *Iron Glory*'s crash site before morning. And the Tinker had been right: the ship ran quiet as it flew over the countryside. The only light came from the moon and stars above, and the glowing red eyes of the wolves below. Unless the *Iron Glory* had keen-eyed scouts posted around the ship, no one would see them coming.

After another hour, they could see the ship. From the air, it was hard to miss. The *Iron Glory* had torn up a substantial portion of the ground in the crash.

"She used to be so beautiful," Stella told the Tinker, her heart twisting. "Now she'll never fly again."

The Tinker angled the ornithopter toward the ground. "Never say never—don't forget, we olarans are fairly experienced machinists," he said jovially. "Now, hold on tight!"

Stella grabbed the metal cage and braced herself as

the craft spiraled down and came in for a bone-jarring landing, skidding across the field several yards from the *Iron Glory*. Blades of tall grass whipped through the cage and against Stella's legs as they slid to a stop.

The ornithopter's engine sputtered and died. Stella spent a moment just being grateful they were back on solid ground again. Then she unbuckled her safety harness and eagerly climbed out of the craft. The Tinker fussed over his control panel a bit longer before joining her.

In the tall grasses, the craft was rather hidden, and the pair only had to wait a few moments for the pack of wolves to catch up. Stella took off the invisibility suit—what was left of it—and stashed it under her seat. Then, with the wolves in tow and looking like the strangest rescue party ever formed, they hiked the rest of the way to the *Iron Glory*.

Stella's hands shook as she went over the plan she'd concocted during the flight. If the Tinker's wolves didn't intimidate the Faceless man into backing down, she knew she'd only have one chance to surprise him with her secret weapon. But she dearly hoped he *would* back down and that none of this would be necessary.

Stella slowed the group's pace as the wreckage rose up before them, looking for signs of people. The wolves slunk low to the ground, their bellies making soft swishing sounds over the grass. A makeshift camp had been set up outside the wreckage, with a handful of medical tents to house wounded crew members, but Stella saw none of the ship's scouts anywhere in the area.

"Something's not right," she whispered to the Tinker. "We should have been stopped by now."

But no one confronted them. They got all the way to the first row of tents before a voice called out, "Stop! Who goes there?"

A lone guard stepped out of the shadows to block their path. He was human, with long, stringy brown hair, a face full of exhaustion, and a bandaged wound on his neck. When his gaze fell on the Tinker and his mechanical wolves, the man jumped and took an involuntary step back.

"It's all right!" Stella called out, holding up her hands to keep the man from panicking. "We're here to help!"

At the sound of the raised voices, four more crew members emerged from the medical tents and gathered around Stella and the Tinker. None of them looked like they should be out of bed, and some had been injured so badly they could barely stand. They kept their distance from the wolves, but Stella could see the scientists casting curious glances in their direction.

"Where is everyone else?" Stella demanded, addressing the guard. "Captain Keeler and First Officer Drea— I need to warn them about the Faceless man."

And she had to find Cyrus and her parents.

The guard shook his head and spat on the ground in disgust. "No need," he said. "Captain and the first officer are scouring the ship for him right now, along with anyone else who isn't wounded or trapped somewhere."

One of the injured crew members, a woman with short red hair and her arm in a sling, spoke up. "Soon as you disappeared, the Faceless man started attacking the crew, catching people alone, trying to pick us off one by one," she said. She cupped the elbow of her injured arm. "He's gotten at least six of us that way. He's relentless."

"He won't stop until you're all dead," the Tinker said, his gaze darkening behind his spectacles.

"What about Cyrus?" Stella pressed the guard. "Do you know if he's still in the medical bay? Are my parents there too?"

"I don't know," the guard admitted. "The captain ordered me out here to keep watch over the wounded in case the Faceless man came for them. I don't know what's going on inside the ship. No one's reported in for over an hour."

"I'll leave one of the wolves out here to help stand guard," the Tinker offered. "We'll take the rest inside. Our first stop will be the medical bay."

The guard's face creased in relief, but it was short-lived as he eyed the big mechanical wolves. "How do they . . . er . . . work?" he asked.

"I'll program one to follow your commands," the

Tinker said. "All you really need to do is point at what you want him to bite."

Stella waited impatiently as the Tinker opened a small panel on the back of a wolf's neck and made some sort of adjustment she couldn't see. She had to stay calm. Help was here. They would bring the rest of the wolves onto the ship, and together they would find the Faceless man. Like the Tinker had said, he didn't stand a chance.

If she repeated the words enough, maybe she would start to believe them.

THIRTY-FIVE

When the Tinker was finished programming the wolf, the small crowd dispersed, with the guard helping the injured crew members back to their tents. Meanwhile, Stella quickly led their rescue party to the ship.

The shortest route to the medical bay that the wolves could fit through was the hole that the boiler had blown in the side of the ship's engine room. So Stella, the Tinker, and the remaining wolves climbed through the gap amid jagged shards of wood and metal, back through the dark remains of the engine room, and out to the corridor and the stairs leading to the medical bay.

Distantly, Stella heard shouts and footsteps echoing in various parts of the ship, but it was impossible to tell what the voices were saying or where exactly they were coming from. She quickened her pace, determined to get to the medical bay. She had to know if Cyrus was alive, and it was as good a place as any to start to find her parents.

When they arrived, they found the room a shambles— worse than it had been after the crash. In addition to the debris littering the floor, tables and cots were overturned all over the room, as if a storm had torn through it.

Or an attack by the Faceless man.

Stella looked around wildly, but there was no sign of her parents. The room appeared to be deserted . . . all except for a small form buried under a pile of blankets in one corner of the room.

Cyrus.

Stella ran across the room, falling to her knees at her friend's side.

"I'm here, Cyrus," she said, pulling back the blankets so she could search for his pulse. "I've brought the Tinker, just like I promised."

There was no response. He was unconscious, but Stella's trembling fingers found a faint pulse still beating at his neck.

The breath left Stella's body in a rush that made her head swim. "He's alive," she said, gesturing frantically for the Tinker to join her. "You can still save him."

The Tinker came over and gently ushered Stella aside so he could examine Cyrus. "Yes," he murmured after a moment, forehead creased in concentration. "Yes, I believe we got here in time. But there's also the matter of the Faceless man."

"I've already thought of that," Stella said, rising to her feet. "I think I know where he is. If he's got my parents and he's trying to evade the captain and his search team, he'll need a good place to hide, somewhere he can see an attack coming."

And the best hiding place on the ship was the cargo bay, where Stella and Cyrus had stowed away for days without anyone being the wiser.

"You stay here and help Cyrus," Stella told the Tinker. "If you see any of the crew, tell them you know me, and tell them I've gone to the cargo bay to rescue my parents."

"I can't let you go alone!" the Tinker said in alarm. "The Faceless man is the olarans' responsibility. As a representative of my people, I should be the one to deal with him."

"I brought you here to save Cyrus!" Stella said, her voice rising. They didn't have time to argue about this. "Don't you understand? If he dies, all this was for nothing! And I don't care what happens to me, as long as I can save my parents. Please, don't try to stop me."

The Tinker pursed his lips, taking in her determined expression. "If you insist on doing this, at least let me send some of the wolves with you," he said. "They'll protect you from the Faceless man."

"Agreed," Stella said. "But please hurry!"

The Tinker quickly went to program the wolves, and after what seemed like an eternity, Stella was on her way to the cargo bay with three of them in tow.

They reached the hallway where she'd first met Cyrus. Stella touched the support column where she'd hidden while she'd watched him use his power. The column had been bent almost in half by the crash.

Cautiously and quietly, they worked their way down the stairs and into the cargo bay itself, but it was slow going. Many of the storage crates had been knocked over and smashed by the crash, and the floor was covered in debris. Eventually, they found a path to the back corner of the bay, to the camp where Stella and Cyrus had hidden for five days at the beginning of their journey, secretly getting to know each other.

"That's far enough," a voice rang out from the corner, yanking Stella from her thoughts.

The Faceless man stepped out from the shadows. He wore the form of the young man Stella had encountered at the top of the crow's nest during the ice storm. Was this his true form, then? Stella found that mattered little. All she cared about was what lay behind the Faceless man. Her parents, bound and gagged, their backs pressed against one of the tall storage crates.

Stella fought the urge to run to them. When they saw her, they uttered choked cries, shaking their heads as their eyes bulged with fear.

The Faceless man's eyes rested on Stella and hardened. "You disobeyed me."

"I do that a lot," Stella said, forcing her attention away from her parents and to the Faceless man. The wolves stood on either side of her, red eyes bright in the dim light of the cargo bay. "If I were you, I'd give up now," she advised. "You tried everything you could to destroy this expedition, but it's time to admit you failed. I've brought back help, and the captain's closing in on you. It's over."

"No," the Faceless man said, his bloodshot eyes defiant, even in the face of the giant wolves. "If I have to give my life, so be it. I'll take as many of you with me as I can. If I don't, you will be the ruin of the olarans. Your people will tear us apart and steal the very essence of what we are!"

"You attacked *us*!" Stella countered. "You would have even killed Cyrus to get what you want. But if you'd taken even a moment to try to understand us, things might have been different."

How could so much blind hatred exist in one person? Stella might almost have felt sorry for the Faceless man, had he not threatened to take everything from her. "This is a new world now," she said, "and you don't get to decide how we're going to live in it."

"You're wrong," the Faceless man snarled. He backed toward her parents, drawing a knife from the waistband of his trousers. There was nothing in his eyes. No fear, no doubt, and no sympathy.

It was time for Stella to make her move. The blood thundered in her ears, and her right hand trembled, but she took a single step forward.

"The alagant's representatives are coming," she said, hoping to distract him. "They're going to help the *Iron Glory*. If you'll let my parents go and surrender, the captain will turn you over to them. You can give them all the warnings about our people that you want."

She waited, hardly daring to breathe. When the Faceless man glanced down at her parents, Stella took another step forward. When he looked back at her, the determination in his eyes wavered for just a second.

Stella risked another step, moving slowly, keeping her hands at her sides so she wouldn't scare the Faceless man, and so that he wouldn't see the way she had her thumb pressed into the center of her right palm.

"Stay where you are!" the Faceless man barked. He brandished the knife and started to turn toward Stella's mother.

That was more than Stella could take.

She tightened her grip on the Lazuril rod in her right hand.

It was wrapped in one of the sleeves of the invisibility suit, the ends hastily stitched together in flight using the Tinker's tools. To all appearances, she held nothing at all in her hands.

"Protect them!" Stella shouted, and let the wolves loose.

The Faceless man tensed as the wolves ate up the distance between them in seconds. He turned, slashing the knife at Stella's mother, but at the last minute, one of the wolves tackled him, knocking him off his feet as the other two put their giant bodies protectively in front of Stella's parents. The knife skittered away behind a crate.

Before the Faceless man could recover, Stella darted forward, and in the same motion, she activated the Lazuril rod. There was a brief flash of blue, sparks spitting from its tip, before it connected with the Faceless man's chest.

A jolt of pain traveled up Stella's arm to her shoulder. The Lazuril rod sparked and burned through the invisibility suit, illuminating the Faceless man's wide, bloodshot eyes for a brief instant before the shock of the weapon knocked him prone. And just like that, he lay unconscious on the cargo bay floor.

Stella dropped the Lazuril rod and fell to her knees, clutching her arm, but the pain wasn't as bad as it had been on top of the crow's nest when she'd grabbed the exposed rod with her bare hand. She might end up with another burn on her hand, but that was a small price to pay.

As the pain slowly ebbed, she pushed to her feet and ran over to her parents, removing their gags and yanking and tearing at the ropes that bound them until they were both free and could throw their arms around Stella.

And that was all it took. The tears Stella had been holding back finally broke free. The three of them stood in a group, crying and hugging, and for the first time since the crash, Stella felt like her world was put back together again.

⇒ THIRTY-SIX ⇒

The captain and several crew members burst into the cargo bay while Stella was still holding on to her parents, the three mechanical wolves standing guard over the unconscious Faceless man.

"Eliza, Martin," the captain called out in concern. "Are you all right?"

"We're fine," Stella's father said, walking over to him. "Stella got here just in time."

The captain eyed the wolves with some trepidation. "We spoke to the Tinker," he explained. "He said you all were down here, confronting the Faceless man." The captain gestured to two of the crew he'd brought with him and then to the unconscious man. "Secure him," he commanded.

The wolves backed away as the crew approached, taking the Faceless man into custody.

"How is Cyrus?" Stella asked, finally pulling away from her mother. "Is he going to be all right?"

"I don't know," the captain said, turning to Stella's parents. "For now, let's get you all out of here. There are more wounded who need attention."

"Of course," Stella's mother said, her professional mask slipping back into place. "Lead on."

They made their way back to the medical bay, with Stella quickly filling the captain and her parents in on everything that had happened since she'd left the ship, including the fact that help from the alagant was on the way.

When they arrived at the medical bay, the Tinker was still working on Cyrus. Thin wires ran from two different machines the Tinker had brought to Cyrus's body and attached with small round pads to his chest and arms. The Tinker was checking the settings on the machines, but he looked up when Stella and the others entered the room.

"How is he?" Stella asked at once, crossing the room to Cyrus's side. She glanced at the strange machines. "Is he going to be all right?"

"It's still early yet in the procedure," the Tinker said. He saw her studying the equipment and tried to explain. "The machine stimulates mechanical activity in olarans. It's a delicate process because it requires equilibrium—too much regenerative energy can damage our organic components. Too little, and it won't be enough to bring him back."

"Do you have the balance right?" Stella asked, her throat dry with fear.

"I believe I do," the Tinker said solemnly, "but there are no guarantees in medicine. Time will tell."

Stella knew that all too well. She would have to trust in the Tinker's judgment.

"Stella," her mother said, coming up and putting a hand on Stella's shoulder. "Your father and I have to check on the crew outside, and there are still some who've been injured or trapped in other parts of the ship, but we'll be back when we can to check on Cyrus." Her gaze fell on the Tinker. "It looks as if he's in good hands here."

Distracted, Stella pulled her attention away from Cyrus long enough to introduce her parents to the Tinker.

"Healers, the both of you?" The Tinker looked delighted as he shook her parents' hands. "What a remarkable family. When we have more time, I would love to talk to you both. One of the things we hoped to accomplish when we came in contact with your people was to learn more about your medical treatments. We hoped to study with your doctors who specialized in certain areas of medicine."

"We'd be happy to talk," Stella's father said. "But for now, if you'll excuse us, we have to see to the crew."

"Of course, of course," the Tinker said, stepping back while Stella gave her parents another quick hug. Then they left the medical bay with the captain, leaving her and the Tinker to wait and see if the procedure on Cyrus would be successful.

Now that the fear and excitement of the battle with the Faceless man had passed, time seemed to slow, and with each passing minute, Stella's restlessness grew. Her injured wrist still ached, and there was a new blister forming on her hand where she'd held the Lazuril rod, but she couldn't bring herself to leave Cyrus's side long enough to even go get a bandage.

The worst of it was that she couldn't tell if the machines were doing Cyrus any good. He was still deathly pale. She wasn't allowed to touch him to check his pulse, so she had no idea what was going on inside his body.

Finally, about twenty minutes later, the Tinker turned a switch on one of the machines and sat back with a sigh. "The machines have done their work," he said. "All that's left is to wait and see if he wakes up on his own. If he does, that's a *very* hopeful sign."

Stella nodded, watching the rise and fall of Cyrus's chest. Footsteps approaching the medical bay made her look up. The captain re-entered the room, followed this time by First Officer Drea.

"Is everything all right?" Stella asked, noting the concerned set to the captain's face.

"I hope so," the captain replied, glancing at the Tinker. "Our scouts just spotted three airships headed this way from the west, flying fast."

"That would be the palace guard and the alagant's representatives," the Tinker affirmed. He flicked a switch on each of the machines and stood up. "If you don't mind, I should be there with you to meet them. They won't all speak your language, but this will be recorded, in our history books at least, as the first official meeting of our two peoples."

"What about Cyrus?" Stella asked. "Is it all right for you to leave him?"

"I won't be gone long," the Tinker assured her. "He needs to rest, and if I'm not mistaken, so do you."

"I'm all right," Stella said. Her voice shook with pent-up emotion. Cyrus was close to coming back—she could feel it.

She knelt next to Cyrus and helped the Tinker remove the pads and wires while the captain sent Drea outside to be ready to greet the approaching ships.

"Would you like to come with me to meet the delegation?" the Tinker asked Stella as he worked. His eyes twinkled. "I know they're going to want to meet you."

Stella had to admit she was curious about the olarans headed their way. Would they all be as open-minded and compassionate as the Tinker? How would the *Iron Glory*'s crew react? After all, this was what they'd been dreaming about since the expedition began, but so many things had happened since then. Would the meeting be full of hope, or fear and mistrust? Part of Stella wanted to be there to see it, but she shook her head. "I want to wait with Cyrus until he wakes up," she said.

"Of course." The Tinker smiled fondly and squeezed her shoulder. "History may say what it likes about this encounter between our peoples, but I'm glad I got the chance to meet you first, Stella. You've brought me on quite an adventure, one that I hope is just beginning. I'm deeply grateful to you."

Stella's cheeks warmed. "Thank you," she said. "And thank you for trusting me."

≈ THIRTY-SEVEN ≈

During the next hour, Stella's parents received a new wave of patients, crew members who'd been attacked by the Faceless man or trapped in various parts of the ship. Some were seriously injured, but many were simply exhausted and dehydrated. Stella's mother took the latter group outside to the tents to get them food and water.

Stella kept out of the way and sat in a chair by Cyrus's bed. They'd moved him to a cot after the Tinker's procedure was finished, but he still hadn't woken. After a while, her father came over with a bowl of hot soup and a bandage.

"Both for you," he said, smiling at her. "And remember to drink water."

The bandage helped dull the fiery pain of the blister, and the soup made her sleepy. Stella wasn't sure what time it was or even what day anymore. *What do the olarans call the days here?* she wondered. She would have to ask Cyrus. She would also have to rest sometime, but she didn't want to leave the medical bay.

Despite her best efforts, she must have nodded off, because she woke to a familiar soft chuckle.

"That has to be the most uncomfortable position in the history of sleep," Cyrus said, his voice groggy but still managing to be playful. "I think the cargo bay was better."

Stella sat up, the muscles in her neck screaming in protest. There was a pillow propped on the chair arm, and she'd been lying against that, curled into a tight ball. She put her feet down on the floor and leaned forward to seize her friend's hand. "You're all right," she said, a wave of relief flowing over her. "I thought we were going to lose you."

"So did I," Cyrus admitted, sitting up in bed and rubbing his eyes. "To tell you the truth, I'm a little bit shocked that I'm still alive. How did it happen?"

"The Tinker saved you," Stella said. She quickly filled him in on everything that had happened since his last message from the beetle. Cyrus's eyes lit up when she described her flight on the ornithopter and the Tinker's pack of mechanical wolves. He whistled in amazement when she told him how the Tinker had helped her modify the invisibility suit to conceal the Lazuril rod.

"Stella Glass, you are without a doubt the most incredible explorer who ever set foot in Kovall," Cyrus said, a huge grin spreading across his face.

Stella shook her head. "You were the amazing one," she said. "You were willing to die to save the ship."

They stared at each other in silence for a minute while Stella thought of all the things they'd been through since she and Cyrus had snuck on board the *Iron Glory*. How many times disaster had been just an inch away, how many times they'd almost lost each other.

How much meeting him had changed her.

Thinking all this, Stella met his eyes and smiled. "Cyrus, you are without a doubt the most important friend I've ever had," she said quietly.

Cyrus's face softened. He reached for her hand, but just then, Captain Keeler and Drea walked back into the medical bay. Stella jumped and sat back in her chair, cheeks on fire all over again.

"I'm glad to see you're all right, Cyrus," the captain said, not appearing to notice Stella's embarrassment. "Every person on this ship owes you and Stella their life. We can't ever thank you properly or make up for our treatment of you when we first met, but I hope that we can start over. I'd be grateful for a second chance."

He held out his hand to Cyrus. Cyrus shook it, and now his face was as red as Stella's. He mumbled that it wasn't necessary, that he was glad everyone was all right.

Stella didn't catch the rest. Her attention was drawn to the doorway, where another group of people had appeared.

There were four of them, and they wore ceremonial uniforms, with tailored burgundy coats that fell to their knees, fastened with small, ornate silver clasps. Pinned to their chests was some kind of symbol. From a distance, it looked like a starburst, and the metal glimmered in a way that reminded Stella of aletheum.

The olaran delegation had arrived.

The two olarans in front were older. There was a woman who looked to be in her late sixties. Her thick white hair hung loosely around her face, and she had dark, penetrating gray eyes. The man standing next to her looked about twenty years younger, smooth-shaven and bald. Both of them wore serious, almost severe expressions.

Then the man looked across the room and saw Cyrus.

His expression told Stella everything she needed to know, even more than the resemblance, which became clearer the longer she looked at him. This man was Cyrus's father.

The room went very quiet then. The captain stepped back, but, for a moment, Cyrus and his father simply stared at each other. It was as if they were looking from across the gulf of the Hiterian Mountains and beyond. Cyrus's hands clutched his blanket. His chest rose and fell, his breath coming in quick, unsteady gasps.

"Danaala," he said hoarsely in his own language.

Stella didn't know what the word meant, but she could guess.

Father.

That word and three long strides brought the man into the room and over to his son's bedside. He dropped to his knees, wrapped his arms around Cyrus, and pulled him into a tight hug. It took Stella a moment to realize that they were both crying, quiet, joyful tears that shook their shoulders as they held each other up.

Stella rose from her chair and stepped back, giving them as much privacy as she could in the cramped medical bay.

The other three olarans had entered the room and were talking to Drea and Captain Keeler. Every now and then, the older woman glanced at Stella, and once she smiled at her. Stella smiled back tentatively. She was suddenly nervous, feeling out of place. She wished her parents were here.

The woman said something to Drea that Stella didn't hear, and the sarnun beckoned to Stella. Hesitantly, she made her way over to them.

"Stella, this is the alagant's personal guard and representative, Leandral," Drea introduced her.

"It is a pleasure to meet you, Stella," Leandral said warmly. Her use of the Trader's Speech was smooth and practiced. "The alagant regrets she cannot be here to meet you at this time, but I carry a message of greetings and welcome to your people. We also wanted you to know that we have taken the Faceless man into our custody, and we give you our promise that neither he nor any other olaran will threaten you again.

"We are eager to bring you and the rest of the crew of the *Iron Glory* to Kovall as soon as you are able, for a personal audience with the alagant," Leandral went on. "The Tinker is also eager to meet with all of you, and to help with the repair and rebuilding of your ship. We hope that a bright future lies ahead of both our peoples."

Before Stella could reply to the speech, a hand touched her shoulder. Turning, she was surprised to see Cyrus's father, his eyes still wet with tears.

Lifting his hand and placing it over the starburst symbol pinned to his chest, Cyrus's father sank into a deep bow right in front of Stella. One by one, the other olarans in the room followed suit, until they were all bowing to her.

Stella's cheeks burned. She didn't know what to do. She'd never expected this. Should she bow in return? Curtsy? But her feet might as well have been nailed to the floor. She couldn't move. All she could do was stand there in shock while the olaran representatives paid their respects.

Cyrus's father stood up straight and gazed down at her. He looked like he wanted to say something. His brown eyes were full of emotion and held the same kindness that Cyrus's did. Seeing them finally gave Stella the courage to speak.

"Antya," she said, greeting him in the olaran language, and then, in her own added, "I'm happy to meet you, sir." Her voice quavered only a little. "Cyrus has told me a lot about you."

His lips curved in a smile that made the resemblance between father and son even stronger. "I'm told your name is Stella," he said in her language. His voice was elegant and measured, with a slight accent. "Is that right?"

"That's right," she said. "Stella Glass."

He nodded solemnly, as if her name was something precious. "Stella, you've brought my family back to life." His elegant voice cracked. "We can never repay you for what you've done."

A tear slid down Stella's cheek. She wiped it away and shook her head. "Cyrus saved me too, saved all of us," she said, looking around at the scattered crew.

He smiled, and the pride in his eyes shone clearly. "Your actions have given our peoples a chance to come together," he said. "I look forward to getting to know all of you better in the coming days."

Overwhelmed again, Stella couldn't speak. Cyrus's father reached for her hand, turned her palm up, and placed a small metal object into it.

Cyrus's messenger beetle.

Then he said something in his own language.

Confused, Stella waited for him to translate, but it was Cyrus who spoke up.

"'From today, may we always be connected,'" he said.

A lump rose in Stella's throat. "May we always be connected," she said, meeting Cyrus's eyes as she repeated the words.

EPILOGUE

"You know we're going to be late," Stella said in exasperation.

The sun was high and bright in the sky, the wind warm on their faces as Stella and Cyrus stood side by side at the gates of Kovall.

The last several days had been a whirlwind of activity. The city had sent more supplies and even more people to help the *Iron Glory* and its crew recover from the crash. In fact, most of the wreckage had already been transported via Kovall's airships to the Tinker's estate. The *Iron Glory*'s scientists and engineers had taken up temporary residence there too. Teams of humans, sarnuns, chamelins, and olarans were already hard at work on reconstructing the ship. And according to Cyrus, the Tinker was giddy with excitement at being able to study with them. All his hard work organizing the expeditions was finally paying off, and he couldn't have been happier.

Meanwhile, Stella and her parents had been invited to stay with Cyrus's family, and they'd gladly accepted. Cyrus was recovering, and he still spent a good deal of time resting in bed on the orders of the Tinker, but he was getting stronger every day.

Captain Keeler, Drea, and the command crew had been spending most of their time at the royal palace in meetings with the alagant and her diplomatic staff. In fact, they'd sent a message just yesterday that Stella was to come to the palace to meet with the olaran queen. They were supposed to have been on their way twenty minutes ago, but Cyrus had taken them to the city gates instead.

Stella crossed her arms. "Are you throwing me out of the city?" she teased. "Bored with me already, so you're booting me out?"

He grinned. "Tiresome as you are, no, that's not why we're here." He took her hand and drew her to the side of the main thoroughfare, out of the way of traffic flowing into and out of the bustling city. His face turned serious. "There was something I didn't get a chance to tell you that day I woke up in the medical bay."

Stella's forehead creased as she thought back to that day. There had been so many emotions wrapped up in that moment that it had been overwhelming. "What is it?" she asked.

Instead of answering, Cyrus reached out and wrapped his arms around Stella, setting his chin on her shoulder.

Stella's heart began to beat very fast as she stood in his arms. Thinking about all the hugs she'd shared with her family, this was yet another new one for her. This was Cyrus. A person she'd known only for a short time, but long enough to know she would cross the world for him.

"Stella, you said I was your most important friend." Cyrus's voice cracked. "I wanted to tell you I feel the same way. Thank you for keeping your promise." His shoulders shook. "You . . . you brought me home."

Stella had no words, but she didn't need any. She just hugged Cyrus back fiercely, letting her feelings speak for her. When he finally pulled away, he wiped his eyes quickly with the back of his hand.

"Are you ready to go?" Stella asked, smiling and taking his hand.

He nodded and returned her smile, a grin that went all the way up to his eyes. "I pictured this moment in my head, you know—the two of us standing at these gates. I dreamed about it, the way I dreamed of coming home when I didn't know how I'd ever get here. But now that we are here, there's something I've wanted to say to you ever since we crossed the Hiterian Mountains," he said, looking at her meaningfully.

With his free hand, he gestured to the city beyond

the gates, the wonder of it spreading out before them like a new adventure waiting to happen. "Welcome to Kovall, Stella Glass."

Stella beamed and squeezed his hand as they walked into the city together. "Welcome home," she said.

GLOSSARY OF OLARAN WORDS

alagant: queen
antya: hello or good day
danaala: father
lazuril: living light
sinhave: goodbye
tictan: beetle

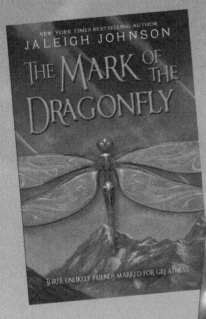

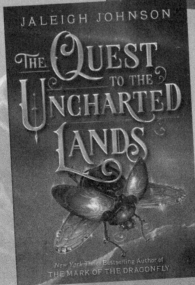

ACKNOWLEDGMENTS

I've been living in Solace for almost six years now, and this book is the culmination of that time spent in the company of characters I couldn't wait for readers to meet. But a separate cast of amazing individuals made this world and these stories possible.

To my amazing team at Delacorte Press, let me thank you for your dedication, and for delivering on every promise you ever made and more. Krista Marino, Monica Jean, and Beverly Horowitz, as well as everyone on the marketing and publicity teams, and the designers and artists who gave me such amazing covers and maps, EVERYONE who got these books out in the world: I can't give you all enough virtual hugs.

Thank you to Sara Megibow, extraordinary agent and all-around wonderful person. I've been surrounded by an incredible group of people in publishing, and you are the center of that circle.

My writing group has been with me for the entire six-year process. Elizabeth, Gary, and Kelly, I can't thank you enough for sticking with me to the end.

A special thanks to all the readers who have sent me artwork, stories, and notes showing their love of Solace. You made the world come alive in new ways with your creativity and joy, and that makes this author so happy.

To my mom, my dad, and Jeff, I've only ever wanted to make you proud of me. Thank you for everything.

And finally, this is for my husband, Tim. You know you own my heart. You're my partner—my Gee, my Ozben, my Cyrus. I love you.

ABOUT THE AUTHOR

Jaleigh Johnson is the *New York Times* bestselling author of *The Mark of the Dragonfly*, *The Secrets of Solace*, and *The Quest to the Uncharted Lands*. A lifelong reader, gamer, and moviegoer, she loves nothing better than to escape into fictional worlds and take part in fantastic adventures.

Jaleigh lives and writes in the wilds of the Midwest, but you can visit her online at jaleighjohnson.com or follow @JaleighJohnson on Twitter.

TURN THE PAGE
FOR A SPECIAL PREVIEW
OF ANOTHER ADVENTURE
IN THE WORLD OF SOLACE.

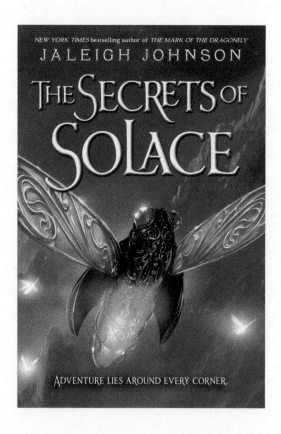

NEW YORK TIMES bestselling author of THE MARK OF THE DRAGONFLY
JALEIGH JOHNSON
THE SECRETS OF SOLACE
ADVENTURE LIES AROUND EVERY CORNER.

≽ ONE ≼

"Apprentices, quiet!" The excited chatter in the classroom almost drowned out Tolwin's exasperated shout. "You'd think that none of you had ever seen a simple box before."

From her seat near the back of the classroom, Lina Winterbock snorted in amusement. An archivist, even a junior apprentice like her, knew there was no such thing as "a simple box." Not when that box had been shipped from the meteor fields up north.

The classroom for Archival Studies was an amphitheater, the desks arranged in a semicircle on stone tiers carved out of the cavern's natural rock formations. At the bottom, in the teaching pit, there was a scarred oak table and a podium beside it for the teacher. The box that had caused the pandemonium sat in the middle of the table. Lina's teacher, the archivist Tolwin, stood behind the podium. His apprentice and assistant, Simon, stood at Tolwin's side, scowling at all the noise. Though to be fair, the sour expression could just be Simon's version of a smile. With him, it was hard to tell.

As Tolwin swept his gaze over the fifty-odd students assembled in the classroom, Lina turned her attention away from the box and sank as low in her seat as she could manage without actually falling to the floor. It didn't matter. The teacher's sharp eyes found her anyway and narrowed as his lips pressed into a thin line of displeasure. Lina forced herself to stare back at him without flinching, but it wasn't easy. Tolwin's glare felt like a spider skittering down her spine. A large, hairy spider with fangs.

Given the *incident* last year, Tolwin's reaction to her wasn't that surprising, but Lina kept hoping maybe he would fall and hit his head and somehow forget the whole unpleasant business. Normally, she would never wish a head injury on anyone, but it might make her days in Archival Studies a bit easier.

Lina released a tense breath as Tolwin finally looked away from her, and she eagerly refocused her attention on the mysterious box. What *was* Tolwin hiding in there? Some new bit of technology? A painting? Or maybe even a manuscript? Mystery poured from the depths of the box, filling Lina's mind and quickening her heart.

Where do you come from? How far have you traveled? What secrets do you hold?

Lina had never been to the meteor fields or the scrap towns where all these strange objects were gathered. They were located far to the north of the archivists' strongholds, in the Merrow Kingdom. But she'd heard plenty of stories of the violent meteor storms that ravaged the land up there. For reasons that even the wisest of the archivists hadn't been able to discover, the boundary between their world of Solace and other lands was thin in the meteor fields, and on the night of each full moon, it dissolved completely. With no barrier, objects from other worlds tumbled from the sky in clouds of poisonous green dust. It was the poorest people in the north, the scrappers, who bravely took on the task of harvesting these meteorites. They cleaned up whatever objects were still intact and sold them at local trade markets to make money to live on.

The scrappers' best customers were the archivists, who bought up as many of these otherworldly artifacts as they could. They paid special attention to any object that might reveal hints of what life was like in unknown worlds. It was the archivists' mission to preserve the artifacts and record whatever knowledge they gleaned from them, both for its own sake and because they believed that the more people learned about these other worlds, the more they would come to understand their own. It was a unique calling, one that, even as an apprentice, made Lina's life very different from the lives of people living in other lands.

"I said *quiet!*" Tolwin barked, shaking Lina from her thoughts. Anger deepened the crisscrossing lines on her instructor's face. His bushy brown-gray hair even seemed unhappy. As he glared at the students, the noise level in the room gradually dropped to a quiet murmur. "Today I'm going to conduct a hands-on experiment, the purpose of which is to test your understanding of the archivist principles you've been taught so far." Tolwin gestured to the box on the table. "You're all wondering what I've got in here, yes? I hear you whispering about it, trying to guess which division it came from."

Naturally, Lina thought. It was the first thing any archivist would wonder. The six general divisions—Flora, Fauna, Technology, Language/Literature, Cultural Artifacts, and Medicine—formed the basis for all the archivists' work. At the end of their long years of study and apprenticeship, each of the students in this room would end up working in one of those divisions.

Tolwin rubbed his hands together as if to build suspense. "All I will tell you, to start, is that there is an object inside the box that was discovered in the meteor fields only two weeks ago."

An astonished hush fell over the classroom at this announcement, and Lina sat up straighter in her seat.

Apprentices rarely got the opportunity to *see*, let alone *study*, an object newly recovered from the meteor fields. That privilege was usually reserved for the senior archivists.

"Well, now that we've finally achieved silence," Tolwin said dryly, "we can begin the lesson. First, I will require a volunteer. Simon, would you care to select someone?"

Hands shot up all over the room as the students squirmed in their seats and shot pleading looks at Tolwin's apprentice. They all wanted to be the first to examine the object inside the box.

Only Lina sat with her hands folded tight on top of her desk. All the while, her heart banged against her ribs, begging her with each unsteady beat to raise her hand and volunteer. But, curious as she was about the secrets and wonders contained within the box, she didn't trust Tolwin. She didn't trust anyone who made her feel spider legs on her spine.

And then Simon said something that made her heart stand still. "I think . . . I think Lina Winterbock looks eager to volunteer."

Lina's stomach dropped, and she caught the malicious glint in Simon's eyes as he motioned for her to come down and join them in the teaching pit.

"Ah yes, I believe you're right." Tolwin glanced up at her, and the slightest of smiles curved his thin lips.

"Come down and stand in front of the table here, Miss Winterbock."

Lina's mind raced even as she slid her chair away from her desk with a quiet scraping sound. All eyes in the classroom fixed on her, which automatically brought a deep flush of embarrassment to her cheeks.

At times like this, Lina wished more than anything that she could look across the room and meet the eyes of a best friend, someone who would giggle and stick her tongue out at Tolwin when his back was turned, and who would mouth a few encouraging words to her while she faced down the teacher. She'd even settle for a temporary friend, one who appeared under only the direst of circumstances. She wasn't picky.

Focus, Lina.

Whatever game Tolwin and Simon were playing, the way Lina saw it, she had three possible countermoves. She could refuse to volunteer, which would thwart Tolwin but also probably get her kicked out of class. There was always the option of feigning sickness. Lina considered it as she stood up and made her way down the stairs. All she had to do was clutch her stomach and run out of the room as if she were about to vomit. If she played it up enough, Tolwin might even believe her.

But that would give him the satisfaction of knowing that he'd scared her off.